"Don't believe everything you read about me," Brad said easily.

"Who says I've been reading about you?"

"Come on, Meg. You expected me to drink Jack Daniel's straight from the bottle. That's hype—part of the bad-boy image. My manager cooked it up."

"You haven't been to rehab?"

He grinned. "Nope. Never trashed a hotel room, spent a weekend in jail or done any of the rest of the stuff you believe."

"Really?"

"Really." Brad pushed back his chair, returned to the jukebox and dropped a few coins in the slot. An old Johnny Cash ballad poured softly into the otherwise silent bar.

Brad started in her direction. He held out a hand to her.

Meg went to him. Automatically.

He drew her into his arms, holding her close but easy, and they danced without moving their feet. As the song ended, Brad propped his chin on top of Meg's head and sighed. "I've missed you."

Dear Reader,

A lot of you have asked for Meg McKettrick's story, and here it is. What happens when a McKettrick butts heads with an O'Ballivan? Well, sparks fly, for one thing. Saddle up and ride with Meg, Brad and me, along with some familiar faces from earlier books, on an adventure of romance, humor and excitement in *The McKettrick Way*. I promise you'll enjoy the journey, whether the McKettricks and O'Ballivans are old friends or new.

I also wanted to tell you about a special group of people with whom I've recently become involved. It is the Humane Society of the United States (HSUS), specifically their Pets for Life program.

The Pets for Life program is one of the best ways to help your local shelter, which is to help keep animals out of shelters in the first place. Keep a collar and tag on your pet all the time; be a responsible pet owner; spay or neuter your pet and don't give up when things don't go perfectly. If your dog digs in the yard or your cat scratches the furniture know that these are problems that can be addressed. You can find all the information about these—and many other common problems—at www.petsforlife.org. This campaign is focused on keeping pets and their people together for a lifetime.

As many of you know, my own household includes two dogs, two cats and four horses, so this is a cause that is near and dear to my heart. I hope you'll get involved along with me.

With love,

Paula Swift Miller

LINDA LAEL MILLER

THE McKETTRICK Way

SPECIAL EDITION®

Published by Silhouette Books

America's Publisher of Contemporary Romance

SILHOUETTE BOOKS

ISBN-13: 978-0-373-24867-4
ISBN-10:   0-373-24867-9

THE McKETTRICK WAY

This edition published by arrangement with Harlequin Books S.A.

® and TM are trademarks of Harlequin Books S.A., used under license. Trademarks indicated with ® are registered in the United States Patent and Trademark Office, the Canadian Trade Marks Office and in other countries.

Visit Silhouette Books at www.eHarlequin.com

Printed in U.S.A.

Books by Linda Lael Miller

LINDA LAEL MILLER

The daughter of a town marshal, Linda Lael Miller grew up in rural Washington. The self-confessed barn goddess was inspired to pursue a career as an author after an elementary school teacher said the stories she was writing might be good enough to be published.

Linda broke into publishing in the early 1980s. She is now a *New York Times* bestselling author of more than sixty contemporary, romantic suspense and historical novels, including *The Man from Stone Creek, A Wanted Man* and *Deadly Gamble.* When not writing, Linda enjoys riding her horses and playing with her cats and dogs. Through her Linda Lael Miller Scholarships for Women, she provides grants to women who seek to improve their lot in life through education.

For more information about Linda, her scholarships and her novels, visit www.lindalaelmiller.com.

In memory of my dad, Grady "Skip" Lael.
Happy trails, Cowboy.

Chapter One

Brad O'Ballivan opened the driver's-side door of the waiting pickup truck, tossed his guitar case inside and turned to wave a farewell to the pilot and crew of the private jet he hoped never to ride in again.

A chilly fall wind slashed across the broad, lonesome clearing, rippling the fading grass, and he raised the collar of his denim jacket against it. Pulled his hat down a little lower over his eyes.

He was home.

Something inside him resonated to the Arizona high country, and more particularly to Stone Creek Ranch, like one prong of a perfectly balanced tuning fork. The sensation was peculiar to the place—he'd never felt it in his sprawling lakeside mansion outside Nashville, on the periphery of a town called Hendersonville, or at the villa in Mexico, or any of the other fancy digs where he'd hung his hat over the years since he'd turned his back on the spread—and so much more—to sing for his supper.

His grin was slightly ironic as he stood by the truck and watched the jet soar back into the sky. His retirement from the country music scene, at the age of thirty-five and the height of his success, had caused quite a media stir. He'd sold the jet and the big houses and most of what was in them, and given away the rest, except for the guitar and the clothes he was wearing. And he knew he'd never regret it.

He was through with that life. And once an O'Ballivan was through with something, that was the end of it.

The jet left a trail across the sky, faded to a silver spark, and disappeared.

Brad was about to climb into the truck and head for the ranch house, start coming to terms with things there, when he spotted a familiar battered gray Suburban jostling and gear-grinding its way over the rough road that had never really evolved beyond its beginnings as an old-time cattle trail.

He took off his hat, even though the wind nipped at the edges of his ears, and waited, partly eager, partly resigned.

The old Chevy came to a chortling stop a few inches from the toes of his boots, throwing up a cloud of red-brown dust, and his sister Olivia shut the big engine down and jumped out to round the hood and stride right up to him.

"You're back," Olivia said, sounding nonplussed. The eldest of Brad's three younger sisters, at twenty-nine, she'd never quite forgiven him for leaving home—much less getting famous. Practical to the bone, she was small, with short, glossy dark hair and eyes the color of a brand-new pair of jeans, and just as starchy. Olivia was low-woman-on-thetotem-pole at a thriving veterinary practice in the nearby town of Stone Creek, specializing in large animals, and Brad knew she spent most of her workdays in a barn someplace, or out on the range, with one arm shoved up where the sun didn't shine, turning a crossways calf or colt.

"I'm delighted to see you, too, Doc," Brad answered dryly.

With an exasperated little cry, Olivia sprang off the soles of her worn-out boots to throw her arms around his neck, knocking his hat clear off his head in the process. She hugged him tight, and when she drew back, there were tears on her dirt-smudged cheeks, and she sniffled self-consciously.

"If this is some kind of publicity stunt," Livie said, once she'd rallied a little, "I'm never going to forgive you." She bent to retrieve his hat, handed it over.

God, she was proud. She'd let him pay for her education, but returned every other check he or his accountant sent with the words *NO THANKS* scrawled across the front in thick black capitals.

Brad chuckled, threw the hat into the pickup, to rest on top of the guitar case. "It's no stunt," he replied. "I'm back for good. Ready to 'take hold and count for something,' as Big John used to say."

The mention of their late grandfather caused a poignant and not entirely comfortable silence to fall between them. Brad had been on a concert tour when the old man died of a massive coronary six months before, and he'd barely made it back to Stone Creek in time for the funeral. Worse, he'd had to leave again right after the services, in order to make a sold-out show in Chicago. The large infusions of cash he'd pumped into the home place over the years did little to assuage his guilt.

How much money is enough? How famous do you have to

be? Big John had asked, in his kindly but irascible way, not once but a hundred times. *Come home, damn it. I need you. Your little sisters need you. And God knows, Stone Creek Ranch needs you.*

Shoving a hand through his light brown hair, in need of trimming as always, Brad thrust out a sigh and scanned the surrounding countryside. "That old stallion still running loose out here, or did the wolves and the barbed wire finally get him?" he asked, raw where the memories of his grandfather chafed against his mind, and in sore need of a distraction.

Livie probably wasn't fooled by the dodge, but she was gracious enough to grant Brad a little space to recover in, and he appreciated that. "We get a glimpse of Ransom every once in a while," she replied, and a little pucker of worry formed between her eyebrows. "Always off on the horizon some-where, keeping his distance."

Brad laid a hand on his sister's shoulder. She'd been fas-cinated with the legendary wild stallion since she was little. First sighted in the late nineteenth century and called King's Ransom because that was what he was probably worth, the animal was black and shiny as wet ink, and so elusive that some people maintained he wasn't flesh and blood at all, but spirit, a myth believed for so long that thought itself had made him real. The less fanciful maintained that Ransom was one in a long succession of stallions, all descended from that first mysterious sire. Brad stood squarely in this camp, as Big John had, but he wasn't so sure Livie took the same rational view.

"They're trying to trap him," she said now, tears glisten-ing in her eyes. "They want to pen him up. Get samples of his DNA. Turn him out to stud, so they can sell his babies."

"Who's trying to trap him, Liv?" Brad asked gently. It was

cold, he was hungry, and setting foot in the old ranch house, without Big John there to greet him, was a thing to get past.

"Never mind," Livie said, bucking up a little. Setting her jaw. "You wouldn't be interested."

There was no point in arguing with Olivia O'Ballivan, DVM, when she got that look on her face. "Thanks for bringing my truck out here," Brad said. "And for coming to meet me."

"I didn't bring the truck," Livie replied. Some people would have taken the credit, but Liv was half again too stubborn to admit to a kindness she hadn't committed, let alone one she considered unwarranted. "Ashley and Melissa did that. They're probably at the ranch house right now, hanging streamers or putting up a Welcome Home, Brad banner or something. And I only came out here because I saw that jet and figured it was some damn movie star, buzzing the deer."

Brad had one leg inside the truck, ready to hoist himself into the driver's seat. "That's a problem around here?" he asked, with a wry half grin. "Movie stars buzzing deer in Lear jets?"

"It happens in Montana all the time," Livie insisted, plainly incensed. She felt just as strongly about snowmobiles and other off-road vehicles.

Brad reached down, touched the tip of her nose with one index finger. "This isn't Montana, shortstop," he pointed out. "See you at home?"

"Another time," Livie said, not giving an inch. "After all the hoopla dies down."

Inwardly, Brad groaned. He wasn't up for hoopla, or any kind of celebration Ashley and Melissa, their twin sisters, might have cooked up in honor of his return. Classic between-a-rock-and-a-hard-place stuff—he couldn't hurt their feelings, either.

"Tell me they're not planning a party," he pleaded.

Livie relented, but only slightly. One side of her mouth quirked up in a smile. "You're in luck, Mr. Multiple Grammy Winner. There's a McKettrick baby shower going on over in Indian Rock as we speak, and practically the whole county's there."

The name McKettrick unsettled Brad even more than the prospect of going home to banners, streamers and a collection of grinning neighbors, friends and sisters. "Not Meg," he muttered, and then blushed, since he hadn't intended to say the words out loud.

Livie's smile intensified, the way it did when she had a solid hand at gin rummy and was fixing to go out and stick him with a lot of aces and face cards. She shook her head. "Meg's back in Indian Rock for good, rumor has it, and she's still single," she assured him. "Her sister Sierra's the one having a baby."

In a belated and obviously fruitless attempt to hide his relief at this news, Brad shut the truck door between himself and Livie and, since the keys were waiting in the ignition, started up the rig.

Looking smug, Livie waved cheerily, climbed back into the Suburban and drove off, literally in a cloud of dust.

Brad sat waiting for it to settle.

The feelings took a little longer.

"Go haunt somebody else!" Meg McKettrick whispered to the ghost cowboy riding languidly in the passenger seat of her Blazer, as she drove past Sierra's new house, on the outskirts of Indian Rock, for at least the third time. Both sides of the road were jammed with cars, and if she didn't find a parking place soon, she'd be late for the baby shower. If not the actual *baby*. "Pick on Keegan—or Jesse—or Rance—*anybody* but me!"

"They don't need haunting," he said mildly. He looked nothing like the august, craggy-faced, white-haired figure in his portraits, grudgingly posed for late in his long and vigorous life. No, Angus McKettrick had come back in his prime, square-jaw handsome, broad shouldered, his hair thick and golden brown, his eyes intensely blue, at ease in the charm he'd passed down to generations of male descendents.

Still flustered, Meg found a gap between a Lexus and a minivan, wedged the Blazer into it, and turned off the ignition with a twist of one wrist. Tight-tipped, she jumped out of the rig, jerked open the back door, and reached for the festively wrapped package on the seat. "I've got news for you," she sputtered. "*I* don't need haunting, either!"

Angus, who looked to Meg as substantial and "real" as anybody she'd ever encountered, got out and stood on his side of the Blazer, stretching. "So you say," he answered, in a lazy drawl. "All of *them* are married, starting families of their own. Carrying on the McKettrick name."

"Thanks for the reminder," Meg bit out, in the terse undertone she reserved for arguments with her great-great-however-many-greats grandfather. Clutching the gift she'd bought for Travis and Sierra's baby, she shouldered both the back and driver's doors shut.

"In my day," Angus said easily, "you'd have been an old maid."

"Hello?" Meg replied, without moving her mouth. Over her long association with Angus McKettrick—which went back to her earliest childhood memories—she'd developed her own brand of ventriloquism, so other people, who couldn't see him, wouldn't think she was talking to herself. "This *isn't* 'your day.' It's mine. Twenty-first century, all the way. Women don't define themselves by whether they're married or not." She paused, sucked in a calming breath. "Here's an idea—why don't you wait in the car? Or, better yet, go ride some happy trail."

Angus kept pace with her as she crossed the road, clomping along in his perpetually muddy boots. As always, he wore a long, cape-shouldered canvas coat over a rough-spun shirt of butternut cotton and denim trousers that weren't quite jeans. The handle of his ever-present pistol, a long-barreled Colt .45, made a bulge behind his right coat pocket. He wore a hat only when there was a threat of rain, and since the early-October weather was mild, he was bare-headed that evening.

"It might be your testy nature that's the problem," Angus ruminated. "You're downright pricklish, that's what you are. A woman ought to have a little sass to her, to spice things up a mite. You've got more than your share, though, and it ain't becoming."

Meg ignored him, and the bad grammar he always affected when he wanted to impart folksy wisdom, as she tromped up the front steps, shuffling the bulky package in her arms to jab at the doorbell. *Here comes your nineteenth noncommittal yellow layette,* she thought, wishing she'd opted for the sterling baby rattles instead. If Sierra and Travis knew the sex of their unborn child, they weren't telling, which made shopping even more of a pain than normal.

The door swung open and Eve, Meg and Sierra's mother, stood frowning in the chasm. "It's about time you got here," she said, pulling Meg inside. Then, in a whisper, "Is he with you?"

"Of course he is," Meg answered, as her mother peered past her shoulder, searching in vain for Angus. "He never misses a family gathering."

Eve sniffed, straightened her elegant shoulders. "You're late," she said. "Sierra will be here any minute!"

"It's not as if she's going to be surprised, Mom," Meg said, setting the present atop a mountain of others of a suspiciously similar size and shape. "There must be a hundred cars parked out there."

Eve shut the door smartly and then, before Meg could shrug out of her navy blue peacoat, gripped her firmly by the shoulders. "You've lost weight," she accused. "And there are dark circles under your eyes. Aren't you sleeping well?"

"I'm fine," Meg insisted. And she *was* fine—for an old maid.

Angus, never one to be daunted by a little thing like a closed door, materialized just behind Eve, looked around at his assembled brood with pleased amazement. The place was jammed with McKettrick cousins, their wives and husbands, their growing families.

Something tightened in the pit of Meg's stomach.

"Nonsense," Eve said. "If you could have gotten away with it, you would have stayed home today, wandering around that old house in your pajamas, with no makeup on and your hair sticking out in every direction."

It was true, but beside the point. With Eve McKettrick for a mother, Meg couldn't get away with much of anything. "I'm here," she said. "Give me a break, will you?"

She pulled off her coat, handed it to Eve, and sidled into the nearest group, a small band of women. Meg, who had spent all her childhood summers in Indian Rock, didn't recognize any of them.

"It's all over the tabloids," remarked a tall, thin woman wearing a lot of jewelry. "Brad O'Ballivan is in rehab again."

Meg caught her breath at the name, and nearly dropped the cup of punch someone shoved into her hands.

"Nonsense," a second woman replied. "Last week those rags were reporting that he'd been abducted by aliens."

"He's handsome enough to have fans on other planets," observed a third, sighing wistfully.

Meg tried to ease out of the circle, but it had closed around her. She felt dizzy.

"My cousin Evelyn works at the post office over in Stone Creek," said yet another woman, with authority. "According to her, Brad's fan mail is being forwarded to the family ranch, just outside of town. He's not in rehab, and he's not on another planet. He's *home*. Evelyn says they'll have to build a second barn just to hold all those letters."

Meg smiled rigidly, but on the inside, she was scrambling for balance.

Suddenly, woman #1 focused on her. "You used to date Brad O'Ballivan, didn't you, Meg?"

"That—that was a long time ago," Meg said as graciously as she could, given that she was right in the middle of a panic attack. "We were just kids, and it was a summer thing—" Frantically, she calculated the distance between Indian Rock and Stone Creek—a mere forty miles. Not nearly far enough.

"I'm sure Meg has dated a lot of famous people," one of the other women said. "Working for McKettrickCo the way she did, flying all over the place in the company jet—"

"Brad wasn't famous when I knew him," Meg said lamely.

"You must miss your old life," someone else commented.

While it was true that Meg was having some trouble shifting from full throttle to a comparative standstill, since the family conglomerate had gone public a few months before, and her job as an executive vice president had gone with it, she *didn't* miss the meetings and the sixty-hour workweeks all that much. Money certainly wasn't a problem; she had a trust fund, as well as a personal investment portfolio thicker than the Los Angeles phone book.

A stir at the front door saved her from commenting.

Sierra came in, looking baffled.

"Surprise!" the crowd shouted as one.

The surprise is on me, Meg thought bleakly. *Brad O'Bal-livan is back.*

Brad shoved the truck into gear and drove to the bottom of the hill, where the road forked. Turn left, and he'd be home in five minutes. Turn right, and he was headed for Indian Rock.

He had no damn business going to Indian Rock.

He had nothing to say to Meg McKettrick, and if he never set eyes on the woman again, it would be two weeks too soon.

He turned right.

He couldn't have said why.

He just drove.

At one point, needing noise, he switched on the truck radio, fiddled with the dial until he found a country-western station. A recording of his own voice filled the cab of the pickup, thundering from all the speakers.

He'd written that ballad for Meg.

He turned the dial to Off.

Almost simultaneously, his cell phone jangled in the pocket of his jacket; he considered ignoring it—there were a number of people he didn't want to talk to—but suppose it was one of his sisters calling? Suppose they needed help?

He flipped the phone open, not taking his eyes off the curvy mountain road to check the caller ID panel first. "O'Ballivan," he said.

"Have you come to your senses yet?" demanded his manager, Phil Meadowbrook. "Shall I tell you again just *how much* money those people in Vegas are offering? They're willing to build you your own *theater,* for God's sake. This is a three-year gig—"

"Phil?" Brad broke in.

"Say yes," Phil pleaded.

"I'm retired."

"You're thirty-five," Phil argued. "*Nobody* retires at thirty-five!"

"We've already had this conversation, Phil."

"Don't hang up!"

Brad, who'd been about to thumb the off button, sighed.

"What the hell are you going to do in Stone Creek, Arizona?" Phil demanded. "Herd cattle? Sing to your horse? Think of the money, Brad. Think of the women, throwing their underwear at your feet—"

"I've been working real hard to repress that image," Brad said. "Thanks a lot for the reminder."

"Okay, forget the underwear," Phil shot back, without missing a beat. "But think of the money!"

"I've already got more of that than I need, Phil, and so do you, so spare me the riff where your grandchildren are homeless waifs picking through garbage behind the supermarket."

"I've used that one, huh?" Phil asked.

"Oh, yeah," Brad answered.

"What are you doing, right this moment?"

"I'm headed for the Dixie Dog Drive-In."

"The *what?*"

"Goodbye, Phil."

"What are you going to do at the Dixie-Whatever Drive-In that you couldn't do in Music City? Or Vegas?"

"You wouldn't understand," Brad said. "And I can't say I blame you, because I don't really understand it myself."

Back in the day, he and Meg used to meet at the Dixie Dog,

by tacit agreement, when either of them had been away. It had been some kind of universe-thing, purely intuitive. He guessed he wanted to see if it still worked—and he'd be damned if he'd try to explain that to Phil.

"Look," Phil said, revving up for another sales pitch, "I can't put these casino people off forever. You're riding high right now, but things are bound to cool off. I've got to tell them *something*—"

"Tell them 'thanks, but no thanks,'" Brad suggested. This time, he broke the connection.

Phil, being Phil, tried to call twice before he finally gave up.

Passing familiar landmarks, Brad told himself he ought to turn around. The old days were gone, things had ended badly between him and Meg anyhow, and she wasn't going to be at the Dixie Dog.

He kept driving.

He went by the Welcome To Indian Rock sign, and the Roadhouse, a popular beer-and-burger stop for truckers, tourists and locals, and was glad to see the place was still open. He slowed for Main Street, smiled as he passed Cora's Curl and Twirl, squinted at the bookshop next door. That was new.

He frowned. Things changed, places changed.

What if the Dixie Dog had closed down?

What if it was boarded up, with litter and sagebrush tumbling through a deserted parking lot?

And what the hell did it matter, anyhow?

Brad shoved a hand through his hair. Maybe Phil and everybody else was right—maybe he was crazy to turn down the Vegas deal. Maybe he *would* end up sitting in the barn, serenading a bunch of horses.

He rounded a bend, and there was the Dixie Dog, still open. Its big neon sign, a giant hot dog, was all lit up and going through its corny sequence—first it was covered in red squiggles of light, meant to suggest catsup, and then yellow, for mustard. There were a few cars lined up in the drive-through lane, a few more in the parking lot.

Brad pulled into one of the slots next to a speaker and rolled down the truck window.

"Welcome to the Dixie Dog Drive-In," a youthful female voice chirped over the bad wiring. "What can I get you today?"

Brad hadn't thought that far, but he was starved. He peered at the light-up menu box under the chunky metal speaker. Then the obvious choice struck him and he said, "I'll take a Dixie Dog," he said. "Hold the chili and onions."

"Coming right up" was the cheerful response. "Anything to drink?"

"Chocolate shake," he decided. "Extra thick."

His cell phone rang again.

He ignored it again.

The girl thanked him and roller-skated out with the order about five minutes later.

When she wheeled up to the driver's-side window, smiling, her eyes went wide with recognition, and she dropped the tray with a clatter.

Silently, Brad swore. Damn if he hadn't forgotten he was famous.

The girl, a skinny thing wearing too much eye makeup, immediately started to cry. "I'm sorry!" she sobbed, squatting to gather up the mess.

"It's okay," Brad answered quietly, leaning to look down at her, catching a glimpse of her plastic name tag. "It's okay, Mandy. No harm done."

"I'll get you another dog and a shake right away, Mr. O'Ballivan!"

"Mandy?"

She stared up at him pitifully, sniffling. Thanks to the copious tears, most of the goop on her eyes had slid south. "Yes?"

"When you go back inside, could you not mention seeing me?"

"But you're Brad O'Ballivan!"

"Yeah," he answered, suppressing a sigh. "I know."

She was standing up again by then, the tray of gathered debris clasped in both hands. She seemed to sway a little on her rollers. "Meeting you is just about the most important thing that's ever happened to me in my whole entire *life*. I don't know if I could keep it a secret even if I tried!"

Brad leaned his head against the back of the truck seat and closed his eyes. "Not forever, Mandy," he said. "Just long enough for me to eat a Dixie Dog in peace."

She rolled a little closer. "You wouldn't happen to have a picture you could autograph for me, would you?"

"Not with me," Brad answered. There were boxes of publicity pictures in storage, along with the requisite T-shirts, slick concert programs and other souvenirs commonly sold on the road. He never carried them, much to Phil's annoyance.

"You could sign this napkin, though," Mandy said. "It's only got a little chocolate on the corner."

Brad took the paper napkin, and her order pen, and scrawled his name. Handed both items back through the window.

"Now I can tell my grandchildren I spilled your lunch all over the pavement at the Dixie Dog Drive-In, and here's my proof." Mandy beamed, waggling the chocolate-stained napkin.

"Just imagine," Brad said. The slight irony in his tone was wasted on Mandy, which was probably a good thing.

"I won't tell anybody I saw you until you drive away," Mandy said with eager resolve. "I *think* I can last that long."

"That would be good," Brad told her.

She turned and whizzed back toward the side entrance to the Dixie Dog.

Brad waited, marveling that he hadn't considered incidents like this one before he'd decided to come back home. In retrospect, it seemed shortsighted, to say the least, but the truth was, he'd expected to be—Brad O'Ballivan.

Presently, Mandy skated back out again, and this time, she managed to hold on to the tray.

"I didn't tell a soul!" she whispered. "But Heather and Darlene *both* asked me why my mascara was all smeared." Efficiently, she hooked the tray onto the bottom edge of the window.

Brad extended payment, but Mandy shook her head.

"The boss said it's on the house, since I dumped your first order on the ground."

He smiled. "Okay, then. Thanks."

Mandy retreated, and Brad was just reaching for the food when a bright red Blazer whipped into the space beside his. The driver's-side door sprang open, crashing into the metal speaker, and somebody got out, in a hurry.

Something quickened inside Brad.

And in the next moment, Meg McKettrick was standing practically on his running board, her blue eyes blazing.

Brad grinned. "I guess you're not over me after all," he said.

Chapter Two

After Sierra had opened all her shower presents, and cake and punch had been served, Meg had felt the old, familiar tug in the middle of her solar plexus and headed straight for the Dixie Dog Drive-In. Now that she was there, standing next to a truck and all but nose to nose with Brad O'Ballivan through the open window, she didn't know what to do—or say.

Angus poked her from behind, and she flinched.

"Speak up," her dead ancestor prodded.

"Stay out of this," she answered, without thinking.

Puzzlement showed in Brad's affably handsome face. "Huh?"

"Never mind," Meg said. She took a step back, straightened. "And I am *so* over you."

Brad grinned. "Damned if it didn't work," he marveled. He climbed out of the truck to stand facing Meg, ducking around the tray hooked to the door. His dark-blond hair was artfully rumpled, and his clothes were downright ordinary.

"*What* worked?" Meg demanded, even though she knew.

Laughter sparked in his blue-green eyes, along with considerable pain, and he didn't bother to comment.

"What are you doing here?" she asked.

Brad spread his hands. Hands that had once played Meg's body as skillfully as any guitar. Oh, yes. Brad O'Ballivan knew how to set all the chords vibrating.

"Free country," he said. "Or has Indian Rock finally seceded from the Union with the ranch house on the Triple M for a capitol?"

Since she felt a strong urge to bolt for the Blazer and lay rubber getting out of the Dixie Dog's parking lot, Meg planted her feet and hoisted her chin. *McKettricks*, she reminded herself silently, *don't run*.

"I heard you were in rehab," she said, hoping to get under his hide.

"That's a nasty rumor," Brad replied cheerfully.

"How about the two ex-wives and that scandal with the actress?"

His grin, insouciant in the first place, merely widened. "Unfortunately, I can't deny the two ex-wives," he said. "As for the actress—well, it all depends on whether you believe her version or mine. Have you been following my career, Meg McKettrick?"

Meg reddened.

"Tell him the truth," Angus counseled. "You never forgot him."

"No," Meg said, addressing both Brad *and* Angus.

Brad looked unconvinced. He was probably just egotistical enough to think she logged onto his Web site regularly, bought all his CDs and read every tabloid article about him that she could get her hands on. Which she did, but that was *not* the point.

"You're still the best-looking woman I've ever laid eyes on," he said. "That hasn't changed, anyhow."

"I'm not a member of your fan club, O'Ballivan," Meg informed him. "So hold the insincere flattery, okay?"

One corner of his mouth tilted upward in a half grin, but his eyes were sad. He glanced back toward the truck, then met Meg's gaze again. "I don't flatter anybody," Brad said. Then he sighed. "I guess I'd better get back to Stone Creek."

Something in his tone piqued Meg's interest.

Who was she kidding?

Everything about him piqued her interest. As much as she didn't want that to be true, it was.

"I was sorry to hear about Big John's passing," she said. She almost touched his arm, but managed to catch herself just short of it. If she laid a hand on Brad O'Ballivan, who knew what would happen?

"Thanks," he replied.

A girl on roller skates wheeled out of the drive-in to collect the tray from the window edge of Brad's truck, her cheeks pink with carefully restrained excitement. "I might have said something to Heather and Darleen," the teenager confessed, after a curious glance at Meg. "About you being who you are and the autograph and everything."

Brad muttered something.

The girl skated away.

"I've gotta go," Brad told Meg, looking toward the drive-in. Numerous faces were pressed against the glass door; in another minute, there would probably be a stampede. "I don't suppose we could have dinner together or something? Maybe tomorrow night? There are—well, there are some things I'd like to say to you."

"Say yes," Angus told her.

"I don't think that would be a good idea," Meg said.

"A drink, then? There's a redneck bar in Stone Creek—"

"Don't be such a damned prig," Angus protested, nudging her again.

"I'm not a prig."

Brad frowned, threw another nervous look toward the drive-in and all those grinning faces. "I never said you were," he replied.

"I wasn't—" Meg paused, bit her lower lip. *I wasn't talking to you. No, siree, I was talking to Angus McKettrick's ghost.* "Okay," she agreed, to cover her lapse. "I guess one drink couldn't do any harm."

Brad climbed into his truck. The door of the drive-in crashed open, and the adoring hordes poured out, screaming with delight.

"Go!" Meg told him.

"Six o'clock tomorrow night," Brad reminded her. He backed the truck out, made a narrow turn to avoid running over the approaching herd of admirers and peeled out of the lot.

Meg turned to the disappointed fans. "Brad O'Ballivan," she said diplomatically, "has left the building."

Nobody got the joke.

The sun was setting, red-gold shot through with purple, when Brad crested the last hill before home and looked down on Stone Creek Ranch for the first time since his grandfather's funeral. The creek coursed, silvery-blue, through the middle of the land. The barn and the main house, built by Sam O'Ballivan's own hands and shored up by every generation to

follow, stood as sturdy and imposing as ever. Once, there had
been two houses on the place, but the one belonging to Major
John Blackstone, the original landowner, had been torn down
long ago. Now a copse of oak trees stood where the major had
lived, surrounding a few old graves.

Big John was buried there, by special dispensation from
the Arizona state government.

A lump formed in Brad's throat. *You see that I'm laid to
rest with the old-timers when the bell tolls,* Big John had told
him once. *Not in that cemetery in town.*

It had taken some doing, but Brad had made it happen.

He wanted to head straight for Big John's final resting
place, pay his respects first thing, but there was a cluster of
cars parked in front of the ranch house. His sisters were
waiting to welcome him home.

Brad blinked a couple of times, rubbed his eyes with a
thumb and forefinger, and headed for the house.

Time to face the proverbial music.

Meg drove slowly back to the Triple M, going the long way
to pass the main ranch house, Angus's old stomping grounds,
in the vain hope that he would decide to haunt it for a while,
instead of her. A descendant of Angus's eldest son, Holt, and
daughter-in-law Lorelei, Meg called their place home.

As they bumped across the creek bridge, Angus assessed
the large log structure, added onto over the years, and well-
maintained.

Though close, all the McKettricks were proud of their particular branch of the family tree. Keegan, who occupied the
main house now, along with his wife, Molly, daughter, Devon,
and young son, Lucas, could trace his lineage back to Kade,
another of Angus's four sons.

Rance, along with his daughters, was Rafe's progeny. He and the girls and his bride, Emma, lived in the grandly rustic structure on the other side of the creek from Keegan's place.

Finally, there was Jesse. He was Jeb's descendant, and resided, when he wasn't off somewhere participating in a rodeo or a poker tournament, in the house Jeb had built for his wife, Chloe, high on a hill on the southwestern section of the ranch. Jesse was happily married to a hometown girl, the former Cheyenne Bridges, and like Keegan's Molly and Rance's Emma, Cheyenne was expecting a baby.

Everybody, it seemed to Meg, was expecting a baby.

Except her, of course.

She bit her lower lip.

"I bet if you got yourself pregnant by that singing cowboy," Angus observed, "he'd have the decency to make an honest woman out of you."

Angus had an uncanny ability to tap into Meg's wavelength; though he swore he couldn't read her mind, she wondered sometimes.

"Great idea," she scoffed. "And for your information, I *am* an honest woman."

Keegan was just coming out of the barn as Meg passed; he smiled and waved. She tooted the Blazer's horn in greeting.

"He sure looks like Kade," Angus said. "Jesse looks like Jeb, and Rance looks like Rafe." He sighed. "It sure makes me lonesome for my boys."

Meg felt a grudging sympathy for Angus. He'd ruined a lot of dates, being an almost constant companion, but she loved him. "Why can't you be where they are?" she asked softly. "Wherever that is."

"I've got to see to you," he answered. "You're the last holdout."

"I'd be all right, Angus," she said. She'd asked him about the afterlife, but all he'd ever been willing to say was that there was no such thing as dying, just a change of perspective. Time wasn't linear, he claimed, but simultaneous. The "whole ball of string," as he put it, was happening at once—past, present and future. Some of the experiences the women in her family, including herself and Sierra, had had up at Holt's house lent credence to the theory.

Sierra claimed that, before her marriage to Travis and the subsequent move to the new semi-mansion in town, she and her young son, Liam, had shared the old house with a previous generation of McKettricks—Doss and Hannah and a little boy called Tobias. Sierra had offered journals and photograph albums as proof, and Meg had to admit, her half sister made a compelling case.

Still, and for all that she'd been keeping company with a benevolent ghost since she was little, Meg was a left-brain type.

When Angus didn't comment on her insistence that she'd get along fine if he went on to the great roundup in the sky, or whatever, Meg tried again. "Look," she said gently, "when I was little, and Sierra disappeared, and Mom was so frantic to find her that she couldn't take care of me, I really needed you. But I'm a grown woman now, Angus. I'm independent. I have a life."

Out of the corner of her eye, she saw Angus's jaw tighten. "That Hank Breslin," he said, "was no good for Eve. No better than *your* father was. Every time the right man came along, she was so busy cozying up to the *wrong* one that she didn't even notice what was right in front of her."

Hank Breslin was Sierra's father. He'd kidnapped Sierra, only two years old at the time, when Eve served him with divorce papers, and raised her in Mexico. For a variety of reasons, Eve hadn't reconnected with her lost daughter until recently. Meg's own father, about whom she knew little, had died in an accident a month before she was born. Nobody liked to talk about him—even his name was a mystery.

"And you think I'll make the same mistakes my mother did?" Meg said.

"Hell," Angus said, sparing her a reluctant grin, "right now, even a *mistake* would be progress."

"With all due respect," Meg replied, "having you around all the time is not exactly conducive to romance."

They started the long climb uphill, headed for the house that now belonged to her and Sierra. Meg had always loved that house—it had been a refuge for her, full of cousins. Looking back, she wondered why, given that Eve had rarely accompanied her on those summer visits, had instead left her daughter in the care of a succession of nannies and, later, aunts and uncles.

Sierra's kidnapping had been a traumatic event, for certain, but the problems Eve had subsequently developed because of it had left Meg relatively unmarked. She hadn't been lonely as a child, mainly because of Angus.

"I'll stay clear tomorrow night, when you go to Stone Creek for that drink," Angus said.

"You like Brad."

"Always did. Liked Travis, too. 'Course, I knew he was meant for your sister, that they'd meet up in time."

Meg and Sierra's husband, Travis, were old friends. They'd tried to get something going, convinced they were perfect for each other, but it hadn't worked. Now that Travis and Sierra were together, and ecstatically happy, Meg was glad.

"Don't get your hopes up," she said. "About Brad and me, I mean."

Angus didn't reply. He appeared to be deep in thought. Or maybe as he looked out at the surrounding countryside, he was remembering his youth, when he'd staked a claim to this land and held it with blood and sweat and sheer McKettrick stubbornness.

"You must have known the O'Ballivans," Meg reflected, musing. Like her own family, Brad's had been pioneers in this part of Arizona.

"I was older than dirt by the time Sam O'Ballivan brought his bride, Maddie, up from Haven. Might have seen them once or twice. But I knew Major Blackstone, all right." Angus smiled at some memory. "He and I used to arm wrestle sometimes, in the card room back of Jolene Bell's Saloon, when we couldn't best each other at poker."

"Who won?" Meg asked, smiling slightly at the image.

"Same as the poker," Angus answered with a sigh. "We'd always come out about even. He'd win half the time, me the other half."

The house came in sight, the barn towering nearby. Angus's expression took on a wistful aspect.

"When you're here," Meg ventured, "can you see Doss and Hannah and Tobias? Talk to them?"

"No," Angus said flatly.

"Why not?" Meg persisted, even though she knew Angus didn't want to pursue the subject.

"Because they're not dead," he said. "They're just on the other side, like my boys."

"Well, I'm not dead, either," Meg said reasonably. She refrained from adding that she could have shown him their graves, up in the McKettrick cemetery. Shown him his own, for that matter. It would have been unkind, of course, but there was another reason for her reluctance, too. In some version of that cemetery, given what he'd told her about time, there was surely a headstone with *her* name on it.

"You wouldn't understand," Angus told her. He always said that, when she tried to find out how it was for him, where he went when he wasn't following her around.

"Try me," she said.

He vanished.

Resigned, Meg pulled up in front of the garage, added onto the original house sometime in the 1950s, and equipped with an automatic door opener, and pushed the button so she could drive in.

She half expected to find Angus sitting at the kitchen table when she went into the house, but he wasn't there.

What she needed, she decided, was a cup of tea.

She got Lorelei's teapot out of the built-in china cabinet and set it firmly on the counter. The piece was legendary in the family; it had a way of moving back to the cupboard of its own volition, from the table or the counter, and vice versa.

Meg filled the electric kettle at the sink and plugged it in to heat.

Tea was not going to cure what ailed her.

Brad O'Ballivan was back.

Compared to that, ghosts, the mysteries of time and space, and teleporting teapots seemed downright mundane.

And she'd agreed, like a fool, to meet him in Stone Creek for a drink. What had she been thinking?

Standing there in her kitchen, Meg leaned against the counter and folded her arms, waiting for the tea water to boil. Brad had hurt her so badly, she'd thought she'd never recover. For years after he'd dumped her to go to Nashville, she'd barely been able to come back to Indian Rock, and when she had, she'd driven straight to the Dixie Dog, against her will, sat in some rental car, and cried like an idiot.

There are some things I'd like to say to you, Brad had told her, that very day.

"What things?" she asked now, aloud.

The teakettle whistled.

She unplugged it, measured loose orange pekoe into Lorelei's pot and poured steaming water over it.

It was just a drink, Meg reminded herself. An innocent drink.

She should call Brad, cancel gracefully.

Or, better yet, she could just stand him up. Not show up at all. Just as he'd done to her, way back when, when she'd loved him with all her heart and soul, when she'd believed he meant to make a place for her in his busy, exciting life.

Musing, Meg laid a hand to her lower abdomen.

She'd stopped believing in a lot of things when Brad O'Ballivan ditched her.

Maybe he wanted to apologize.

She gave a teary snort of laughter.

And maybe he really had fans on other planets.

A rap at the back door made her start. Angus? He never knocked—he just appeared. Usually at the most inconvenient possible time.

Meg went to the door, peered through the old, thick panes of greenish glass, saw Travis Reid looming on the other side. She wrestled with the lock and let him in.

"I'm here on reconnaissance," he announced, taking off his cowboy hat and hanging it on the peg next to the door. "Sierra's worried about you, and so is Eve."

Meg put a hand to her forehead. She'd left the baby shower abruptly to go meet Brad at the Dixie Dog Drive-In. "I'm sorry," she said, stepping back so Travis could come inside. "I'm all right, really. You shouldn't have come all the way out here—"

"Eve tried your cell—which is evidently off—and Sierra left three or four messages on voice mail," he said with a nod toward the kitchen telephone. "Consider yourself fortunate that I got here before they called out the National Guard."

Meg laughed, closed the door against the chilly October twilight, and watched as Travis took off his sheepskin-lined coat and hung it next to the hat. "I was just feeling a little—overwhelmed."

"Overwhelmed?" She'd been *possessed*.

Travis went to the telephone, punched in a sequence of numbers and waited. "Hi, honey," he said presently, when Sierra answered. "Meg's alive and well. No armed intruders. No bloody accident. She was just—overwhelmed."

"Tell her I'll call her later," Meg said. "Mom, too."

"She'll call you later," Travis repeated dutifully. "Eve, too." He listened again, promised to pick up a gallon of milk and a loaf of bread on the way home and hung up.

Knowing Travis wasn't fond of tea, Meg offered him a cup of instant coffee, instead.

He accepted, taking a seat at the table where generations of McKettricks, from Holt and Lorelei on down, had taken their meals. "What's really going on, Meg?" he asked quietly, watching her as she poured herself some tea and joined him.

"What makes you think anything is going on?"

"I know you. We tried to fall in love, remember?"

"Brad O'Ballivan's back," she said.

Travis nodded. "And this means—?"

"Nothing," Meg answered, much too quickly. "It means nothing. I just—"

Travis settled back in his chair, folded his arms, and waited.

"Okay, it was a shock," Meg admitted. She sat up a little straighter. "But you already knew."

"Jesse told me."

"And nobody thought to mention it to me?"

"I guess we assumed you'd talked to Brad."

"Why would I do that?"

"Because—" Travis paused, looked uncomfortable. "It's no secret that the two of you had a thing going, Meg. Indian Rock and Stone Creek are small places, forty miles apart. Things get around."

Meg's face burned. She'd thought, she'd truly believed, that no one on earth knew Brad had broken her heart. She'd pretended it didn't matter that he'd left town so abruptly. Even laughed about it. Gone on to finish college, thrown herself into that first entry-level job at McKettrickCo. Dated other men, including the then-single Travis.

And she hadn't fooled anyone.

"Are you going to see him again?"

Meg pressed the tips of her fingers hard into her closed eyes. Nodded. Then shook her head from side to side.

Travis chuckled. "Make a decision, Meg," he said.

"We're supposed to have a drink together tomorrow night, at a cowboy bar in Stone Creek. I don't know why I said I'd meet him—after all this time, what do we have to say to each other?"

"'How've ya been?'" Travis suggested.

"I *know* how he's been—rich and famous, married twice, busy building a reputation that makes Jesse's look tame," she said. "I, on the other hand, have been a workaholic. Period."

"Aren't you being a little hard on yourself? Not to mention

Brad?" A grin quirked the corner of Travis's mouth. "Comparing him to *Jesse?*"

Jesse had been a wild man, if a good-hearted, well-intentioned one, until he'd met up with Cheyenne Bridges. When he'd fallen, he'd fallen hard, and for the duration, the way bad boys so often do.

"Maybe Brad's changed," Travis said.

"Maybe not," Meg countered.

"Well, I guess you *could* leave town for a while. Stay out of his way." Travis was trying hard not to smile. "Volunteer for a space mission or something."

"I am *not* going to run," Meg said. "I've always wanted to live right here, on this ranch, in this house. Besides, I intend to be here when the baby comes."

Travis's face softened at the mention of the impending birth. Until Sierra came along, Meg hadn't thought he'd ever settle down. He'd had his share of demons to overcome, not the least of which was the tragic death of his younger brother. Travis had blamed himself for what happened to Brody. "Good," he said. "But what do you actually *do* here? You're used to the fast lane, Meg."

"I take care of the horses," she said.

"That takes, what—two hours a day? According to Eve, you spend most of your time in your pajamas. She thinks you're depressed."

"Well, I'm not," Meg said. "I'm just—catching up on my rest."

"Okay," Travis said, drawing out the word.

"I'm not drinking alone and I'm not watching soap operas," Meg said. "I'm vegging. It's a concept my mother doesn't understand."

"She loves you, Meg. She's worried. She's not the enemy."

"I wish she'd go back to Texas."

"Wish away. She's not going anywhere, with a grand-child coming."

At least Eve hadn't taken up residence on the ranch; that was some comfort. She lived in a small suite at the only hotel in Indian Rock, and kept herself busy shopping, day trading on her laptop and spoiling Liam.

Oh, yes. And nagging Meg.

Travis finished his coffee, carried his cup to the sink, rinsed it out. After hesitating for a few moments, he said, "It's this thing about seeing Angus's ghost. She thinks you're obsessed."

Meg made a soft, strangled sound of frustration.

"It's not that she doesn't believe you," Travis added.

"She just thinks I'm a little crazy."

"No," Travis said. "Nobody thinks that."

"But I should get a life, as the saying goes?"

"It would be a good idea, don't you think?"

"Go home. Your pregnant wife needs a gallon of milk and a loaf of bread."

Travis went to the door, put on his coat, took his hat from the hook. "What do *you* need, Meg? That's the question."

"Not Brad O'Ballivan, that's for sure."

Travis grinned again. Set his hat on his head and turned the doorknob. "Did I mention him?" he asked lightly.

Meg glared at him.

"See you," Travis said. And then he was gone.

"He puts me in mind of that O'Ballivan fella," Angus announced, nearly startling Meg out of her skin.

She turned to see him standing over by the china cabinet. Was it her imagination, or did he look a little older than he had that afternoon?

"Jesse looks like Jeb. Rance looks like Rafe. Keegan looks like Kade. You're seeing things, Angus."

"Have it your way," Angus said.

Like any McKettrick had ever said *that* and meant it.

"What's for supper?"

"What do you care? You never eat."

"Neither do you. You're starting to look like a bag of bones."

"If I were you, I wouldn't make comments about bones. Being dead and all, I mean."

"The problem with you young people is, you have no respect for your elders."

Meg sighed, got up from her chair at the table, stomped over to the refrigerator and selected a boxed dinner from the stack in the freezer. The box was coated with frost.

"I'm sorry," Meg said. "Is that a hint of silver I see at your temples?"

Self-consciously, Angus shifted his weight from one booted foot to the other. "If I'm going gray," he scowled, "it's on account of you. None of my boys ever gave me half as much trouble as you, or my Katie, either. And they were plum full of the dickens, all of them."

Meg's heart pinched. Katie was Angus's youngest child, and his only daughter. He rarely mentioned her, since she'd caused some kind of scandal by eloping on her wedding day—with someone other than the groom. Although she and Angus had eventually reconciled, he'd been on his deathbed at the time.

"I'm *all right,* Angus," she told him. "You can go. Really."

"You eat food that could be used to drive railroad spikes into hard ground. You don't have a husband. You rattle around in this old house like some—ghost. I'm not leaving until I know you'll be happy."

"I'm happy *now.*"

Angus walked over to her, the heels of his boots thumping on the plank floor, took the frozen dinner out of her hands, and carried it to the trash compactor. Dropped it inside.

"Damn fool contraption," he muttered.

"That was my supper," Meg objected.

"Cook something," Angus said. "Get out a skillet. Dump some lard into it. Fry up a chicken." He paused, regarded her darkly. "You *do* know how to cook, don't you?"

Chapter Three

Jolene's, built on the site of the old saloon and brothel where Angus McKettrick and Major John Blackstone used to arm wrestle, among other things, was dimly lit and practically empty. Meg paused on the threshold, letting her eyes adjust and wishing she'd listened to her instincts and cancelled; now there would be no turning back.

Brad was standing by the jukebox, the colored lights flashing across the planes of his face. Having heard the door open, he turned his head slightly to acknowledge her arrival with a nod and a wisp of a grin.

"Where is everybody?" she asked. Except for the bartender, she and Brad were alone.

"Staying clear," Brad said. "I promised a free concert in the high school gym if we could have Jolene's to ourselves for a couple of hours."

Meg nearly fled. If it hadn't been against the McKettrick code, as inherent to her being as her DNA, she would have given in to the urge and called it good judgment.

"Have a seat," Brad said, drawing back a chair at one of the tables. Nothing in the whole tavern matched, not even the bar stools, and every stick of furniture was scarred and scratched. Jolene's was a hangout for honky-tonk angels; the winged variety would surely have given the place a wide berth.

"What'll it be?" the bartender asked. He was a squat man, wearing a muscle shirt and a lot of tattoos. With his handle-bar mustache, he might have been from Angus's era, instead of the present day.

Brad ordered a cola as Meg forced herself across the room to take the chair he offered.

Maybe, she thought, as she asked for an iced tea, the rumors were true, and Brad was fresh out of rehab.

The bartender served the drinks and quietly left the saloon, via a back door.

Brad, meanwhile, turned his own chair around and sat astraddle it, with his arms resting across the back. He wore jeans, a white shirt open at the throat and boots, and if he hadn't been so breathtakingly handsome, he'd have looked like any cowboy, in any number of scruffy little redneck bars scattered all over Arizona.

Meg eyed his drink, since doing that seemed slightly less dangerous than looking straight into his face, and when he chuckled, she felt her cheeks turn warm.

Pride made her meet his gaze. "What?" she asked, running damp palms along the thighs of her oldest pair of jeans. She'd made a point of *not* dressing up for the encounter—no perfume, and only a little mascara and lip gloss. War paint,

Angus called it. Her favorite ghost had an opinion on everything, it seemed, but at least he'd honored his promise not to
horn in on this interlude, or whatever it was, with Brad.

"Don't believe everything you read," Brad said easily,
settling back in his chair. "Not about me, anyway."

"Who says I've been reading about you?"

"Come on, Meg. You expected me to drink Jack Daniel's
straight from the bottle. That's hype—part of the bad-boy
image. My manager cooked it up."

Meg huffed out a sigh. "You haven't been to rehab?"

He grinned. "Nope. Never trashed a hotel room, spent a
weekend in jail, or any of the rest of the stuff Phil wanted
everybody to believe about me."

"Really?"

"Really." Brad pushed back his chair, returned to the
jukebox, and dropped a few coins in the slot. An old Johnny
Cash ballad poured softly into the otherwise silent bar.

Meg took a swig of her iced tea, in a vain effort to steady
her nerves. She was no teetotaler, but when she drove, she
didn't drink. Ever. Right about then, though, she wished she'd
hired a car and driver so she could get sloshed enough to
forget that being alone with Brad O'Ballivan was like having
her most sensitive nerves bared to a cold wind.

He started in her direction, then stopped in the middle of
the floor, which was strewn with sawdust and peanut shells.
Held out a hand to her.

Meg went to him, just the way she'd gone to the Dixie Dog
Drive-In the day before. Automatically.

He drew her into his arms, holding her close but easy, and
they danced without moving their feet.

As the song ended, Brad propped his chin on top of Meg's
head and sighed. "I've missed you," he said.

Meg came to her senses.

Finally.

She pulled back far enough to look up into his face.

"Don't go there," she warned.

"We can't just pretend the past didn't happen, Meg," he reasoned quietly.

"Yes, we can," she argued. "Millions of people do it, every day. It's called denial, and it has its place in the scheme of things."

"Still a McKettrick," Brad said, sorrow lurking behind the humor in his blue eyes. "If I said the moon was round, you'd call it square."

She poked at his chest with an index finger. "Still an O'Ballivan," she accused. "Thinking you've got to explain the shape of the moon, as if I couldn't see it for myself."

The jukebox in Jolene's was an antique; it still played 45s, instead of CDs. Now a record flopped audibly onto the turntable, and the needle scratched its way into Willie Nelson's version of "Georgia."

Meg stiffened, wanting to pull away.

Brad's arms, resting loosely around her waist, tightened slightly.

Over the years, the McKettricks and the O'Ballivans, owning the two biggest ranches in the area, had been friendly rivals. The families were equally proud and equally stubborn—they'd had to be, to survive the ups and downs of raising cattle for more than a century. Even when they were close, Meg and Brad had always identified strongly with their heritages.

Meg swallowed. "Why did you come back?" she asked, without intending to speak at all.

"To settle some things," Brad answered. They were swaying to the music again, though the soles of their boots were still rooted to the floor. "And you're at the top of my list, Meg McKettrick."

"You're at the top of mine, too," Meg retorted. "But I don't think we're talking about the same kind of list."

He laughed. God, how she'd missed that sound. How she'd missed the heat and substance of him, and the sun-dried laundry smell of his skin and hair...

Stop, she told herself. She was acting like some smitten fan or something.

"You bought me an engagement ring," she blurted, without intending to do anything of the kind. "We were supposed to elope. And then you got on a bus and went to Nashville and married what's-her-name!"

"I was stupid," Brad said. "And scared."

"No," Meg replied, fighting back furious tears. "You were *ambitious.* And of course the bride's father owned a recording company—"

Brad closed his eyes for a moment. A muscle bunched in his cheek. "Valerie," he said miserably. "Her name was Valerie."

"Do you really think I give a damn what her name was?"

"Yeah," he answered. "I do."

"Well, you're wrong!"

"That must be why you look like you want to club me to the ground with the nearest blunt object."

"I got over you like that!" Meg told him, snapping her fingers. But a tear slipped down her cheek, spoiling the whole effect.

Brad brushed it away gently with the side of one thumb. "Meg," he said. "I'm so sorry."

"Oh, that changes everything!" Meg scoffed. She tried to move away from him again, but he still wouldn't let her go.

One corner of his mouth tilted up in a forlorn effort at a

grin. "You'll feel a lot better if you forgive me." He curved the fingers of his right hand under her chin, lifted. "For old times' sake?" he cajoled. "For the nights when we went skinny-dipping in the pond behind your house on the Triple M? For the nights we—"

"No," Meg interrupted, fairly smothering as the memories wrapped themselves around her. "You don't deserve to be forgiven."

"You're right," Brad agreed. "I don't. But that's the thing about forgiveness. It's all about grace, isn't it? It's supposed to be undeserved."

"Great logic if you're on the *receiving* end!"

"I had my reasons, Meg."

"Yeah. You wanted bright lights and big money. Oh, and fast women."

Brad's jaw tightened, but his eyes were bleak. "I couldn't have married you, Meg."

"Pardon my confusion. You gave me an engagement ring and proposed!"

"I wasn't thinking." He looked away, faced her again with visible effort. "You had a trust fund. I had a mortgage and a pile of bills. I laid awake nights, sweating blood, thinking the bank would foreclose at any minute. I couldn't dump that in your lap."

Meg's mouth dropped open. She'd known the O'Ballivans weren't rich, at least, not like the McKettricks were, but she'd never imagined, even once, that Stone Creek Ranch was in danger of being lost.

"They wanted that land," Brad went on. "The bankers, I mean. They already had the plans drawn up for a housing development."

"I didn't know—I would have helped—"

"Sure," Brad said. "You'd have helped. And I'd never have been able to look you in the face again. I had one chance, Meg. Valerie's dad had heard my demo and he was willing to give me an audition. A fifteen-minute slot in his busy day. I tried to tell you—"

Meg closed her eyes for a moment, remembering. Brad had told her he wanted to postpone the wedding until after his trip to Nashville. He'd promised to come back for her. She'd been furious and hurt—and keeping a secret of her own—and they'd argued....

She swallowed painfully. "You didn't call. You didn't write—"

"When I got to Nashville, I had a used bus ticket and a guitar. If I'd called, it would have been collect, and I wasn't *about* to do that. I started half a dozen letters, but they all sounded like the lyrics to bad songs. I went to the library a couple of times, to send you an e-mail, but beyond 'how are you?' I just flat-out didn't know what to say."

"So you just hooked up with Valerie?"

"It wasn't like that."

"I'm assuming she was a rich kid, just like me? I guess you didn't mind if *she* saved the old homestead with a chunk of her trust fund."

Brad's jawline tightened. "*I* saved the ranch," he said. "Most of the money from my first record contract went to paying down the mortgage, and it was still a struggle until I scored a major hit." He paused, obviously remembering the much leaner days before he could fill the biggest stadiums in the country with devoted fans, swaying to his music in the darkness, holding flickering lighters aloft in tribute. "I didn't love Valerie, and she didn't love me. She was a rich kid, all right. Spoiled and lonesome, neglected in the ways rich kids so often are, and she was in big trouble. She'd gotten herself pregnant by some married guy who wanted nothing to do with her. She figured her dad would kill her if he found out, and given his temper, I tended to agree. So I married her."

Meg made her way back to the table and sank into her chair. "There was…a baby?"

"She miscarried. We divorced amicably, after trying to make it work for a couple of years. She's married to a dentist now, and really happy. Four kids, at last count." Brad joined Meg at the table. "Do you want to hear about the second marriage?"

"I don't think I'm up to that," Meg said weakly.

Brad's hand closed over hers. "Me, either," he replied. He ducked his head, in a familiar way that tugged at Meg's heart, to catch her eye. "You all right?"

"Just a little shaken up, that's all."

"How about some supper?"

"They serve supper here? At Jolene's?"

Brad chuckled. "Down the road, at the Steakhouse. You can't miss it—it's right next to the sign that says, Welcome To Stone Creek, Arizona, Home Of Brad O'Ballivan."

"Braggart," Meg said, grateful that the conversation had taken a lighter turn.

He grinned engagingly. "Stone Creek has always been the home of Brad O'Ballivan," he said. "It just seems to mean more now than it did when I left that first time."

"You'll be mobbed," Meg warned.

"The whole town could show up at the Steakhouse, and it wouldn't be enough to make a mob."

"Okay," Meg agreed. "But you're buying."

Brad laughed. "Fair enough," he said.

Then he got up from his chair and summoned the bartender, who'd evidently been cooling his heels in a storeroom or office.

The floor felt oddly spongy beneath Meg's feet, and she was light-headed enough to wonder if there'd been some alcohol in that iced tea after all.

The Steakhouse, unlike Jolene's, was jumping. People called out to Brad when he came in, and young girls pointed and giggled, but most of them had been at the welcome party Ashley and Melissa had thrown for him on the ranch the night before, so some of the novelty of his being back in town had worn off.

Meg drew some glances, though—all of them admiring, with varying degrees of curiosity mixed in. Even in jeans, boots and a plain woolen coat over a white blouse, she looked like what she was—a McKettrick with a trust fund and an impressive track record as a top-level executive. When McKettrickCo had gone public, Brad had been surprised when she didn't turn up immediately as the CEO of some corporation. Instead, she'd come home to hibernate on the Triple M, and he wondered why.

He wondered lots of things about Meg McKettrick.

With luck, he'd have a chance to find out everything he wanted to know.

Like whether she still laughed in her sleep and ate cereal with yogurt instead of milk and arched her back like a gymnast when she climaxed.

Since the Steakhouse was no place to think about Meg having one of her noisy orgasms, Brad tried to put the image out of his mind. It merely shifted to another part of his anatomy.

They were shown to a booth right away, and given menus and glasses of water with the obligatory slices of fresh lemon rafting on top of the ice.

Brad ordered a steak, Meg a Caesar salad.

The waitress went away, albeit reluctantly.

"Okay," Brad said, "it's my turn to ask questions. Why did you quit working after you left McKettrickCo?"

Meg smiled, but she looked a little flushed, and he could tell by her eyes that she was busy in there, sorting things and putting them in their proper places. "I didn't need the money. And I've always wanted to live full-time on the Triple M, like Jesse and Rance and Keegan. When I spent summers there, as a child, the only way I could deal with leaving in the fall to go back to school was to promise myself that one day I'd come home to stay."

"You love it that much?" Given his own attachment to Stone Creek Ranch, Brad could understand, but at the same time, the knowledge troubled him a little, too. "What do you do all day?"

Her mouth quirked in a way that made Brad want to kiss her. And do a few other things, too. "You sound like my mother," she said. "I take care of the horses, ride sometimes—"

He nodded. Waited.

She didn't finish the sentence.

"You never married." He hadn't meant to say that. Hadn't meant to let on that he'd kept track of her all these years, mostly on the Internet, but through his sisters, too.

She shook her head. "Almost," she said. "Once. It didn't work out."

Brad leaned forward, intrigued and feeling pretty damn territorial, too. "Who was the unlucky guy? He must have been a real jackass."

"You," she replied sweetly, and then laughed at the expression on his face.

He started to speak, then gulped the words down, sure they'd come out sounding as stupid as the question he'd just asked.

"I've dated a lot of men," Meg said.

The orgasm image returned, but this time, he wasn't Meg's

partner. It was some other guy bringing her to one of her long, exquisite, clawing, shouting, bucking climaxes, not him. He frowned.

"Maybe we shouldn't talk about my love life," she suggested.

"Maybe not," Brad agreed.

"Not that I exactly have one."

Brad felt immeasurably better. "That makes two of us."

Meg looked unconvinced. Even squirmed a little on the vinyl seat.

"What?" Brad prompted, enjoying the play of emotions on her face. He and Meg weren't on good terms—too soon for that—but it was a hopeful sign that she'd met him at Jolene's and then agreed to supper on top of it.

"I saw that article in *People* magazine. 'The Cowboy with the Most Notches on His Bedpost,' I think it was called?"

"I thought we weren't going to talk about our love lives. And would you mind keeping your voice down?"

"We agreed not to talk about *mine,* if I remember correctly, which, as I told you, is nonexistent. And to avoid the subject of your second wife—at least, for now."

"There have been women," Brad said. "But that bedpost thing was all Phil's idea. Publicity stuff."

The food arrived.

"Not that I care if you carve notches on your bedpost," Meg said decisively, once the waitress had left again.

"Right," Brad replied, serious on the outside, grinning on the inside.

"Where is this Phil person from, anyway?" Meg asked, mildly disgruntled, her fork poised in midair over her salad. "Seems to me he has a pretty skewed idea on the whole cowboy mystique. Rehab. Trashing hotel rooms. The notch thing."

"There's a 'cowboy mystique'?"

"You know there is. Honor, integrity, courage—those are the things being a cowboy is all about."

Brad sighed. Meg was a stickler for detail; good thing she hadn't gone to law school, like she'd once planned. She probably would have represented his second ex-wife in the divorce and stripped his stock portfolio clean. "I tried. Phil works freestyle, and he sure knew how to pack the concert halls."

Meg pointed the fork at him. "*You* packed the concert halls, Brad. You and your music."

"You like my music?" It was a shy question; he hadn't quite dared to ask if she liked *him* as well. He knew too well what the answer might be.

"It's...nice," she said.

Nice? Half a dozen Grammies and CMT awards, weeks at number one on every chart that mattered, and she thought his music was "nice"?

Whatever she thought, Brad finally concluded, that was all she was going to give up, and he had to be satisfied with it.

For now.

He started on the steak, but he hadn't eaten more than two bites when there was a fuss at the entrance to the restaurant and Livie came storming in, striding right to his table.

Sparing a nod for Meg, Brad's sister turned immediately to him. "He's hurt," she said. Her clothes were covered with straw and a few things that would have upset the health department, being that she was in a place where food was being served to the general public.

"Who's hurt?" Brad asked calmly, sliding out of the booth to stand.

"Ransom," she answered, near tears. "He got himself cut up in a tangle of rusty barbed wire. I'd spotted him with binoculars, but before I could get there to help, he'd torn free and headed for the hills. He's hurt bad, and I'm not going to be able to get to him in the Suburban—we need to saddle up and go after him."

"Liv," Brad said carefully, "it's dark out."

"He's *bleeding,* and probably weak. The wolves could take him down!" At the thought of that, Livie's eyes glistened with moisture. "If you won't help, I'll go by myself."

Distractedly, Brad pulled out his wallet and threw down the money for the dinner he and Meg hadn't gotten a chance to finish.

Meg was on her feet, the salad forgotten. "Count me in, Olivia," she said. "That is, if you've got an extra horse and some gear. I could go back out to the Triple M for Banshee, but by the time I hitched up the trailer, loaded him and gathered the tack—"

"You can ride Cinnamon," Olivia told Meg, after sizing her up as to whether she'd be a help or a hindrance on the trail. "It'll be cold and dark up there in the high country," she added. "Could be a long, uncomfortable night."

"No room service?" Meg quipped.

Livie spared her a smile, but when she turned to Brad again, her blue eyes were full of obstinate challenge. "Are you going or not—cowboy?"

"Hell, yes, I'm going," Brad said. Riding a horse was a thing you never forgot how to do, but it had been a while since he'd been in the saddle, and that meant he'd be groaning-sore before this adventure was over. "What about the stock on the Triple M, Meg? Who's going to feed your horses, if this takes all night?"

"They're good till morning," Meg answered. "If I'm not back by then, I'll ask Jesse or Rance or Keegan to check on them."

Livie led the caravan in her Suburban, with Brad following in his truck, and Meg right behind, in the Blazer. He was worried about Ransom, and about Livie's obsession with the animal, but there was one bright spot in the whole thing.

He was going to get to spend the night with Meg McKettrick, albeit on the hard, half-frozen ground, and the least he could do, as a gentleman, was share his sleeping bag—and his body warmth.

"Right smart of you to go along," Angus commented, appearing in the passenger seat of Meg's rig. "There might be some hope for you yet."

Meg answered without moving her mouth, just in case Brad happened to glance into his rearview mirror and catch her talking to nobody. "I thought you were giving me some elbow room on this one," she said.

"Don't worry," Angus replied. "If you go to bed down with him or something like that, I'll skedaddle."

"I'm not going to 'bed down' with Brad O'Ballivan."

Angus sighed. Adjusted his sweat-stained cowboy hat. Since he usually didn't wear one, Meg read it as a sign bad weather was on its way. "Might be a good thing if you did. Only way to snag some men."

"I will not dignify that remark with a reply," Meg said, flooring the gas pedal to keep up with Brad, now that they were out on the open road, where the speed limit was higher. She'd never actually been to Stone Creek Ranch, but she knew where it was. Knew all about King's Ransom, too. Her cousin Jesse, practically a horse-whisperer, claimed the animal was nothing more than a legend, pieced together around a hundred campfires, over as many years, after all the lesser tales had been told.

Meg wanted to see for herself.

Wanted to help Olivia, whom she'd always liked but barely knew.

Spending the night on a mountain with Brad O'Ballivan didn't enter into the decision at all. Much.

"Is he real?" she asked. "The horse, I mean?"

Angus adjusted his hat again. "Sure he is," he said, his voice quiet, but gruff. Sometimes a look came into his eyes, a sort of hunger for the old days and the old ways.

"Is there anything you can do to help us find him?"

Angus shook his head. "You've got to do that yourselves, you and the singing cowboy and the girl."

"Olivia is not a girl. She's a grown woman and a veterinarian."

"She's a snippet," Angus said. "But there's fire in her. That O'Ballivan blood runs hot as coffee brewed on a cook-stove in hell. She needs a man, though. The knot in *her* lasso is way too tight."

"I hope that reference wasn't sexual," Meg said stiffly, "because I do *not* need to be carrying on that type of conversation with my dead multi-great grandfather."

"It makes me feel old when you talk about me like I helped Moses carry the commandments down off the mountain," Angus complained. "I was young once, you know. Sired four strapping sons and a daughter by three different women— Ellie, Georgia and Concepcion. And I'm not dead, neither. Just…different."

Olivia had stopped suddenly for a gate up ahead, and Meg nearly rear-ended Brad before she got the Blazer reined in.

"Different as in dead," Meg said, watching through the windshield, in the glow of her headlights, as Brad got out of his truck and strode back to speak to her, leaving the driver's-side door gaping behind him.

He didn't look angry—just earnest.

"If you want to ride with me," he said when Meg had buzzed down her window, "fine. But if you're planning to drive this rig up into the bed of my truck, you might want to wait until I park it in a hole and lower the tailgate."

"Sorry," Meg said after making a face.

Brad shook his head and went back to his truck. By then, Olivia had the gate open, and he drove ahead onto an unpaved road winding upward between the juniper and Joshua trees clinging to the red dirt of the hillside.

"What was that about?" Meg mused, following Brad and Olivia's vehicles through the gap and not really addressing Angus, who answered, nonetheless.

"Guess he's prideful about the paint on that fancy jitney of his," he said. "Didn't want you denting up his buggy."

Meg didn't comment. Angus was full of the nineteenth-century equivalent of "woman driver" stories, and she didn't care to hear any of them.

They topped a rise, Olivia still in the lead, and dipped down into what was probably a broad valley, given what little Meg knew about the landscape on Stone Creek Ranch. Lights glimmered off to the right, revealing a good-size house and a barn.

Meg was about to ask if Angus had ever visited the ranch when he suddenly vanished.

She shut off the Blazer, got out and followed Brad and Olivia toward the barn. She wished it hadn't been so dark— it would have been interesting to see the place in the daylight.

Inside the barn, which was as big as any of the ones on the Triple M and boasted all the modern conveniences, Olivia and Brad were already saddling horses.

"That's Cinnamon over there," Olivia said with a nod to a

tall chestnut in the stall across the wide breezeway from the one she was standing in, busily preparing a palomino to ride. "His gear's in the tack room, third saddle rack on the right."

Meg didn't hesitate, as she suspected Olivia had expected her to do, but found the tack room and Cinnamon's gear, and lugged it back to his stall. Brad and his sister were already mounted and waiting at the end of the breezeway when Meg led the gelding out, however.

"Need a boost?" Brad asked, in a teasing drawl, saddle leather creaking as he shifted to step down from the big paint he was riding and help Meg mount up.

Cinnamon was a big fella, taller by several hands than any of the horses in Meg's barn, but she'd been riding since she was in diapers, and she didn't need a boost from a "singing cowboy," as Angus described Brad.

"I can do it," she replied, straining to grip the saddle horn and get a foot into the high stirrup. It was going to be a stretch.

In the next instant, she felt two strong hands pushing on her backside, hoisting her easily onto Cinnamon's broad back.

Thanks, Angus, she said silently.

Chapter Four

It was a purely crazy thing to do, setting out on horseback, in the dark, for the high plains and meadows and secret canyons of Stone Creek Ranch, in search of a legendary stallion determined not to be found. It had been way too long since she'd done anything like it, Meg reflected, as she rode behind Olivia and Brad, on the borrowed horse called Cinnamon.

Olivia had brought a few veterinary supplies along, packed in saddle bags, and while Meg was sure Ransom, wounded or not, would elude them, she couldn't help admiring the kind of commitment it took to set out on the journey anyway. Olivia O'Ballivan was a woman with a cause and for that, Meg envied her a little.

The moon was three-quarters full, and lit their way, but the trail grew steadily narrower as they climbed, and the mountainside was steep and rocky. One misstep on the part of a dis-tracted horse and both animal and rider would plunge hundreds of feet into an abyss of shadow, to their very certain and very painful deaths.

When the trail widened into what appeared, in the thin wash of moonlight, to be a clearing, Meg let out her breath, sat a little less tensely in the saddle, loosened her grip on Cinnamon's reins. Brad drew up his own mount to wait for her, while Olivia and her horse shot forward, intent on their mission.

"Do you think we'll find him?" Meg asked. "Ransom, I mean?"

"No," Brad answered, unequivocally. "But Livie was bound to try. I came to look out for her."

Meg hadn't noticed the rifle in the scabbard fixed to Brad's saddle before, back at the O'Ballivan barn, but it stood out in sharp relief now, the polished wooden stock glowing in a silvery flash of moonlight. He must have seen her eyes widen; he patted the scabbard as he met her gaze.

"You're expecting to shoot something?" Meg ventured. She'd been around guns all her life—they were plentiful on the Triple M—but that didn't mean she liked them.

"Only if I have to," Brad said, casting a glance in the di-rection Olivia had gone. He nudged his horse into motion, and Cinnamon automatically kept pace, the two geldings moving at an easy trot.

"What would constitute having to?" Meg asked.

"Wolves," Brad answered.

Meg was familiar with the wolf controversy—environmen-talists and animal activists on the one side, ranchers on the other. She wanted to know where Brad stood on the subject. He was well-known for his love of all things finned, feathered and furry—but that might have been part of his carefully constructed persona, like the notched bedpost and the trashed hotel rooms.

"You wouldn't just pick them off, would you? Wolves, I mean?"

"Of course not," Brad replied. "But wolves are predators, and Livie's not wrong to be concerned that they'll track Ransom and take him down if they catch the blood-scent from his wounds."

A chill trickled down Meg's spine, like a splash of cold water, setting her shivering. Like Brad, she came from a long line of cattle ranchers, and while she allowed that wolves had a place in the ecological scheme of things, like every other creature on earth, she didn't romanticize them. They were not misunderstood *dogs,* as so many people seemed to think, but hunters, savagely brutal and utterly ruthless, and no one who'd ever seen what they did to their prey would credit them with nobility.

"Sharks with legs," she mused aloud. "That's what Rance calls them."

Brad nodded, but didn't reply. They were gaining on Olivia now; she was still a ways ahead, and had dismounted to look at something on the ground.

Both Brad and Meg sped up to reach her.

By the time they arrived, Olivia's saddle bags were open beside her, and she was holding a syringe up to the light. Because of the darkness, and the movements of the horses, a few moments passed before Meg focused on the animal Olivia was treating.

A dog lay bloody and quivering on its side.

Brad was off his horse before Meg broke the spell of shock that had descended over her and dismounted, too. Her stomach rolled when she got a better look at the dog; the poor creature, surely a stray, had run afoul of either a wolf or coyote pack, and it was purely a miracle that he'd survived.

Meg's eyes burned.

Brad crouched next to the dog, opposite Olivia, and stroked the animal with a gentleness that altered something deep down inside Meg, causing a grinding sensation, like the shift of tectonic plates far beneath the earth.

"Can he make it?" he asked Olivia.

"I'm not sure," Olivia replied. "At the very least, he needs stitches." She injected the contents of the syringe into the animal's ruff. "I sedated him. Give the medicine a few minutes to work, and then we'll take him back to the clinic in Stone Creek."

"What about the horse?" Meg asked, feeling helpless, a bystander with no way to help. She wasn't used to it. "What about Ransom?"

Olivia's eyes were bleak with sorrow when she looked up at Meg. She was a veterinarian; she couldn't abandon the wounded dog, or put him to sleep because it would be more convenient than transporting him back to town, where he could be properly cared for. But worry for the stallion would prey on her mind, just the same.

"I'll look for him tomorrow," Olivia said. "In the daylight."

Brad reached across the dog, laid a hand on his sister's shoulder. "He's been surviving on his own for a long time, Liv," he assured her. "Ransom will be all right."

Olivia bit her lower lip, nodded. "Get one of the sleeping bags, will you?" she said.

Brad nodded and went to unfasten the bedroll from behind his saddle. They were miles from town, or any ranch house.

"How did a dog get all the way out here?" Meg asked, mostly because the silence was too painful.

"He's probably a stray," Olivia answered, between sooth-ing murmurs to the dog. "Somebody might have dumped him, too, down on the highway. A lot of people think dogs and cats can survive on their own—hunt and all that non-sense."

Meg drew closer to the dog, crouched to touch his head. He appeared to be some kind of lab-retriever mix, though it was hard to tell, given that his coat was saturated with blood. He wore no collar, but that didn't mean he didn't have a mi-crochip—and if he did, Olivia would be able to identify him immediately, once she got him to the clinic. Though from the looks of him, he'd be lucky to make it that far.

Brad returned with the sleeping bag, unfurling it. "Okay to move him now?" he asked Olivia.

Olivia nodded, and she and Meg sort of helped each other to their feet. "You mount up," Olivia told Brad. "And we'll lift him."

Brad whistled softly for his horse, which trotted obe-diently to his side, gathered the dangling reins, and swung up into the saddle.

Meg and Olivia bundled the dog, now mercifully uncon-scious, in the sleeping bag and, together, hoisted him high enough so Brad could take him into his arms. They all rode slowly back down the trail, Brad holding that dog as tenderly as he would an injured child, and not a word was spoken the whole way.

When they got back to the ranch house, where Olivia's Suburban was parked, Brad loaded the dog into the rear of the vehicle.

"I'll stay and put the horses away," Meg told him. "You'd better go into town with Olivia and help her get him inside the clinic."

Brad nodded. "Thanks," he said gruffly.

Olivia gave Meg an appreciative glance before scrambling into the back of the Suburban to ride with the patient, ambulance-style. Brad got behind the wheel.

Once they'd driven off, Meg gathered the trio of horses and led them into the barn. There, in the breezeway, she removed their saddles and other tack and let the animals show her which stalls were their own. She checked their hooves for stones, made sure their automatic waterers were working, and gave them each a flake of hay. All the while, her thoughts were with Brad, and the stray dog lying in the back of Olivia's rig.

A part of her wanted to get into the Blazer and head straight for Stone Creek, and the veterinary clinic where Olivia worked, but she knew she'd just be in the way. Brad could provide muscle and moral support, if not medical skills, but Meg had nothing to offer.

With the O'Ballivans' horses attended to, she fired up the Blazer and headed back toward Indian Rock. She covered the miles between Stone Creek Ranch and the Triple M in a daze, and was a little startled to find herself at home when she pulled up in front of the garage door.

Leaving the Blazer in the driveway, Meg went into the barn to look in on Banshee and the four other horses who resided there. On the Triple M, horses were continually rotated between her place, Jesse's, Rance's and Keegan's, depending on what was best for the animals. Now they blinked at her, sleepily surprised by a late-night visit, and she paused to stroke each one of their long faces before starting for the house.

Angus fell into step with her as she crossed the side yard, headed for the back door.

"The stallion's all right," he informed her. "Holed up in one of the little canyons, nursing his wounds."

"I thought you said you couldn't help find him," Meg said, stopping to stare up at her ancestor in the moonlight.

"Turned out I was wrong," Angus drawled. His hat was gone; the bad weather he'd probably been expecting hadn't materialized.

"Mark the calendar," Meg teased. "I just heard a McKettrick admit to being wrong about something."

Angus grinned, waited on the small, open back porch while she unlocked the kitchen door. In his day, locks hadn't been necessary. Now the houses on the Triple M were no more immune to the rising crime rate than anyplace else.

"I've been wrong about plenty in my life," Angus said. "For one thing, I was wrong to leave Holt behind in Texas, after his mother died. He was just a baby, and God knows what I'd have done with him on the trail between there and the Arizona Territory, but I should have brought him, nonetheless. Raised him with Rafe and Kade and Jeb."

Intrigued, Meg opened the door, flipped on the kitchen lights and stepped inside. All of this was ancient family history to her, but to Angus, it was immediate stuff. "What else were you wrong about?" she asked, removing her coat and hanging it on the peg next to the door, then going to the sink to wash her hands.

Angus took a seat at the head of the table. In this house, it would have been Holt's place, but Angus was in the habit of taking the lead, even in small things.

"I ever tell you I had a brother?" he asked.

Meg, about to brew a pot of tea, stopped and stared at him, stunned out of her fatigue. "No," she said. "You didn't." The McKettricks were raised on legend and lore, cut their teeth on it; the brother came as news. "Are you telling me there could be a whole other branch of the family out there?"

"Josiah got on fine with the ladies," Angus reminisced. "It would be my guess his tribe is as big as mine."

Meg forgot all about the tea-brewing. She made her way to the table and sat down heavily on the bench, gaping at Angus.

"Don't fret about it," he said. "They'd have no claim on this ranch, or any of the take from that McKettrickCo outfit."

Meg blinked, still trying to assimilate the revelation. "No one has *ever* mentioned that you had a brother," she said. "In all the diaries, all the letters, all the photographs—"

"They wouldn't have said anything about Josiah," Angus told her, evidently referring to his sons and their many descendents. "They never knew he existed."

"Why not?"

"Because he and I had a falling-out, and I didn't want anything to do with him after that. He felt the same way."

"Why bring it up now—after a century and a half?"

Angus shifted uncomfortably in his chair and, for a moment, his jawline hardened. "One of them's about to land on your doorstep," he said after a long, molar-grinding silence. "I figured you ought to be warned."

"*Warned?* Is this person a serial killer or a crook or something?"

"No," Angus said. "He's a lawyer. And that's damn near as bad."

"As a family, we haven't exactly kept a low profile for the last hundred or so years," Meg said slowly. "If Josiah has as many descendants as you do, why haven't any of them contacted us? It's not as if McKettrick is a common name, after all."

"Josiah took another name," Angus allowed, after more jaw-clamping. "That's what we got into it about, him and me."

"Why would he do that?" Meg asked.

Angus fixed her with a glare. Clearly, even after all the time that passed, he hadn't forgiven Josiah for changing his name and for whatever had prompted him to do that.

"He went to sea, when he was hardly more than a boy," Angus said. "When he came back home to Texas, years later, he was calling himself by another handle and running from the law. Hinted that he'd been a pirate."

"A *pirate?*"

"Left Ma and me to get by on our own, after Pa died," Angus recalled bitterly, looking through Meg to some long-ago reality. "Rode out before they'd finished shoveling dirt into Pa's grave. I ran down the road after him—he was riding a big buckskin horse—but he didn't even look back."

Tentatively, Meg reached out to touch Angus's arm. Clearly, Josiah had been the elder brother, and Angus a lot younger. He'd adored Josiah McKettrick—that much was plain—and his leaving had been a defining event in Angus's life. So defining, in fact, that he'd never acknowledged the other man's existence.

Angus bristled. "It was a long time ago," he said.

"What name did he go by?" Meg asked. She knew she wasn't going to sleep, for worrying about the injured dog and the stallion, and planned to spend the rest of the night at the computer, searching on Google for members of the heretofore unknown Josiah-side of the family.

"I don't rightly recall," Angus said glumly.

Meg knew he was lying. She also knew he wasn't going to tell her his brother's assumed name.

She got up again, went back to brewing tea.

Angus sat brooding in silence, and the phone rang just as Meg was pouring boiling water over the loose tea leaves in the bottom of Lorelei's pot.

Glancing at the caller ID panel, she saw no name, just an unfamiliar number with a 615 area code.

"Hello?"

"He's going to recover," Brad said.

Tears rushed to Meg's eyes, and her throat constricted. He was referring to the dog, of course. And using the cell phone he'd carried when he still lived in Tennessee. "Thank God," she managed to say. "Did Olivia operate?"

"No need," Brad answered. "Once she'd taken X-rays and run a scan, she knew there were no internal injuries. He's pretty torn up—looks like a baseball with all those stitches—but he'll be okay."

"Was there a microchip?"

"Yeah," Brad said after a charged silence. "But the phone number's no longer in service. Livie ran an Internet search and found out the original owner died six months ago. Who knows where Willie's been in the meantime."

"Willie?"

"The dog," Brad explained. "That's his name. Willie."

"What's going to happen to Willie now?"

"He'll be at the clinic for a while," Brad said. "He's in pretty bad shape. Livie will try to find out if anybody adopted him after his owner died, but we're not holding out a lot of hope on that score."

"He'll go to the pound? When he's well enough to leave the clinic?"

"No," Brad answered. He sounded as tired as Meg felt. "If nobody has a prior claim on him, he'll come to live with me. I could use a friend—and so could he." He paused. "I hope I didn't wake you or anything."

"I was still up," Meg said, glancing in Angus's direction only to find that he'd disappeared again.

"Good," Brad replied.

A silence fell between them. Meg knew there was something else Brad wanted to say, and that she'd want to hear it. So she waited.

"I'm riding up into the high country again first thing in the morning," he finally said. "Looking for Ransom. I was wondering if—well—it's probably a stupid idea, but—"

Meg waited, resisting an urge to rush in and finish the sentence for him.

"Would you like to go along? Livie has a full schedule tomorrow—one of the other vets is out sick—and she wants to keep an eye on Willie, too. She's going to obsess about this horse until I can tell her he's fine, so I'm going to find him if I can."

"I'd like to go," Meg said. "What time are you leaving the ranch?"

"Soon as the sun's up," Brad answered. "You're sure? The country's pretty rough up there."

"If you can handle rough country, O'Ballivan, so can I."

He chuckled. "Okay, McKettrick," he said.

Meg found herself smiling. "I'll be there by 6:00 a.m., unless that's too early. Shall I bring my own horse?"

"Six is about right," Brad said. "Don't go to the trouble of trailering another horse—you can ride Cinnamon. Dress warm, though. And bring whatever gear you'd need if we had to spend the night for some reason."

Alone in her kitchen, Meg blushed. "See you in the morning," she said.

"'Night," Brad replied.

"Good night," Meg responded—long after Brad had hung up.

Giving up on the tea and, at least for that night, researching Josiah McKettrick, and having decided she needed to at least *try* to sleep, since tomorrow would be an eventful day, Meg locked up, shut off the lights and went upstairs to her room.

After getting out a pair of thermal pajamas, she took a long shower in the main bathroom across the hall, brushed her teeth, tamed her wet hair as best she could and went to bed.

Far from tossing and turning, as she'd half expected, she dropped into an immediate, consuming slumber, so deep she remembered none of her dreams.

Waking, she dressed quickly, in jeans and a sweatshirt, over a set of long underwear, made of some miraculous microfiber and bought for skiing, and finished off her ensemble with two pairs of socks and her sturdiest pair of boots. She shoved toothpaste, a brush and a small tube of moisturizer into a plastic storage bag, rolled up a blanket, tied it tightly with twine from the kitchen junk drawer and breakfasted on toast and coffee.

She called Jesse on her cell phone as she climbed into the Blazer, after feeding Banshee and the others. Cheyenne, Jesse's wife, answered on the second ring.

"Hi, it's Meg. Is Jesse around?"

"Sleeping," Cheyenne said, yawning audibly.

"I woke you up," Meg said, embarrassed.

"Jesse's the lay-abed in this family," Cheyenne responded warmly. "I've been up since four. Is anything wrong, Meg? Sierra and the baby—?"

"They're fine, as far as I know," Meg said, anxious to reassure Cheyenne and, at the same time, very glad she'd gotten Jesse's wife instead of Jesse himself. He'd look after her horses if she asked, but he'd want to know where she was going, and if she replied that she and Brad O'Ballivan were riding off into the sunrise together, he'd tease her unmercifully. "Look, Cheyenne, I need a favor. I'm going on a—on a trail ride with a friend, and I'll probably be back tonight, but—"

"Would this 'friend' be the famous Brad O'Ballivan?"

"Yes," Meg said, but reluctantly, backing out of the driveway and turning the Blazer around to head for Stone Creek. It was still dark, but the first pinkish gold rays of sunlight were rimming the eastern hills. "Cheyenne, will you ask Jesse to check on my horses if he doesn't hear from me by six or so tonight?"

"Of course," Cheyenne said. "So you're going riding with Brad, and it might turn into an overnight thing. Hmmmmm—"

"It isn't anything romantic," Meg said. "I'm just helping him look for a stallion that might be hurt, that's all."

"I see," Cheyenne said sweetly.

"Just out of curiosity, what made you jump to the conclusion that the friend I mentioned was Brad?"

"It's all over town that you and country music's baddest bad boy met up at the Dixie Dog Drive-In the other day."

"Oh, great," Meg breathed. "I guess that means Jesse knows, then. And Rance and Keegan."

Cheyenne laughed softly, but when she spoke, her voice was full of concern. "Rance and Jesse are all for finding Brad and punching his lights out for hurting you so badly all those years ago, but Keegan is the voice of reason. He says give Brad a week to prove himself, *then* punch his lights out."

"The McKettrick way," Meg said. Her cousins were as protective as brothers would have been, and she loved them. But in terms of her social life, they weren't any more help than Angus had been.

"We'll talk later," Cheyenne said practically. "You're probably driving."

"Thanks, Chey," Meg answered.

When she got to Stone Creek Ranch, Brad came out of the house to greet her. He was dressed for the trail in jeans, boots, a work shirt and a medium-weight leather coat.

Meg's breath caught at the sight of him, and she was glad of the mechanics of parking and shutting off the Blazer, because it gave her a few moments to gather her composure.

Normally, she was unflappable.

She'd handled some of the toughest negotiations during her career with McKettrickCo, without so much as a flutter of nerves, but there was something about Brad that erased all the years she'd spent developing a thick skin and a poker face.

He opened the Blazer door before she was quite ready to face him.

"Hungry?" he asked.

"I had toast and coffee at home," Meg answered.

"That'll never hold you till lunch," he said. "Come on inside. I've got some *real* food on the stove."

"Okay," Meg said, because short of sitting stubbornly in the car, she couldn't think of a way to avoid accepting his invitation.

The O'Ballivan house, like the ones on the Triple M, was large and rustic, and it exuded a sense of rich history. The porch wrapped around the whole front of the structure, and the back door was on the side nearest the barn. Meg followed Brad up the porch steps in front and around to another entrance.

The kitchen was big, and except for the wooden floors, which looked venerable, the room showed no trace of the old days. The countertops were granite, the cupboards gleamed, and the appliances were ultramodern, as were the furnishings.

Meg felt strangely let down by the sheer glamour of the place. All the kitchens on the Triple M had been modernized, of course, but in all cases, the original wood-burning stoves had been incorporated, and the tables all dated back to Holt, Rafe, Kade and Jeb's time, if not Angus's.

If Brad noticed her reaction, he didn't mention it. He dished up an omelet for her, and poured her a cup of coffee.

"You cook?" Meg teased, washing her hands at the gleaming stainless steel sink.

"I'm a fair hand in a kitchen," Brad replied modestly. "Dig in. I'll go saddle the horses while you eat."

Meg nodded, sat down and tackled the omelet.

It was delicious, and so was the coffee, but she felt uncomfortable sitting alone in that kitchen, as fancy as it was. She kept wondering what Maddie O'Ballivan would think, if she could see it, or even Brad's mother. Surely if things had been as difficult financially as Brad had let on the night before, at Jolene's, the renovations were fairly recent.

Having eaten as much as she could, Meg rinsed her plate, stuck it into the dishwasher, along with her fork and coffee cup, and hurried to the back door. Brad was out in front of the barn, the big paint ready to ride, tightening the cinch on Cinnamon's saddle. He picked her rolled blanket up off the ground and tied it on behind.

"Not much gear," he said. "Do you know how cold it gets up there?"

"I'll be fine," Meg said.

Brad merely shook his head. His own horse was restless, and the rifle was in evidence, too, looking ominous in the worn scabbard.

"That's quite a kitchen," Meg said as Brad gave her a leg up onto Cinnamon's back.

"Big John said it was a waste of money," Brad recalled, smiling to himself as he mounted up. "That was my granddad."

Meg knew who Big John O'Ballivan was—everybody in the county did—but she didn't point that out. If Brad wanted to talk about his family, to pass the time, that was fine with

Meg. She nudged Cinnamon to keep pace with Brad's horse as they crossed a pasture, headed for the hills beyond.

"He raised you and your sisters, didn't he?" she asked, though she knew that, too.

"Yes," Brad said, and the set of his jaw reminded her of the way Angus's had looked, when he told her about his estranged brother.

Meg's curiosity spiked, but she didn't indulge it. "I take it Willie's still on the mend?"

Brad's grin was as dazzling as the coming sunrise would be. "Olivia called just before you showed up," he said with a nod. "Willie's going to be fine. In a week or two, I'll bring him home."

Remembering the way Brad had handled the dog, with such gentleness and such strength, Meg felt a pinch in the center of her heart. "You plan on staying, then?"

He tossed her a thoughtful look. "I plan on staying," he confirmed. "I told you that, didn't I?"

You also told me we'd get married and you'd love me forever.

"You told me," she said.

"Would this be a good time to tell you about my second wife?"

Meg considered, then shook her head, smiling a little. "Probably not."

"Okay," Brad said, "then how about my sisters?"

"Good idea." Meg had known Olivia slightly, but there was a set of twins in the family, too. She'd never met them.

"Olivia has a thing for animals, as you can see. She needs to get married and channel some of that energy into having a family of her own, but she's got a cussed streak and runs off every man who manages to get close to her. Ashley and Melissa—the twins—are fraternal. Ashley's pretty down-home—she runs a bed-and-breakfast in Stone Creek. Melissa's clerking in a law office in Flagstaff."

"You're close to them?"

"Yes," Brad said, expelling a long breath. "And, no. Olivia resents my leaving home— I can't seem to get it through her head that we wouldn't have *had* a home if I hadn't gone to Nashville. The twins are ten years younger than I am, and seem to see me more as a visiting celebrity than their big brother."

"When Olivia needed help," Meg reminded him, "she came to you. So maybe she doesn't resent you as much as you think she does." There was something really different about Olivia O'Ballivan, Meg thought, looking back over the night before, but she couldn't quite figure out what it was.

"I hope you're right," Brad said. "It's fine to love animals—I'm real fond of them myself. But Olivia carries it to a whole new place. So much so that there's no room in her life for much of anything—or anybody—else."

"She's a veterinarian, Brad," Meg said reasonably. "It's natural that animals are her passion."

"To the exclusion of everything else?" Brad asked.

"She'll be fine," Meg said. "When Olivia meets the right man, she'll make room for him. Just wait and see."

Brad looked unconvinced. He raised his chin and said, "If we're going to find that horse, we'd better move a little faster."

Meg nodded in agreement and Cinnamon fell in behind Brad's gelding as they started the twisting, perilous climb up the mountainside.

Chapter Five

Looking for that wild stallion was a fool's errand, and Brad knew it. As he'd told Meg, his primary reason for undertaking the quest was to keep Olivia from doing it. Now he wondered how many times, during his long absence, his little sister had climbed this mountain alone, at all hours of the day and night, and in all seasons of the year.

The thought made him shudder.

The country above Stone Creek was as rugged as it had ever been. Wolves, coyotes and even javelinas were plentiful, as were rattlesnakes. There were deep crevices in the red earth, some of them hidden by brush, and they'd swallowed many a hapless hiker. But the worst threat was probably the weather—at that elevation, blizzards could strike literally without warning, even in July and August. It was October now, and that only increased the danger.

Meg, shivering in her too-light coat, rode along beside him without complaint. Being a McKettrick, he thought, with a sad smile turned entirely inward, she'd freeze to death before she'd admit she was cold.

Inviting her along had been a purely selfish act, and Brad regretted it. Too many things could happen, most of them bad.

They'd been traveling for an hour or so when he stopped alongside a creek to rest the horses. High banks on either side sheltered them from the wind, and Meg got a chance to warm up.

Brad opened his saddlebags and brought out a long-sleeved thermal shirt, extended it to Meg. She hesitated a moment— that damnable McKettrick pride again—then took the shirt and pulled it on, right over the top of her coat.

The effect was comically unglamorous.

"Where's a Starbucks when you need one?" she joked.

Brad grinned. "There's an old line shack up the trail a ways," he told her. "Big John always kept it stocked with supplies, in case a hiker got stranded and needed shelter. It's not Starbucks, but I'll probably be able to rustle up a pot of coffee and some lunch. If you don't mind the survivalist packaging."

Meg's relief was visible, though she wouldn't have expressed it verbally, Brad knew. "We didn't need to bring the blankets and other gear then," she reasoned. "If there's a line shack, I mean."

"You've been living in the five-star lane for too long," Brad replied, but the jibe was a gentle one. "A while back, some hunters were trespassing on this land—Big John posted No Hunting signs years ago—and a snowstorm came up. They were found, dead of exposure, about fifty feet from the shack."

She shivered. "I remember," she said, and for a moment, her blue eyes looked almost haunted. The story had been a gruesome one, and she obviously *did* remember—all too clearly.

"We're not all that far from the ranch," Brad said. "It would probably be best if I took you back."

Meg's gaze widened, and grew more serious. "And you'd turn right around and come back up here to look for Ransom?"

"Yes," Brad answered, resigned.

"Alone."

He nodded. Once, Big John would have made the journey with him. Now there was no one.

"I'm staying," Meg said and shifted slightly, as if planting her feet. "You *invited* me to come along, in case you've forgotten."

"I shouldn't have. If anything happened to you—"

"I'm a big girl, Brad," she interrupted.

He looked her over, and—as always—liked what he saw. Liked it so much that his throat tightened and he had a hard time swallowing so he could hold up his end of the conversation. "You probably weigh a hundred and thirty pounds wrapped in a blanket and dunked into a lake. And despite your illustrious heritage, you're no match for a pack of wolves, a sudden blizzard, or a chasm that reaches halfway to China."

"If you can do it," Meg said, "*I* can do it."

Brad shoved a hand through his hair, exasperated even though he knew it was his own fault that Meg was in danger. After all, he *had* asked her to come along, half hoping the two of them would end up sharing a sleeping bag.

What the hell had he been thinking?

The pertinent question, he decided, was what had he been thinking *with*—not his brain, certainly.

"We'd better get moving again," she told him, when he

didn't speak. Before they'd left the ranch, he'd given her a pair of binoculars on a neck strap; now she pulled them out from under the donated undershirt, her coat, and whatever was beneath that. "We have a horse to find."

Brad nodded, cupped his hands to give her a leg up onto Cinnamon's back. She paused for a moment, deciding, before setting her left foot in the stirrup of his palms.

"This is a tall horse," she said, a little flushed.

"We should have named him Stilts instead of Cinnamon," Brad allowed, amused. Meg, like the rest of her cousins, had virtually grown up on horseback, as had he and Olivia and the twins. She'd interpret even the smallest courtesy—the offer of a boost, for instance—as an affront to her riding skills.

Forty-five minutes later, Meg, using the binoculars, spotted Ransom on the crest of a rocky rise.

"There he is!" she whispered, awed. "Wait till I tell Jesse he's real!"

After a few seconds, she lifted the binoculars off her neck by the strap and handed them across to Brad.

Brad drew in a breath, struck by the magnificence of the stallion, the defiance and barely restrained power. A moment or so passed before he thought to scan the horse for wounds. It was hard to tell, given the distance, even with binoculars, but Ransom wasn't limping, and Brad didn't see any blood. He could report to Olivia, in all honesty, that the object of her equine obsession was holding his own.

Before lowering the binoculars, Brad swept them across the top of that rise, and that was when he saw the two mares. He chuckled. Ransom had himself a harem, then.

He watched them a while, then gave the binoculars back to Meg, with a cheerful, "He has company."

Meg's face glowed. "They're beautiful," she whispered, as if afraid to startle the horses and send them fleeing, though they were well over a mile away, by Brad's estimation. "And Ransom. He knows we're here, Brad. It's almost as if he wanted to let us see that he's all right."

Brad raised his coat collar against a chilly breeze and wished he'd worn his hat. He'd considered it that morning, but it had seemed like an affectation, a way of asserting that he was still a cowboy, by his own standards if not those of the McKettricks. "He knows," he agreed finally, "but it's more likely that he's taunting us. Catch-me-if-you-can. That's what he'd say if he could talk."

Meg's entire face was glowing. In fact, Brad figured if he could strip all those clothes off her, that glow would come right through her skin and be enough to warm him until he died of old age.

"How about that coffee?" she said, grinning.

After seeing Brad's kitchen on Stone Creek Ranch, Meg had expected the "line shack" to be a fancy log A-frame with a Jacuzzi and Internet service. It was an actual *shack,* though, made of weathered board. There was a lean-to on one side, to shelter the horses, but no barn, with hay stored inside. Brad gave the animals grain from a sealed metal bin, and filled two water buckets for them from a rusty old pump outside.

Meg might have gone inside and started the fire, so they could brew the promised coffee, but she was mesmerized, watching Brad. It was as though the two of them had somehow gone back in time, back to when all the earlier McKettricks and O'Ballivans were still in the prime of their lives.

Once, there had been several shacks like that one on the

Triple M, far from the barns and bunkhouses. Ranch hands, riding the far-flung fence lines, or just traveling overland for some reason, used to spend the night in them, take refuge there when the weather was bad. Eventually, those tiny buildings had become hazards, rather than havens, and they'd been knocked down and burned.

"Pretty decrepit," Brad said, leading the way into the shack.

Things skittered inside, and the smell of the place was faintly musty, but Brad soon had a good fire going in the ancient potbellied stove. There was no furniture at all, but shelves, made of old wooden crates stacked on top of each other, held cups, food in airtight silver packets, cans of coffee.

The whole place was about the size of Meg's downstairs powder room on the Triple M.

"I'd offer you a chair," Brad said, grinning, "but obviously there aren't any. Make yourself at home while I rinse out these cups at the pump and fill the coffeepot."

Meg examined the plank floor, sat down cross-legged, and reveled in the warmth beginning to emanate from the wood-burning stove. The shack, inadequate as it was, offered a welcome respite from the cold wind outside. The hunters Brad had mentioned probably wouldn't have died if they'd been able to reach it. She remembered the news story; the facts had been bitter and brutal.

Like Stone Creek Ranch, the Triple M was posted, and hunting wasn't allowed. Still, people trespassed constantly, and Rance, Keegan and Jesse enforced the boundaries—mostly in a peaceful way. Just the winter before, though, Jesse had caught two men running deer with snowmobiles on the high meadow above his house, and he'd scared them off with a rifle shot aimed at the sky. Later, he'd tracked the pair to a tavern in Indian Rock—strangers to the area, they'd laughed at his warning—and put both of them in the hospital. He might have killed them, in fact, if Keegan hadn't gotten wind of the fight and come to break it up, and even with his help, it took the local marshal, Wyatt Terp, his deputy, and half the clientele in the bar to get Jesse off the second snowmobiler. He'd already pulverized the first one.

There was talk about filing assault charges against Jesse, and later it was rumored that there might be lawsuits, but nothing ever came of either. Meg, along with everybody else in Indian Rock, doubted the snowmobilers would ever set foot in town again, let alone on the Triple M.

But there was always, as Keegan liked to say, a fresh supply of idiots.

Brad came in with the cups and the full coffeepot, shoving the door closed behind him with one shoulder. Again, Meg had a sense of having stepped right out of the twenty-first century and into the nineteenth.

Despite cracks between the board walls, the shack was warm.

Brad set the coffeepot on the stove, measured ground beans into it from a can, and left it to boil, cowboy-style. No basket, no filter.

Then he emptied two of the crates being used as cupboards and dragged them over in front of the stove, so he and Meg could sit on them.

Overhead, thunder rolled across the sky, loud as a freight train.

Meg stiffened. "Rain?"

"Snow," Brad said. "I saw a few flakes drift past while I was outside. Soon as we've warmed up a little and fortified ourselves with caffeine and some grub, we'd better make for the low-country."

Had there been any windows, Meg would have gotten up to

look out of one of them. She could open the door a crack, but the thought of being buffeted by the rising wind stopped her.

By reflex, she scrambled to extract her cell phone from her coat pocket, flipped it open.

"No service," she murmured.

"I know," Brad said, smiling a little as he rose off the crate he'd been sitting on to add wood to the stove. Fortunately, there seemed to be an adequate supply of that. "I tried to call Olivia and let her know Ransom was still king of the hill a few minutes ago. Nothing."

Another round of thunder rattled the roof, and out in the lean-to, the horses fussed in alarm.

"Be right back," Brad said, heading for the door.

When he returned, he had a bedroll and Meg's pitifully insufficient blanket with him. And the horses were quiet.

"Just in case," he said when Meg's gaze landed, alarmed, on the overnight gear. "It's snowing pretty hard."

Meg, feeling foolish for sitting on her backside while Brad had been tending to the horses and fetching their gear inside, stood to lift the lid off the coffeepot and peek inside. The water was about to boil, but it would be a few minutes before the grounds settled to the bottom and they could drink the stuff.

"Relax, Meg," Brad said quietly. "There's still a chance the snow will ease up before dark."

At once tantalized and full of dread at the prospect of spending the night alone in a line shack with Brad O'Balli-van, Meg paced back and forth in front of the stove.

She knew what would happen if they stayed.

She'd known when she accepted Brad's invitation. Known when she set out for Stone Creek Ranch before dawn.

And he probably had, too.

She shoved both hands into her hair and paced faster.

"Meg," Brad said, sitting leisurely on his upended crate, *"relax."*

"You knew," she accused, stopping to shake a finger at him. "You knew we'd be stuck here!"

"So did you," Brad replied, unruffled.

Meg went to the door, wrenched it open and looked out, oblivious to the cold. The snow was coming down so hard and so fast that she couldn't see the pine trees towering less than a hundred yards from where she stood.

Attempting to travel under those conditions would be suicide.

Brad came and helped her shut the door again.

On the other side of the wall, in the lean-to, the horses made no sound.

Meg was standing too close to Brad, no question about it. But when she tried to move, she couldn't.

They looked into each other's eyes.

The very atmosphere zinged around them.

If Brad had kissed her then, she wouldn't have had the will to do anything but kiss him right back, but he didn't. "I'd better get some drinking water," he said, turning away and reaching for a bucket. "While I can still find my way back from the pump."

He went out.

Meg, needing something to do, pushed the coffeepot to the back of the stove so it wouldn't boil over and then examined a few of the food packets, evidently designed for post-apocalyptic dinner parties. The expiration dates were fifty years in the future.

"Spaghetti à la the Starship Enterprise," she muttered. There was Beef Wellington, too, and even meat loaf. At least they wouldn't starve.

Not right away, anyhow.

They'd starve *slowly.*

If they didn't freeze to death first.

Meg tried her cell phone again.

Still no service.

It was just as well, she supposed. Cheyenne knew her approximate location. Jesse would feed her horses, and if her absence was protracted, he and Keegan and Rance were sure to come looking for her. In the meantime, though, there would be a lot of room for speculation about what might be going on up there in the high country. And Jesse wouldn't miss a chance to tease her about it.

She was still holding the phone when Brad came in again, carrying a bucket full of water. He looked so cold that Meg almost went to put her arms around him.

Instead, she poured him a cup of hot coffee, still chewy with grounds, and handed it to him as soon as he'd set the bucket down.

"I don't suppose there's a generator," she said because the shack was darkening, even though it wasn't noon yet, and by nightfall, she wouldn't be able to see the proverbial hand in front of her face.

He favored her with a tilted grin. "Just a couple of battery-operated lamps and a few candles. We'll want to conserve the batteries, of course."

"Of course," Meg said, and smiled determinedly, hoping that would distract Brad from the little quaver in her voice.

"We don't have to make love," Brad said, lingering by the stove and taking slow, appreciative sips from his coffee. "Just because we're alone in a remote line shack during what may be the snowstorm of the century."

"You are not making me feel better."

That grin again. It was saucy, but it had a wistful element. "Am I making you feel *something?*"

"Nothing discernible," Meg lied. In truth, all her nerves felt supercharged, and her body was remembering, against strict orders from her mind, the weight and warmth of Brad's hands, caressing her bare skin.

"I used to be pretty good at it. Making you feel things, that is."

"Brad," Meg said, "don't."

"Okay," he said.

Meg was relieved, but at the same time, she wished he hadn't given up quite so easily.

"You wanted coffee," Brad remarked. "Have some."

Meg filled a cup for herself. Scooted her crate an inch or two farther from Brad's and sat down.

The shadows deepened and the shack seemed to grow even smaller than it was, pressing her and Brad closer together. And then closer still.

"This," Meg said, inspired by desperation, "would be a good time to talk about your second wife. Since we've been putting it off for a while."

Brad chuckled, fished in his saddlebags, now lying on the floor at his feet, and brought out a deck of cards. "I was thinking more along the lines of gin rummy," he said.

"What was her name again?"

"What was whose name?"

"Your second wife."

"Oh, her."

"Yeah, her."

"Cynthia. Her name is Cynthia. And I don't want to talk about her right now. Either we reminisce, or we play gin rummy, or—"

Meg squirmed. "Gin rummy," she said decisively. "There is no reason at all to bring up the subject of sex."

"Did I?"

"Did you what?"

"Did I bring up the subject of sex?"

"Not exactly," Meg said, embarrassed.

Brad grinned. "We'll get to that," he said. "Sooner or later."

Meg swallowed so much coffee in the next gulp that she nearly choked.

"There are some things I've been wondering about," Brad said easily, watching her over the rim of his metal coffee mug. His eyes smoldered with lazy blue heat.

Outside, the snow-thunder crashed again, but the horses didn't react. They'd probably already settled down for the night, snug in their furry hides and their lean-to.

"I'm hungry," Meg said, reaching for one of the food packets.

Brad went on as though she hadn't spoken at all. "Do you still like to eat cereal with yogurt instead of milk?"

Meg swallowed. "Yes."

"Do you still laugh in your sleep?"

"I—I suppose."

"Do you still arch your back like a bucking horse when you climax?"

Meg's face felt hotter than the old stove, which rocked a little with the heat inside it, crimson blazes glowing through the cracks. "What kind of question is that?"

"A personal one, I admit," Brad said. He might have passed for a choirboy, so innocent was his expression, but his eyes gave him away. They had the old glint of easy confidence in them. He knew he could have her anyplace and anytime he wanted— he was just biding his time. "I'll know soon enough, I guess."

"No," she said.

"No?" He raised an eyebrow.

"No, I don't arch my back when I—I don't arch my back."

"Hmmmm," Brad said. "Why not?"

Because I don't have sex, Meg almost answered, but in the last, teetering fraction of a second, she realized she didn't want to admit that. Not to Brad, the man with all the notches on his bedpost.

"You haven't been sleeping with anybody?" he asked.

"I didn't say that," Meg replied, keeping her distance, mainly because she wanted so much to take Brad's coffee from his hand, set it aside, straddle his thighs and let him work his slow, thorough magic. Peeling away her outer garments, kissing and caressing everything he uncovered.

"Nobody who could make you arch your back?"

Meg was suffused with aching, needy misery. She'd been in fairly close proximity to Brad all morning, and managed to keep her perspective, but now they were alone in a remote shack, and he'd already begun to seduce her. Without so much as a kiss, or a touch of his hand. With Brad O'Ballivan, even gin rummy would qualify as foreplay.

"Something like that," she said. It was a lame answer, and way too honest, but she'd figured if she tossed his ego a bone, the way she might have done to get past a junkyard dog, she'd get a chance to diffuse the invisible but almost palpable charge sparking between them.

"I came across one of Maddie's diaries a few years ago," Brad said, still stripping her with his eyes. Maddie, of course, was his ancestress—Sam O'Ballivan's wife. "She mentioned this line shack several times. She and Sam spent a night here, once, and conceived a child."

That statement should have quelled Meg's passion—unlike Sam and Maddie, she and Brad weren't married, weren't in love. She wasn't using any form of birth control, since there hadn't been a man in her life for nearly a year, and intuition told her that for all Brad's preparations, Brad hadn't brought any condoms along.

Yet, the mention of a baby opened a gash of yearning within Meg, a great, jagged tearing so deep and so dark and so raw that she nearly doubled over with the pain of it.

"Are you all right?" Brad asked, on his feet quickly, taking her elbows in his hands, looking down into her face.

She said nothing. She couldn't have spoken for anything, not in that precise moment.

"What?" Brad prompted, looking worried.

She couldn't tell him that she'd wanted a baby so badly she'd made arrangements with a fertility specialist on several occasions, always losing her courage at the last moment. That she'd almost reached the point of sleeping with strangers, hoping to get pregnant.

In the end, she hadn't been able to go through with that, either.

She'd never known her own father. Oh, she'd lacked for nothing, being a McKettrick. Nothing except the merest acquaintance with the man who'd sired her. He was so anonymous, in fact, that Eve had occasionally referred to him, not knowing Meg was listening, as "the sperm donor."

She wanted more for her own son or daughter. Granted, the baby's father didn't have to be involved in their day-to-day life, or pay child support, or much of anything else. But he had to have a face and a name, so Meg could show her child a photograph, at some point in time, and say, "This is your daddy."

"Meg?" Brad's hands tightened a little on her elbows.

"Panic attack," she managed to gasp.

He pressed her down onto one of the crates, ladled some water from the bucket he'd braved the elements to fill at the pump outside, and held it to her lips.

She sipped.

"Do you need to take a pill or something?"

Meg shook her head.

He dragged the second crate closer, and sat facing her, so their knees touched. "Since when do you get panic attacks?" he asked.

Tears stung Meg's eyes. She rocked a little, hugging herself, and Brad steadied the ladle in her hands, raised it to her mouth again.

She sipped, more slowly this time, and Brad set it aside when she was finished.

"Meg," he repeated. "The panic attacks?"

It only happens when I suddenly realize I want to have a certain man's baby more than I want anything in the world. And when that certain man turns out to be you.

"It's a freak thing," she said. "I've never had one before."

Brad raised an eyebrow—he'd always been perceptive. It was one of the qualities that made him a good songwriter, for example. "I mentioned that Sam and Maddie conceived a child in this line shack, and you started hyperventilating." He leaned forward a little, took both Meg's hands gently in his. "I remember how much you wanted kids when we were together," he mused. "And now your sister is having a baby."

Meg's heart wedged itself into her windpipe. She'd wanted a baby, all right. And she'd conceived one, with Brad, and miscarried soon after he left for Nashville. Not even her mother had known.

She nodded.

Brad stroked the side of her cheek with the backs of his fingers, offering her comfort. She'd never told him about the pregnancy—she'd been saving the news for their wedding night—but now she knew she would have no choice, if they got involved again.

"I'm not jealous of Sierra," she said, anxious to make that clear. "I'm happy for her and Travis."

"I know," Brad said. He drew her from her crate onto his lap; she straddled his thighs. But beyond that, the gesture wasn't sexual. He simply held her, one hand gently pressing her head to his shoulder.

After a little deep breathing, in order to calm herself, Meg straightened and gazed into Brad's face.

"Suppose we had sex," she said softly. Tentatively. "And I conceived a child. How would you react?"

"Well," Brad said after pondering the idea with an expression of wistful amusement on his face, "I guess that would depend on a couple of things." He kissed her neck, lightly. Nibbled briefly at her earlobe.

A hot shudder went through Meg. "Like what?"

"Like whether we were going to raise the baby together or not," Brad replied, still nibbling. When Meg stiffened slightly, he drew back to look into her face again. "What?"

"I was sort of thinking I could just be a single mother," Meg said.

She was off Brad's thighs and plunked down on her crate again so quickly that it almost took her breath away.

"And my part would be what?" he demanded. "Keep my distance? Go on about my business? What, Meg?"

"You have your career—"

"I don't have my career. That part of my life is over. I've told you that."

"You're young, Brad. You're very talented. It's inevitable that you'll want to sing again."

"I don't have to be in a concert hall or a recording studio to sing," he said tersely. "I mean to live on Stone Creek Ranch for good, and any child of *mine* is going to grow up there."

Meg stood her ground. After all, she was a McKettrick. "Any child of *mine* is going to grow up on the Triple M."

"Then I guess we'd better not make a baby," Brad replied. He got up off the crate, went to the stove and refilled his coffee cup.

"Look," Meg said more gently, "we can just let the subject drop. I'm sorry I brought it up at all—I just got a little emotional there for a moment and—"

Brad didn't answer.

They were stuck in a cabin together, at least overnight, and maybe longer. They had to get along, or they'd both go crazy.

She retrieved the pack of cards from the floor, where Brad had set them earlier. "Bet I can take you, O'Ballivan," she said, waggling the box from side to side. "Gin rummy, five-card stud, go fish—name your poison."

He laughed, and the tension was broken—the overt kind, anyway. There was an underground river of the stuff, coursing silently beneath their feet. "Go fish?"

"Lately, I've played a lot of cards—with my nephew, Liam. That's his favorite."

Brad chose rummy. Set a third crate between them for a table top. "You think you can take me, huh?" he challenged. And the look in his eyes, as he dealt the first hand, said *he* planned on doing the taking—and the cards didn't have a thing to do with it.

Chapter Six

It was a wonder to Brad that he could sit there in the middle of that line shack, playing gin rummy with Meg McKettrick, when practically all he'd thought about since coming home to Stone Creek was bedding down with her. She'd practically invited him to father her baby, too.

Whatever his reservations might be where her insistence on raising the child alone was concerned, and on the Triple M to boot, he sure wouldn't have minded the *process* of conceiving it.

So why wasn't he on top of her at that very moment?

He studied his cards solemnly—Meg was going to win this hand, as she had the last half dozen—and pondered the situation. The wind howled around the shack like a million shrieking banshees determined to drive them both out into the freezing cold, making the walls shake. And the light was going, too, even though it wasn't noon yet.

"Play," Meg said impatiently, a spark of mischievous triumph—and something else—dancing in her eyes.

"If I didn't know better," Brad said ruefully, "I'd think you'd stacked the deck. You're going to lay down all your cards and set me again, aren't you?"

She grinned, looking at him coyly over the fan of cards. Even batting her eyelashes. "There's only one way to find out," she teased.

A cowboy's geisha, Brad thought. Later, when he was alone at the ranch, he'd tinker around with the idea, maybe make a song out of it. He might have retired from recording and life on the road, but he knew he'd always make music.

Resigned, he drew a card from the stack, couldn't use it, and tossed it away.

Meg's whole being seemed to twinkle as she took his discard, incorporated it into a grand-slam of a run and went out with a flourish, spreading the cards across the top of the crate.

"McKettrick luck," she said, beaming.

On impulse, Brad put down his cards, leaned across the crate between them and kissed Meg lightly on the mouth. She tensed at first, then responded, giving a little groan when he used his tongue.

Her arms slipped around his shoulders.

He wanted with everything in him to shove cards and crate aside, lay her down, then and there, and have her.

Whoa, he told himself. *Easy. Don't scare her off.*

There were tears in her eyes when she drew back from his kiss, sniffled once, and blinked, as though surprised to find herself alone with him, in the eye of the storm.

Like most men, Brad was always unsettled when a woman

cried. He felt an urgent need to rectify whatever was wrong, and at the same time, knew he couldn't.

Meg swabbed at her cheeks with the back of one hand, straightened her proud McKettrick spine.

"What's the matter?" Brad asked.

"Nothing," Meg answered, averting her gaze.

"You're lying."

"Just hedging a little," she said, trying hard to smile and falling short. "It was like the old days, that's all. The kiss I mean. It brought up a lot of feelings."

"Would it help if I told you I felt the same way?"

"Not really," she said. A thoughtful look came into those fabulous, fathomless eyes of hers.

Brad slid the crate to one side and leaned in close, filled with peculiar suspense. He had to know what was going on in her head. "What?"

"Lots of people have sex," she told him, "without anybody getting pregnant."

"The reverse is also true," he felt honor-bound to say. "Far as I know, making love still causes babies."

"Making love," Meg said, "is not necessarily the same thing as having sex."

Brad cleared his throat, still walking on figurative eggshells. "True," he said very cautiously. Was she messing with him? Setting him up for a rebuff? Meg wasn't a particularly vengeful person, at least as far as he knew, but he'd hurt her badly all those busy years ago. Maybe she wanted to get back at him a little.

"What I have in mind," she told him decisively, "is *sex,* as opposed to making love." A pause. "Of course."

"Of course," he agreed. Hope fluttered in his chest, like a bird flexing its wings and rising, windborne, off a high tree branch. At the same time, he felt stung—Meg was making it clear that any intimacy they might enjoy during this brief time-out-of-time would be strictly for physical gratification. Frenetic coupling of bodies, an emotion-free zone.

Since beggars couldn't be choosers, he was willing to bargain, but the disturbing truth was, he wanted more from Meg than a noncommittal quickie. She wasn't, after all, a groupie to be groped and taken in the back of some tour bus, then forgotten.

She squinted at him, catching something in his expression. "This bothers you?" she asked.

He tried to smile. "If you want to have sex, McKettrick, I'm definitely game. It's just that—"

"What?"

"It might not be a good idea." Was he crazy? Here was the most beautiful woman he'd ever seen, essentially offering herself to him—and he was leaning on the brake lever?

"Okay," she said, and she looked hurt, uncomfortable, suddenly shy.

And that was his undoing. All his noble reluctance went right out the door.

He pulled her onto his lap again.

She hesitated, then wrapped both arms around his neck.

"Are you sure?" he asked her quietly, gruffly. "We're taking a chance here, Meg. We *could* conceive a child—"

The idea filled him with desperate jubilation, strangely mingled with sorrow.

"We could," she agreed, her eyes shining, dark with sultry heat, despite the chill seeping in between the cracks in the plain board walls.

He cupped her chin in his hand, made her look into his face. "Fair warning, McKettrick. If there's a baby, I'm not going to be an anonymous father, content to cut a check once a month and go on about my business as if it had never happened."

She studied him. "You're serious."

He nodded.

"I'll take that chance," she decided, after a few moments of deliberation.

He kissed her again, deeply this time, and when their mouths parted, she looked as dazed as he felt. Once, during a rehearsal before a concert, he'd gotten a shock from an electric guitar with a frayed chord. The jolt he'd taken, kissing Meg just now, made the first experience seem tame.

She was straddling him, and even through their jeans, the insides of her thighs, squeezing against his hips, seemed to sear his skin. She squirmed against his erection, making him groan.

Never in his life had Brad wanted a bed as badly as he did at that moment. It wasn't right to lay Meg down on a couple of sleeping bags, on that cold floor.

But even as he was thinking these disjointed thoughts, he was pulling her shirt up, slipping his hands beneath all that fabric, stroking her bare ribs.

She shivered deliciously, closed her eyes, threw her head back.

"Cold?" Brad asked, worried.

"Anything but," she murmured.

"You're sure?"

"Absolutely sure," Meg said.

He found the catch on her bra, opened it. Cupped both hands beneath her full, warm breasts.

She moaned as he chafed her nipples gently, using the sides of his thumbs.

And that was when they heard the deafening and unmistakable *thwup-thwup-thwup* of helicopter blades, directly above the roof of the line shack.

Meg looked up, disbelieving. Jesse, Rance, or Keegan—or all three. Who else would take a chopper up in weather like that?

Out in the lean-to, the horses whinnied in panic. The walls of the cabin shook as Meg jumped to her feet and righted her bra in almost the same motion. *"Damn!"* she sputtered furiously.

"That had better not be Phil," Brad said ominously. He was standing, too, his gaze fixed on the trembling ceiling.

Meg smoothed her hair, straightened her clothes. "Phil?"

"My manager," Brad reminded her.

"We should be so lucky," Meg yelled, straining to be heard over the sound of the blades. "It's my cousins!"

They both went to the door and peered out, heedless of the blasting cold, made worse by the downdraft from the chopper, Meg ducking under Brad's left arm to see.

Sure enough, the McKettrickCo helicopter, a relic of the corporation days, was settling to the ground, bouncing on its runners in the deepening snow.

"I'll be damned," Brad said with a grin of what looked like rueful admiration, forcing the door shut against the icy wind. At the last second, Meg saw two figures moving toward them at a half crouch.

"I'll kill them," Meg said.

The door rattled on its hinges at the first knock.

Meg stood back while Brad opened it again.

Jesse came through first, followed by Keegan. They wore Western hats pulled low over their faces, leather coats thickly lined with sheep's wool, and attitudes.

"I tried to stop them," Angus said, appearing at Meg's elbow.

"Good job," Meg scoffed, under her breath, without moving her lips.

Angus spread his hands. "They're McKettricks," he reminded her, as though that explained every mystery in the universe, from spontaneous human combustion to the Bermuda Triangle.

"Are you crazy?" Meg demanded of her cousins, storming forward to stand toe-to-toe with Jesse, who was tight-jawed, casting suspicious glances at Brad. "You could have been killed, taking the copter up in a blizzard!"

Brad, by contrast, hoisted the coffeepot off the stove, grinning wryly, and not entirely in a friendly way. "Coffee?" he asked.

Jesse scowled at him.

"Don't mind if I do," Keegan said, pulling off his heavy leather gloves. He tossed Meg a sympathetic glance in the meantime, one that said, *Don't blame me. I'm just here to keep an eye on Jesse.*

Brad found another cup and, without bothering to wipe it out, filled it and handed it to Keegan. "It's good to see you again," he said with a sort of charged affability, but underlying his tone was an unspoken, *Not.*

"I'll just bet," Jesse said, whipping off his hat. His dark blond hair looked rumpled, as though he'd been shoving a hand through it at regular intervals.

"Jesse," Keegan warned quietly.

Meg stood nearly on tiptoe, her nose almost touching Jesse's, her eyes narrowed to slits. "What the *hell* are you doing here?"

Jesse wasn't about to back down, his stance made that clear, and neither was Meg. Classic McKettrick stand-off.

Keegan, used to the family dynamics, and the most diplomatic member of the current generation, eased an arm between them, holding his mug of hot coffee carefully in the other. "To your corners," he said easily, forcing them both to take a step back.

Jesse gave Brad a scathing look—once, they'd been friends—and turned to face Meg again. "I might ask you the same question," he countered. "What the hell are *you* doing here? With *him?*"

Brad cleared his throat, folded his arms. Waited. He looked amused—the expression in his eyes notwithstanding.

"That, Jesse McKettrick," Meg seethed, "is my own business!"

"We came," Keegan interceded, still unruffled but, in his own way, as watchful as Jesse was, "because Cheyenne told us you were up here on horseback. When we got word of the blizzard, we were worried."

Meg threw her arms out, slapped them back against her sides. "Obviously, I'm all right," she said. "Safe and sound."

"I don't know about that," Jesse said, taking Brad's measure again.

A muscle bunched in Brad's jaw, but he didn't speak.

"Get your stuff, if you have any," Jesse told Meg. "We're leaving." He turned to Brad again, added reluctantly, "You'd better come with us. This storm is going to get a lot worse before it gets better."

"Can't leave the horses," Brad said.

Meg was annoyed. Her cousins had landed a helicopter in front of the line shack, in the middle of a blinding white-out, determined to carry her out bodily if they had to, and all he could think about was the horses?

"I'll stay and ride out with you," Jesse told Brad. Whatever his issues with Brad might be, he was a rancher, born and bred. And a rancher never left a horse stranded, whether it was his own or someone else's, if he had any choice in the matter. His blue eyes sliced to Meg's face. "Keegan will get you back to the Triple M."

"Suppose I don't want to go?"

"Better decide," Keegan put in. "This storm is picking up steam as we speak. Another fifteen or twenty minutes, and the four of us will be bunking in here until spring."

Meg searched Jesse's face, glanced at Brad.

He wasn't going to express an opinion one way or the other, apparently, and that galled her. She knew it wasn't cowardice—Brad had never been afraid of a brawl, with her rowdy cousins or anybody else. Which probably meant he was relieved to get out of a sticky situation.

Color flared in her cheeks.

"I'll get my coat," she said, glaring at Brad. Still hoping he'd stop her, send Jesse and Keegan packing.

But he didn't.

She scrambled into her coat with jamming motions of her fists, and got stuck in the lining of one sleeve.

"Call Olivia," Brad said, watching her struggle, one corner of his mouth tilted slightly upward in a bemused smile. "Let her know I'm okay."

Meg nodded once, angrily, and let Keegan shuffle her out into the impossible cold to the waiting helicopter.

"Smooth," Brad remarked, studying Jesse, shutting the door behind Meg and Keegan and offering a brief, silent prayer for their safety. Flying in this weather was a major risk, but if anybody was up to the job, it was Keegan. His father had been a pilot, and all three of the McKettrick boys were as skilled at the controls of a plane or a copter as they were on the back of a horse.

A little of the air went out of Jesse, but not much. "We'd better ride," he said, "if we're going to make it out of here before dark."

"What'd you think I was going to do, Jesse?" Brad asked evenly, reaching for the poker, opening the stove door to bank the fire. "Rape her?"

Jesse thrust a hand through his hair. "It wasn't that," he said, but grudgingly. "Until we spotted the smoke from the line shack chimney, we thought the two of you might still be out there someplace, in a whole lot of trouble."

"You couldn't have just turned the copter toward the Triple M and left well enough alone?" He hadn't shown it in front of Meg, but Brad was about an inch off Jesse. Meg wasn't a kid, and if she'd needed protection, he would have provided it.

Jesse's eyes shot blue fire. "Maybe Meg's ready to forget what you did to her, but I'm not," he said. "She put on a good show back then, but inside, she was a shipwreck. Especially after the miscarriage."

For Brad, the whole world came to a screeching, spark-throwing stop in the space of an instant.

"What miscarriage?"

"Uh-oh," Jesse said.

It was literally all Brad could do not to get Jesse by the lapels and drag an answer out of him. He even took a step toward the door, meaning to stop Meg from leaving, but the copter was already lifting off, shaking the shack, setting the horses to fretting again.

"There—was—a baby?"

"Let's go get those horses ready for a hard ride," Jesse said, averting his gaze. Clearly, he'd assumed Meg had told Brad about the child. Now Jesse was the picture of regret.

"Tell me," Brad pressed.

"You'll have to talk to Meg," Jesse answered, putting his hat on again and squaring his shoulders to go back out into the cold and around to the lean-to. "I've already said more than I should have."

"It was mine?"

Jesse reddened. Yanked up the collar of his heavy coat. "*Of course* it was yours," he said indignantly. "Meg's not the type to play that kind of game."

Brad put on his own coat and yanked on some gloves. He felt strangely apart from himself, as though his spirit had somehow gotten out of step with his body.

Meg had been pregnant when he caught that bus to Nashville.

He knew in his bones it was true.

If he'd been anything but a stupid, ambitious kid, he'd have known it then. By the fragile light in her eyes. By the way she'd touched his arm, as if to get his attention so she could say something important, then drawn back, trembling a little.

He'd still have gone to Nashville—he'd had to, to save Stone Creek from the bankers and developers. But he'd have sent for Meg first thing, swallowed his pride whole if he had to, or thumbed it back to Arizona to be with her.

Tentatively, Jesse laid a hand on Brad's shoulder. Withdrew it again.

After securing the line shack as best they could, they left, made their way to the fitful horses, saddled them in silence.

The roar of the copter's engine and the whipping of the blades made conversation impossible, without a headset, and Meg refused to put hers on.

Keegan concentrated on working the controls, keeping a close watch on the instrument panel. The blizzard had intensified; they were literally flying blind.

Presently, though, visibility increased, and Meg relaxed a little.

Keegan must have been watching her out of the corner of his eye, because he reached over and patted her lightly on the arm. Picked up the second headset and nudged her until she took it, put on the earphones, adjusted the mic.

"I can't believe you did this," she said.

Keegan grinned. His voice echoed through the headset. "Rule number one," he said. "Never leave another McKettrick stuck in a blizzard."

Meg huffed out a sigh. "I was perfectly all right!"

"Maybe," Keegan replied, banking to the northwest, in the direction of the Triple M. "But we didn't have any way of knowing that. Switch on your cell phone. You'll find we left at least half a dozen messages on your voice mail, trying to find out if you were okay."

"What if they don't make it out of that storm?" Meg fretted. Before, she'd just been furious. Now, with a little perspective, she was suddenly assailed by worries, on all sides. The fear was worse than the anger. "What if the horses get lost?"

"Brad knows the trail," Keegan assured her, "and Jesse could ride out of hell if he had to. If they don't show up in a few hours, I'll come back looking for them."

"You're not invincible, you know," Meg said tersely. "Even if you *are* a McKettrick."

"I'll do what I have to do," he told her. "Are you and Brad—well—back on?"

"That is patently none of your affair."

Keegan's grin was damnably endearing. "When has that ever stopped me?"

"No," Meg said, beaten. "We are *not* 'back on.' I was just helping him look for Ransom, that's all."

"Ransom? The stallion?"

"Yes."

"He's real?"

"I've seen him with my own eyes."

"You decided to go chasing a wild horse in the middle of a blizzard?"

"It wasn't snowing when we left Stone Creek Ranch," Meg said, feeling defensive.

"Know what I think?"

"No, but I'm afraid you're going to tell me."

Keegan's grin widened, took on a wicked aspect. "You wanted to sleep with Brad. He wanted to sleep with you. And I use the word *sleep* advisedly. Both of you knew snow's a real possibility in the high country, year 'round. And there's the old line shack, handy as hell."

"*So* none of your business. And who do you think you are, Dr. Phil?"

Keegan chuckled, shook his head once. "It probably won't help," he told her, "but if we'd known we were interrupting a tryst, we'd have stayed clear."

"We were *playing gin rummy.*"

"Whatever."

Meg folded her arms and wriggled deeper into the cold leather seat. "Keegan, I don't have to convince you. And I definitely don't have to explain."

"You're absolutely right. You don't."

By then, they were out of the snow, gliding through a golden autumn afternoon. They passed over the town of Stone Creek, continued in the direction of Indian Rock.

Meg didn't say another word until Keegan set the copter down in the pasture behind her barn, the downdraft making the long grass ripple like an ocean.

"Thanks for the ride," she said tersely, waiting for the blades to slow so she could get out without having her head cut off. "I'd invite you in, but right now, I am seriously pissed off, and the less I see of any of my male relatives, you included, the better."

Keegan cocked a thumb at her. "Got it," he said. "And for the record, I don't give a rat's ass if you're pissed off."

Meg reached across and slugged him in the upper arm, hard, but she laughed a little as she did it. Shook her head. "Goodbye!" she yelled, tossing the headset into his lap.

Keegan signaled her to keep her head down, and watched as she pushed open the door of the copter and leaped to the ground.

Ducking, she headed for the house.

Angus was standing in the kitchen when she let herself in, looking apologetic.

"Thanks a heap for the help," Meg said.

"There's not much I can do with folks who can't see or hear me," Angus replied.

"I get all the luck," Meg answered, pulling off her coat and flinging it in the direction of the hook beside the door.

Angus looked solemn. "You've got trouble," he said.

Meg tensed, instantly alarmed. She'd ridden home from the mountaintop in relative comfort, but the trip would be dangerous on horseback, even for men who'd literally grown up in the saddle. "Jesse and Brad are okay, aren't they?"

"They'll be fine," Angus assured her. "A couple of shots of good whiskey'll fix 'em right up."

"Then what are you talking about?"

"You'll find out soon enough."

"Do you have to be so damned cryptic?"

Angus's grin was reminiscent of Keegan's. "I'm not cryptic," he said. "I can get around just fine."

"Very funny."

He chuckled.

Frazzled, Meg blurted, "First you tell me about your long-lost brother, and how some unknown McKettrick is about to show up. Then you say I've got trouble. Spill it, Angus!"

He sobered. "Jesse let the cat out of the bag. And that's all I'm going to say."

Meg froze. She had only one deep, dark secret, and Jesse couldn't have let it slip because he didn't know what it was.

Did he?

She put one hand to her mouth.

Angus patted her shoulder. "You'd better go out to the barn and feed the horses early. You might be too busy later on."

Meg stared at her ancestor. "Angus McKettrick—"

He vanished.

Typical man.

Meg placed the promised call to Olivia O'Ballivan, got her voice mail and left a message. Next, she started a pot of coffee, then picked her coat up off the floor, put it back on and went out to tend to the livestock.

The work helped to ease her anxiety, but not all that much.

All the while, she was wondering if Jesse had found out about the baby somehow, if he'd told Brad.

You've got trouble, Angus had said, and the words echoed in her mind.

She finished her chores and returned to the house, shedding her coat again and washing her hands at the sink before pouring herself a mug of fresh coffee. She considered lacing it with a generous dollop of Jack Daniel's, to get the chill out of her bones, then shoved the bottle back in the cupboard, unopened.

If Jesse and Brad didn't get home, Keegan wouldn't be the only one to go out looking for them.

She reached for the telephone, dialed Cheyenne's cell number.

"I'm sorry," Cheyenne said immediately, not bothering with a hello. "When I passed your message on to Jesse, about checking on your horses if you didn't call before nightfall, he wanted to know where you'd gone." She paused. "And I told him."

Meg pressed the back of one hand to her forehead and closed her eyes for a moment. If a certain pair of stubborn cowboys got lost in that blizzard, or if Jesse had, as Angus put it, "let the cat out of the bag," the embarrassing scene at the line shack would be the least of her problems.

"There's a big storm in the high country," she said quietly, "and Jesse and Brad are on horseback. Let me know when Jesse gets back, will you?"

Cheyenne drew in an audible breath. "Oh, my God," she whispered. "They're riding in a *blizzard?*"

"Jesse can handle it," Meg said. "And so can Brad. Just the same, I'll rest easier when I know they're home."

Cheyenne didn't answer for a long time. "I'll call," she promised, but she sounded distracted. No doubt she was thinking the same thing Meg was, that it had been reckless enough, flying into a snowstorm in a helicopter. Taking a treacherous trail down off the mountain was even worse.

Meg spoke a few reassuring words, though they sounded hollow even to her, and she and Cheyenne said goodbye.

At loose ends, Meg took her coffee to the study at the front of the house and logged onto the computer. Ran a search on the name Josiah McKettrick, though her mind wasn't on genealogical detective work, and she started over a dozen times.

In the kitchen, she heated a can of soup and ate it mechanically, never tasting a bite. After that, she read for a couple of hours, then she took a long, hot bath, put on clean sweats and padded downstairs again, thinking she'd watch some television. She was trying to focus on a rerun of *Dog the Bounty Hunter* when she heard a car door slam outside.

Boot heels thundered up the front steps.

And then a fist hammered at the heavy wooden door.

"Meg!" Brad yelled. "Open up! *Now!*"

Chapter Seven

Brad looked crazed, standing there on Meg's doorstep. She moved to step out of his way, but before she could, he advanced on her, backing her into the entryway. Kicking the door shut behind him with a hard motion of one foot.

He hadn't stopped to change clothes after the long, cold ride down out of the hills, and he was soaked to the skin. He'd lost his gloves somewhere, and there was a faintly bluish cast to his taut lips.

"Why didn't you tell me about the baby?" he demanded, shaking an index finger under Meg's nose when she collided with the wall behind her, next to Holt and Lorelei's grandfather clock. The ponderous tick-tock seemed to reverberate throughout the known universe.

Meg's worst fears were confirmed in that moment. Jesse

had known about her pregnancy and subsequent miscarriage—and he'd let it slip to Brad.

"Calm down," she said, recovering a little.

Brad gripped her shoulders. If he'd been anyone other than exactly who he was, Meg might have feared for her safety. But this was Brad O'Ballivan. Sure, he'd crushed her heart, but he wasn't going to hurt her physically, she knew that. It was one of the few absolutes.

"Was there a child?"

Meg bit her lower lip. She'd always known she'd have to tell him if they crossed paths again, but she hadn't wanted it to be like this. "Yes," she whispered, that one word scraping her throat raw.

"My baby?"

She felt a sting of indignation, hot as venom, but it passed quickly. "Yes."

"Why didn't you tell me?"

Meg straightened her spine, lifted her chin a notch. "You were in Nashville," she said. "You didn't write. You didn't call. I guess I didn't think you'd be interested."

The blue fury in Brad's eyes dulled visibly; he let go of her shoulders, but didn't step back. She felt cornered, overshadowed—but still not threatened. Oddly, it was more like being shielded, even protected.

He shoved a hand through his hair. "How could I not be interested, Meg?" he rasped bleakly. "You were carrying our baby."

Slowly, Meg put her palms to his cheeks. "I miscarried a few weeks after you left," she said gently. "It wasn't meant to be."

Moisture glinted in his eyes, and that familiar muscle bunched just above his jawline. "Still—"

"Go upstairs and take a hot shower," Meg told him. "I'll fix you something to eat, and we'll talk."

Brad tensed again, then relaxed, though only slightly. Nodded.

"Travis left some clothes behind when he and Sierra moved to town," she went on, when he didn't speak. "I'll get them for you."

With that, she led the way up the stairs, along the hallway to the main bathroom. After pushing the door open and waiting for Brad to enter, she went on to the master bedroom, pulled an old pair of jeans and a long-sleeved T-shirt from a bureau drawer.

Brad was already in the shower when she returned, naked behind the steamy glass door, but clearly visible.

Swallowing a rush of lust, Meg set the folded garments on the lid of the toilet seat, placed a folded towel on top of them and slipped out.

She was cooking scrambled eggs when Brad came down the back stairs fifteen minutes later, barefoot, his hair towel-rumpled, wearing Travis's clothes. Without comment, Meg poured a cup of fresh coffee and held it out to him.

He took it, after a moment's hesitation, and sipped cautiously.

Meg was relieved to see that the hot shower had restored his normal color. Before, he'd been ominously pale.

"Sit down," she said quietly.

He pulled out Holt's chair and sat, watching her as she turned to the stove again. Even with her back turned to him, she could feel his gaze boring into the space between her shoulder blades.

"What happened?" he asked, after a few moments.

She looked back at him briefly before scraping the eggs onto a waiting plate. Didn't speak.

"The miscarriage," he prompted grimly. "What made it happen?"

With a pang, Meg realized he thought it might have been

his fault somehow, her losing their baby. Because he'd gone to Nashville, or because of the fight they'd had before he left.

She'd suffered her own share of guilt over the years, wondering if she could have done something differently, prevented the tragedy. She didn't want Brad to go through the same agony.

"There was no specific incident," she said softly. "I was pregnant, and then I wasn't. It happens, Brad. And it's not always possible to know why."

Brad absorbed that, took another sip of his coffee. "You should have told me."

"I didn't tell anyone," Meg said. "Not even my mother."

"Then how did Jesse know?"

Now that she'd had time to think, the answer was obvious. Jesse had been the one to take her to the hospital that long-ago night. She'd told him it was just a bad case of cramps, but he'd either put two and two together on his own or overheard the nurses and doctors talking.

"He was with me," she said.

"He was, and I *wasn't*," Brad answered.

She set the plate of scrambled eggs in front of him, along with two slices of buttered toast and some silverware. "It wouldn't have changed anything," she said. "Your being there, I mean. I'd still have lost the baby, Brad."

He closed his eyes briefly, like someone taking a hard punch to the solar plexus, determined not to fight back.

"You should have told me," he insisted.

She gave the plate a little push toward him and, reluctantly, he picked up his fork, began to eat. "We've been over that," she said, sitting down on the bench next to the table, angled to face Brad. "What good would it have done?"

"I could have—helped."

"How?"

He sighed. "You went through it alone. That isn't right."

"Lots of things aren't 'right' in this world," Meg reasoned quietly. "A person just has to—cope."

"The McKettrick way," Brad said without admiration. "Some people would call that being bullheaded, not coping."

She propped an elbow on the tabletop, cupped her chin in her hand, and watched as he continued to down the scrambled eggs. "I'd do the same thing all over again," she confessed. "It was hard, but I toughed it out."

"Alone."

"Alone," Meg agreed.

"It must have been a lot worse than 'hard.' You were only nineteen."

"So were you," she said.

"Why didn't you tell your mother?"

Meg didn't have to reflect on that one. From the day Hank Breslin had snatched Sierra and vanished, Eve had been hit by problem after problem—a serious accident, in which she'd been severely injured, subsequent addictions to painkillers and alcohol, all the challenges of steering McKettrickCo through a lot of corporate white water.

"She'd been through enough," she replied simply. Brad's question had been rhetorical—he'd known the McKettrick history all along.

"She'd have strung me up by my thumbs," Brad said. And though he tried to smile, he didn't quite make it. He was still in shock.

"Probably," Meg said.

He'd finished the food, shoved his plate away. "Where do we go from here?" he asked.

"I don't know," she said. "Maybe nowhere."

He moved to take her hand, but withdrew just short of touching her. Scraped back his chair to stand and carry the remains of his meal to the sink. Set the plate and silverware down with a thunk.

"Was our baby a boy or a girl?" he asked gruffly, standing with his back to her.

She saw the tension in his broad shoulders as he awaited her answer. "I didn't ask," she said. "I guess I didn't want to know. And it was probably too early to tell, anyway. I was only a few weeks into the pregnancy."

He turned, at last, to face her, but kept his distance, leaning back against the counter, folding his arms. "Do you ever think about what it would be like if he or she had survived?"

All the time, she thought.

"No," she lied.

"Right," he said, clearly not believing her.

"I'm—I'm sorry, Brad. That you had to find out from someone else, I mean."

"But not for deceiving me in the first place?"

Meg bristled. "I didn't deceive you."

"What do you call it?"

"You were *gone.* You had things to do. If I'd dragged you back here, you wouldn't have gotten your big chance. You would have hated me for that."

At last, he crossed to her, took her chin in his hand. "I couldn't hate you, Meg," he said gravely, choking a little on the words. "Not ever."

For a few moments, they just stared at each other in silence.

Brad was the first to speak again. "I'd better get back to the ranch." Another rueful attempt at a grin. "It's been a bitch of a day."

"Stay," Meg heard herself say. She wasn't thinking of

leading Brad to her bed—not *exclusively* of that, anyhow. He'd just ridden miles through a blizzard on horseback, he'd taken a chill in the process, and the knowledge that he'd fathered a child was painfully new.

He was silent, perhaps at a loss.

"You shouldn't be alone," Meg said. *And neither should I.*

She knew what would happen if he stayed, of course. And she knew it was likely to be a mistake. They'd become strangers to each other over the years apart, living such different lives. It was too soon to run where angels feared to tread.

But she needed him that night, needed him to hold her, if nothing else.

And his need was just as great.

He grinned, though wanly. "How do we know your cousins won't land on the roof in a helicopter?" he asked.

"We don't," Meg said, and sighed. "They meant well, you know."

"Sure they did," he agreed wryly. "They were out to save your virtue."

Meg stood, went to Brad, slipped her arms around his middle. It seemed such a natural thing to do, and yet, at the same time, it was a breathtaking risk. "Stay," she said again.

He held her a little closer, propped his chin on top of her head. Stroked the length of her back with his hands. "Those who don't learn from history," he said, "are condemned to repeat it."

Meg rested her head against his shoulder, breathed in the scent of him. Felt herself softening against the hard heat of his body.

And the telephone rang.

"It might be important," Brad said, setting Meg away from him a little, when she didn't jump to answer.

She picked up without checking the ID panel. "Hello."

"Jesse's home," Cheyenne said, honoring her earlier promise to let Meg know when he returned. "He's half-frozen. I poured a hot toddy down him and put him to bed."

"Thanks for calling, Chey," Meg replied.

"You're all right?" Cheyenne asked shyly.

Wondering how much Jesse had told his wife when he got home, Meg replied that she was fine.

"He told me he and Keegan barged in on you and Brad, up in the mountains somewhere," Cheyenne went on. "I'm sorry, Meg. Maybe I should have kept my mouth shut, but I heard a report of the blizzard on the radio and I—well—I guess I panicked a little."

"Everything's all right, Cheyenne. Really."

"He's there, isn't he? Brad, I mean. He's with you, right now."

"Since I'd rather not have a midnight visit from my cousins," Meg said, "I'm admitting nothing."

Cheyenne giggled. "My lips are zipped. Want to have lunch tomorrow?"

"That sounds good," Meg answered, smiling. Brad was standing behind her by then, sliding his hands under the front of her sweatshirt, stopping just short of her bare breasts. She fought to keep her voice even, her breathing normal. "Good night, Cheyenne."

"I'll meet you in town, at Lucky's Bar and Grill at noon," Cheyenne said. "Call me if you're still in bed or anything like that, and we'll reschedule."

Brad tweaked lightly at Meg's nipples; she swallowed a gasp of pleasure. "See you there," she replied, and hung up quickly.

Brad turned Meg around, gave her a knee-melting kiss and then swept her up into his arms. Carried her to the back stairs.

She directed him to the very bed Holt and Lorelei had shared as man and wife.

He laid her down on the deep, cushy mattress, a shadow figure rimmed in light from the hallway behind him. She couldn't see his face, but she felt his gaze on her, gentle and hungry and so hot it seared her.

Afraid honor might get the better of him, Meg wriggled out of her sweatpants, pulled the top off over her head. Planning to sleep in the well-worn favorites, she hadn't bothered to put on a bra and panties after her bath earlier. Now she was completely naked. Utterly vulnerable.

Brad made a low, barely audible sound, rested one knee on the mattress beside her.

"Hold me," she whispered, and traces of an old song ran through her mind.

Help me make it through the night...

He stripped, maneuvered Meg so she was under the covers and joined her. The feel of him against her, solid and warm and all man, sent an electric rush of dizziness through her, pervading every cell.

She wrapped her arms around his neck and clung—she who never allowed herself to cling to anyone or anything except her own fierce pride.

A long, delicious time passed, without words, without caresses—only the holding.

The decision that there would be no foreplay was a tacit one.

The wanting was too great.

Brad nudged Meg's legs apart gently, settled between them, his erection pressing against her lower belly like a length of steel, heated in a forge.

She moaned and arched her back slightly, seeking him.

He took her with a single long, slow, smooth stroke, nestling into her depths. Held himself still as she gasped in wordless welcome.

He kissed her eyelids.

She squirmed beneath him.

He kissed her cheekbones.

Craving friction, desperate for it, Meg tried to move her hips, but he had her pinned, heavily, delectably, to the bed.

She whimpered.

He nibbled at her earlobes, one and then the other.

She ran her hands urgently up and down his back.

He tasted her neck.

She pleaded.

He withdrew, thrust again, but slowly.

She said his name.

He plunged deep.

And Meg came apart in his arms, raising herself high. Clawing, now at his back, now at the bedclothes, surrendering with a long, continuous, keening moan.

The climax was ferocious, but it was only a prelude to what would follow, and knowing that only increased Meg's need. Her body merged with Brad's, fused to it at the most elemental level, and the instant he began to move upon her she was lost again.

Even as she exploded, like a shattering star, she was aware of his phenomenal self-control, but when she reached her peak, he gave in. She reveled in the flex of his powerful body, the ragged, half groan, half shout of his release. Felt the warmth of his seed spilling inside her—and prayed it would take root.

Finally, he collapsed beside her, his face buried between her neck and the curve of her shoulder, his arms and legs still clenched around her, loosening by small, nearly imperceptible shivers.

Instinctively, Meg tilted her pelvis slightly backward, cradling the warmth.

A long while later, when both their breathing had returned to normal, or some semblance of that, Brad lifted his head. Touched his nose to hers. Started to speak, then thrust out a sigh, instead.

Meg threaded her fingers through his hair. Turned her head so she could kiss his chin.

"Guess you just earned another notch for the bedpost," she said.

He chuckled. "Yeah," he said. "Except this is *your* bed, McKettrick. *You* seduced *me.* I want that on record. Either way, since it's obviously an antique, carving the thing up probably wouldn't be the best idea."

"We're going to regret this in the morning, you know," she told him.

"That's then," he murmured, nibbling at her neck again. "This is now."

"Um-hmm," Meg said. She wanted *now* to last forever.

"I kept expecting a helicopter."

Meg laughed. "Me, too."

Brad lifted his head again, and in the moonlight she could see the smile in his eyes. "Know what?"

"What?"

"I'm glad it happened this way. In a real bed, and not the floor of some old line shack." He kissed her, very lightly. "Although I would have settled for anything I could get."

She pretended to slug him.

He laughed.

She felt him hardening against her, pressed against the outside of her right thigh. Stretching, he found the switch on the bedside lamp and turned it, spilling light over her. The glow of it seemed to seep into her skin, golden. Or was it the other way around? Was *she* the one shining, instead of the lamp?

"God," Brad whispered, "you *are* beautiful."

A tigress before, now Meg felt shy. Turned her head to one side, closed her eyes.

Brad caressed her breasts, her stomach and abdomen and the tops of her thighs; his touch so light, so gentle, that it made her breath catch in her throat.

"Look at me," he said.

She met his eyes. "The light," she protested weakly.

He slid his fingers between the moist curls at the juncture of her thighs. "So beautiful," he said.

She gasped as he made slow, sweet circles, deliberately exciting her. "Brad—"

"What?"

She was conscious of the softness of her belly; knew her breasts weren't as firm and high as he remembered. She wanted more of his lovemaking, and still more, but under the cover of darkness and finely woven sheets and the heirloom quilt Lorelei McKettrick had stitched with her own hands, so many years before. "The *light.*"

He made no move to flip the switch off again, but continued to stroke her, watching her responses. When he slipped his fingers inside her, found her G-spot and plied it expertly, she stopped worrying about the light and became a part of it.

While Meg slept, Brad slipped out of bed, pulled his borrowed clothes back on and retrieved his own from the bathroom where he'd showered earlier. Sat on the edge of the big claw-foot bathtub to pull on his socks and boots, still damp from his ride down the mountainside with Jesse.

Downstairs, he found the old-fashioned thermostat and

turned it up. Dusty heat whooshed from the vents. In the kitchen he switched on the lights, filled and set the coffee-maker. Maybe these small courtesies would make up for his leaving before Meg woke up.

He found a pencil and a memo pad over by the phone, planning to scribble a note, but nothing suitable came to mind, at least not right away.

"Thanks" would be inappropriate.

"Goodbye" sounded too blunt.

Only a jerk would write "See you around."

"I'll call you later"? Too cavalier.

Finally, he settled on, "Horses to feed."

Four of his songs had won Grammies, and all he could come up with was "horses to feed"? He was slipping.

He paused, stood looking up at the ceiling for a few moments, wanting nothing so much as to go back upstairs, crawl in bed with Meg again and make love to her.

Again.

But she'd said they were going to have regrets in the morning, and he didn't want to see those regrets on her face. The two of them would make bumbling excuses, never quite meeting each other's eyes.

And Brad knew he couldn't handle that.

So he left.

Meg stood in her warm kitchen, bundled in a terry-cloth bathrobe and surrounded by the aroma of freshly brewed coffee, peering at the note Brad had left.

Horses to feed.

"The man's a poet," she said out loud.

"Do you think it took?" Angus asked.

Meg whirled to find him standing just behind her, almost

at her elbow. "You scared me!" she accused, one hand pressed to her heart, which felt as though it might scramble up her esophagus to the back of her throat.

"Sorry," Angus said, though there was nothing the least bit contrite about his tone or his expression.

"Do I think *what* took?" Meg had barely sputtered the words when the awful realization struck her: Angus was asking if she thought she'd gotten pregnant, which meant—

Oh, God.

"Tell me you weren't here!"

"What do you take me for?" Angus snapped. "Of *course* I wasn't!"

Meg swallowed. Flushed to the roots of her hair. "But you knew—"

"I saw that singing cowboy leave just before sunup," came the taciturn reply. Now Angus was blushing, too. "Wasn't too hard to guess the rest."

"Will you stop calling him 'that singing cowboy'? He has a name. It's Brad O'Ballivan."

"I know that," Angus said. "But he's a fair hand with a horse, and he croons a decent tune. To my way of thinking, that makes him a singing cowboy."

Meg gave him a look, padded to the refrigerator, jerked open the door and rummaged around for something that might constitute breakfast. She'd cooked the last of the eggs for Brad, and the remaining choices were severely limited. Three green olives floating in a jar, some withered cheese, the arthritic remains of last week's takeout pizza and a carton of baking soda.

"Food doesn't just appear in an icebox, you know," Angus announced. "In my day, you had to hunt it down, or grow it in a garden, or harvest it from a field."

"Yes, and you probably walked ten miles to and from school," Meg said irritably, "uphill both ways."

She was starving. She'd have to hit the drive-through in town, then pick up some groceries. All that before her lunch with Cheyenne.

"I never went to school," Angus replied seriously, not getting the joke. "My ma taught me to read from the Good Book. I learned the rest on my own."

Meg sighed as an answer, shoved the splayed fingers of one hand through her tangled hair. Although she'd been disappointed at first to wake up and find Brad gone, now she was glad he couldn't see her. She looked like—well—a woman who had been having howling, sweaty-sheet sex half the night.

She started for the stairs.

"Make yourself at home," she told Angus, wondering if he'd catch the irony in her tone. For him, "home" was the Great Beyond, or the main ranch house down by the creek.

When she came down again half an hour later, showered and dressed in jeans and a lightweight blue sweater, he was sitting in Holt's chair, waiting for her.

"You ever think about wearing a dress or a skirt?" he asked, frowning.

Meg let that pass. "I've got some errands to run. See you later."

The telephone rang.

Brad?

She checked the caller ID panel.

Her mother.

"Voice mail will pick up," she told Angus.

"Answer it," Angus said sternly.

Meg reached for the receiver. "Hello, Mom. I was just on my way out the door—"

"You'd better sit down," Eve told her.

The pit of Meg's stomach pitched. "Why? Mom, is Sierra all right? Nothing's happened to Liam—"

"Both of them are fine. It's nothing like that."

Meg let out her breath. Leaned against the kitchen counter for support. "What, then?"

"Your father contacted me this morning. He wants to see you."

Meg's knees almost gave out. She'd never met her father, never spoken to him on the telephone or received so much as a birthday or Christmas card from him. She wasn't even sure what his name was—he used so many aliases.

"Meg?"

"I'm here," Meg said. "I don't want to see him."

"I knew I should have talked to you in person," Eve sighed. "But I was so alarmed—"

"Mother, did you hear what I just said? I don't want to see my father."

"He claims he's dying."

"Well, I'm sincerely sorry to hear that, but I still don't want anything to do with him."

"Meg—"

"I mean it, Mother. He's been a nonentity in my life. What could he possibly have to say to me now, after all this time?"

"I don't know," Eve replied.

"And if he wanted to talk to me, why did he call you?" The moment the question left her mouth, Meg wished she hadn't asked it.

"I think he's afraid."

"But he wasn't afraid of you?"

"He's past that, I think," Eve said. She'd been downright secretive on the subject of Meg's father from the first. Now, suddenly, she seemed to be urging Meg to make contact with him. What was going on? "Listen, why don't you stop by the hotel, and I'll make you some breakfast. We'll talk."

"Mom—"

"Blueberry pancakes. Maple-cured bacon. Your favorites."

"All right," Meg said, because as shaken as she was, she could have eaten the proverbial horse. "I'll be there in twenty minutes."

"Good," Eve replied, a little smugly, Meg thought. She was used to getting her way. After all, for almost thirty years, when Eve McKettrick said "jump," everybody reached for a vaulting pole.

"Are you going to ride shotgun?" Meg asked Angus after she'd hung up.

"I wouldn't miss this for anything," Angus said with relish.

Less than half an hour later, Meg was knocking on the front door of her mother's hotel suite.

When it opened, a man stood looking down at her, his expression uncertain and at the same time hopeful. She saw her own features reflected in the shape of his face, the set of his shoulders, the curve of his mouth.

"Hello, Meg," said her long-lost father.

Chapter Eight

After the horses had been fed, Brad turned them out to pasture for the day and made his way not into the big, lonely house, but to the copse of trees where Big John was buried. The old man's simple marker looked painfully new, amid the chipped and moss-covered stone crosses marking the graves of other, earlier O'Ballivans and Blackstones.

Brad had meant to visit the small private cemetery first thing, but between one thing and another, he hadn't managed it until now.

Standing there, in the shade of trees already shedding gold and crimson and rust-colored leaves, he moved to take off his hat, remembered that he wasn't wearing one and crouched to brush a scattering of fallen foliage from the now-sunken mound.

About time you showed up, he heard Big John O'Ballivan's booming voice observe, echoing through the channels of his mind.

Brad gave a lopsided, rueful grin. His eyes smarted, so he blinked a couple of times. "I'm here, old man," he answered hoarsely. "And I mean to stay. Look after the girls and the place. That ought to make you happy."

There was no reply from his grandfather, not even in his head.

But Brad felt like talking, so he did.

"I'm seeing Meg McKettrick again," he said. "Turns out I got her pregnant, back when we were kids, and she lost the baby. I never knew about it until yesterday."

Had Big John been there in the flesh, there'd have been a lecture coming. Brad would have welcomed that, even though the old man could peel off a strip of hide when he was riled.

One more reason why you should have stayed here and attended to business, Big John would have said. And that would have been just the warm-up.

"You never understood," Brad went on, just as if the old man *had* spoken. "We were going to lose Stone Creek Ranch. Maybe you weren't able to face that, but I had to. Everything Sam and Maddie and the ones who came after did to hold on to this place would have been for nothing."

The McKettricks would have stepped in if he'd asked for help, Brad knew that. Meg herself, probably her mother, too. Contrary as that Triple M bunch was, they'd bailed more than one neighbor out of financial trouble, saved dozens of smaller farms and ranches when beef prices bottomed out and things got tough. Even after all this time, though, the thought of going to them with his hat in his hands made the back of Brad's throat scald.

Although the ground was hard, wet and cold, he sat, cross-legged, gazing upon his grandfather's grave through a misty haze. He'd paid a high price for his pride, big, fancy career notwithstanding.

He'd lost the years he might have spent with Meg, the other children that might have come along. He hadn't been around when Big John needed him, and his sisters, though they were all educated, independent women, had been mere girls when he left. Sure, Big John had loved and protected them, in his gruff way, but that didn't excuse *his* absence. He should have been their big brother.

Caught up in these thoughts, and all the emotions they engendered, Brad heard the approaching rig, but didn't look around. Heard the engine shut off, the door slam.

"Hey," Olivia said softly from just behind him.

"Hey," he replied, not ready to look back and meet his sister's gaze.

"Willie's better. I've got him in the truck."

Brad blinked again. "That's good," he said. "Guess I'd better go to town and get him some dog food and stuff."

"I brought everything he needs," Livie said, her voice quiet. She came and sat down beside Brad. "Missing Big John?"

"Every day," Brad admitted. Their mother had hit the road when the twins were barely walking, and their dad had died a year later, herding spooked cattle in a lightning storm. Big John had stepped up to raise four young grandchildren without a word of complaint.

"Me, too," Livie replied softly. "You ever wonder where our mom ended up?"

Brad knew where Della O'Ballivan was—living in a trailer park outside of Independence, Missouri, with the latest in a long line of drunken boyfriends—but he'd never shared that information with his sisters. The story, brought to him by the private detective he'd hired on the proceeds from his first hit record, wasn't a pretty one.

"No," he said in all honesty. "I never wonder." He'd gone to see Della, once he'd learned her whereabouts. She'd been sloshed and more interested in his stardom, and how it might benefit her, than getting to know him. Ironically, she'd refused the help he *had* offered—immediate admission to one of the best treatment centers in the world—standing there in a tattered housecoat and scruffy slippers, with lipstick stains in the deep smoker's lines surrounding her mouth. She hadn't even asked about her daughters or the husband she'd left behind.

"She's probably dead," Livie said with a sigh.

Since Della's existence couldn't be called living, Brad agreed. "Probably," he replied. Except for periodic requests for a check, which were handled by his accountant, Brad never heard from their mother.

"It's why I don't want to get married, you know," Livie confided. "Because I might be like her. Just get on a bus one day and leave."

Just get on a bus one day and leave.

Like he'd done to Meg, Brad reflected, hurting. Maybe he was more like Della than he'd ever want to admit aloud.

"You'd never do that," he told his sister.

"I used to think she'd come home," Livie went on sadly. "To see me play Mary in the Christmas program at church, or when I got that award for my 4-H project, back in sixth grade."

Brad slipped an arm around Livie's shoulders, felt them trembling a little, squeezed. His reaction had been different from Livie's—if Della had come back, especially after their dad was killed, he'd have spit in her face.

"And you figure if you got married and had kids, you'd

just up and leave them? Miss all the Christmas plays and the 4-H projects?"

"I remember her, Brad," Livie said. "Just the lilac smell of her, and that she was pretty, but I remember. She used to sing a lot, hanging clothes out on the line and things like that. She read me stories. And then she was—well—just *gone.* I could never make sense of it. I always figured I must have done something really bad—"

"The flaw was in her, Livie, not you."

"That's the thing about flaws like that. You never know where they're going to show up. Mom probably didn't expect to abandon us."

Brad didn't agree, but he couldn't say so without revealing way too much. The Della he knew was an unmedicated bipolar with a penchant for gin, light on the tonic water. She'd probably married Jim O'Ballivan on a manic high, and decided to hit the road on a low—or vice versa. It was a miracle, by Brad's calculations, that she'd stayed on Stone Creek Ranch as long as she had, far from the bright lights and bigtown bars, where a practicing drunk might enjoy a degree of anonymity.

Coupled with things Big John had said about his daughter-in-law, "man to man" and in strictest confidence, that she'd hidden bottles around the place and slept with ranch hands when there were any around, Brad had few illusions about her morals.

Livie got to her feet, dusting off her jeans as she rose, and Brad immediately did the same.

"I'd better get Willie settled in," she said. "I've got a barn full of sick cows to see to, down the road at the Iversons' place."

"Anything serious?" Brad asked, as Livie headed for the Suburban parked next to his truck, and he kept pace. "The cows, I mean?"

"Some kind of a fever," Livie answered, looking worried. "I drew some random blood samples the last time I was there, and sent them to the university lab in Tempe for analysis. Nothing anybody's ever seen before."

"Contagious?"

Livie sighed. Her small shoulders slumped a little, under the weight of her life's calling, and not for the first time, Brad wished she'd gone into a less stressful occupation than veterinary medicine.

"Possibly," she said.

Brad waited politely until she'd climbed into the Suburban—Willie was curled comfortably in the backseat, in a nest of old blankets—then got behind the wheel of his truck to follow her to the house.

There, he was annoyed to see a black stretch limo waiting, motor purring.

Phil.

Muttering a curse, Brad did his best to ignore the obvious, got out of the truck and strode to Livie's Suburban to hoist Willie out of the backseat and carry him into the house. Livie was on his heels, arms full of rudimentary dog equipment, but she cast a few curious glances toward the stretch.

They entered through the kitchen door. Olivia set the dog bed down in a sunny corner, and Brad carefully lowered Willie onto it.

"Who's in the big car?" Livie asked.

"Probably Phil Meadowbrook," Brad said a little tersely.

"Your manager?" Livie's eyes were wary. She was probably thinking Phil would make an offer Brad couldn't refuse, and he'd leave again.

"*Former* manager."

Willie, his hide criss-crossed with pink shaved strips and stitches, looked up at Brad with luminous, trusting eyes.

Livie was watching him, too. There was something bruised about her expression. She knew him better than Willie did.

"We need you around, Brad," she said at great cost to her pride. "Not just the twins and me, but the whole community. If the Iversons have to put down all those cows, they'll go under. They're already in debt up to their eyeballs—last year, Mrs. Iverson had a bout with breast cancer, and they didn't have insurance."

Brad's jaw tightened, and so did the pit of his stomach. "I'll write a check," he said.

Livie caught hold of his forearm. *"No,"* she said with a vehemence that set him back on his heels a little. "That would make them feel like charity cases. They're good, decent people, Brad."

"Then what do you want me to do?" Half Brad's attention was on the conversation, the other half on the distant closing of the limo door, so he'd probably sounded abrupt.

"Put on a concert," Livie said. "There are half a dozen other families around Stone Creek in similar situations. Divvy up the proceeds, and that will spare everybody's dignity."

Brad frowned down at his sister. "How long has *that* plan been brewing in your busy little head, Dr. Livie?"

She smiled. "Ever since you raised all that money for the animals displaced during Hurricane Katrina," she said.

A knock sounded at the outside door.

Phil's big schnoz was pressed to the screen.

"Gotta go," Livie said. She squatted to give Willie a goodbye pat and ducked out of the kitchen, headed for the front.

"Can I come in?" Phil asked plaintively.

"Would it make a difference if I said no?" Brad shot back.

The screen door creaked open. "Of course not," Phil said, smiling broadly. "I came all the way from New Jersey to talk some sense into your head."

"I could have saved you the trip," Brad answered. "I'm not going to Vegas. I'm not going *anywhere*." He liked Phil, but after the events of the past twenty-four hours, he was something the worse for wear. With his chores done and the overdue visit to Big John's grave behind him, he'd planned to eat something, take a hot shower and fall face-first into his unmade bed.

"Who said anything about Vegas?" Phil asked, the picture of innocent affront. "Maybe I want to deliver a big fat royalty check or something like that."

"And maybe you're full of crap," Brad countered. "I just *got* a 'big, fat royalty check,' according to my accountant. He's fit to be tied because the recording company promised to parcel the money out over at least fifteen years, and it came in a lump sum instead. Says the taxes are going to eat me alive."

Phil sniffled, pretended to wipe tears from his eyes. "Cry me a river, Mr. Country Music," he said. "I belong to the you-can-never-be-too-rich school of thought. Until my niece suffered that bout with anorexia—thank God she recovered—I thought you could never be too thin, either, but that theory's down the swirler."

Brad said nothing.

"What happened to that dog?" Phil asked, after giving Willie the eyeball.

"He was attacked by coyotes—or maybe wolves."

Livie had lugged in a bag of kibble and a couple of bowls, along with the bed Willie was lounging on now, and she'd set two prescription bottles on the counter, too, though Brad hadn't noticed them until now. He busied himself with reading the labels.

"Why anybody'd want to live in a place where a thing like that is even remotely possible, even if he *is* a dog," Phil marveled, "is beyond me."

Willie was to have one of each pill—an antibiotic and a painkiller—morning and night. With food. "A lot of things are beyond you, Phil," Brad said, figuring Olivia must have dosed the dog that morning before leaving the clinic, which meant the medication could wait until suppertime.

"He's pretty torn up. Wouldn't have happened in Music City, to a dog *or* a man."

"Evidently," Brad said, still distracted, "you've repressed the gory memories of my second divorce."

Phil chuckled. "You could give all that extra royalty money you're so worried about to good ole Cynthia," he suggested. "Write it off as an extra settlement and let *her* worry about the taxes."

"You're just full of wisdom today. Something else, too."

Uninvited, Phil drew back a chair at the table and sank into it, one hand pressed dramatically to his heart. "Phew," he sighed. "The old ticker ain't what it used to be."

"Right," Brad said. "I was there for the celebration after your last cardiology workup, remember? You probably have a better heart than I do, so spare me the sympathy plays."

"You have a heart?" Phil countered, raising his bushy gray eyebrows almost to his thinning hairline. Even with plugs, the carpet looked pretty sparse. Phil's pate always reminded Brad of the dolls his sisters had had when they were little, sprouting shocks of hair out of holes in neat little rows. "Couldn't prove it by me."

"Whatever," Brad said, dipping one of Willie's bowls into

the kibble bag, then setting it down, full, where the dog could reach it without getting off his bed. He followed up by filling the other bowl with tap water. Then, on second thought, he dumped that and poured the bottled kind, instead.

"This is something big," Phil said. "That's why I came in person."

"If I let you tell me, will you leave?" By then, Brad was plundering the fridge for the makings of breakfast.

"Got any kosher sausage in there?" the older man asked.

"Sorry," Brad answered. He'd come up with something if Phil stayed, since he couldn't eat in front of the man, but he was still hoping for a speedy departure.

Next, he'd be hanging up a stocking on Christmas Eve, setting out an empty basket the night before Easter.

"Big opportunity," Phil continued. "Very, very big."

"I don't care."

"You don't care? This is a *movie*, Brad. The lead. A *feature,* too. A big Western with cattle and wagons and a cast of dozens. And you won't even have to sing."

"No."

"Two years ago, even a year ago, you would have *killed* for a chance like this!"

"That was then," Brad said, flashing back to the night before, when he'd said practically the same thing to Meg, "and this is now."

"I've got the script in the car. In my briefcase. Solid gold, Brad. It might even be Oscar material."

"Phil," Brad said, turning from the fridge with the makings of a serious omelet in his hands, "what part of 'no' is eluding you? Would it be the *N,* or the *O?*"

"But you'd get to play an *outlaw,* trying to go straight."

"Phil."

"You're really serious about this retirement thing, aren't you?" Phil sounded stunned. Aggrieved. And petulant. "In a year—hell, in *six months*—when you've got all this down-home stuff out of your system, you'll wish you'd listened to me!"

"I listened, Phil. Do you want an omelet?"

"Do I *want an omelet?* Hell, no! I want you to make a damned *movie!*"

"Not gonna happen, Phil."

Phil was suddenly super-alert, like a predator who's just spotted dinner on the hoof. "It's some woman, isn't it?"

Again, he flashed on Meg. The way she'd felt, silky and slick, against him. The way she'd scratched at his back and called his name…

"Maybe," he admitted.

"Do I need to remind you that your romantic history isn't exactly going to inspire a new line of Hallmark valentines?"

Brad sighed. Got out the skillet and set it on the stove. Willie gave him a sidelong look of commiseration from the dog bed.

"If you won't eat an omelet," Brad told Phil, "leave."

"That pretty little thing who sneaked out of here when I came to the door—was that her?"

"That was my sister," Brad said.

Phil raised himself laboriously to his feet, like he was ninety-seven instead of seventy-seven, and all that would save him from a painful and rapid descent into the grave all but yawning at the tips of his gleaming shoes was Brad's signature on a movie contract. "Well, whoever this woman is, I'd like her name. Maybe *she* can get you to see reason."

That made Brad smile. Meg made him see galaxies colliding. Once or twice, during the night, he'd almost seen God. But reason?

Nope.

He plopped a dollop of butter into the skillet.

Phil made a huffy exit, slamming the screen door behind him.

Willie gave a low whine.

"You're right," Brad told the dog. "He'll probably be back."

Meg stood as if frozen in the hallway of Indian Rock's only hotel, wanting to turn and run, but too stunned to move.

She'd just gathered the impetus to flee when her father stuck a hand out. "Ted Ledger," he said, by way of introduction. "Come in and meet your sister, Meg."

Her sister?

It was that, added to a desire to commit matricide, that brought Meg over the threshold and into her mother's simply furnished, elegantly rustic suite.

Eve was nowhere in sight, the coward. But a little girl, ten or twelve years old, sat stiffly on the couch, hands folded in her lap. She was blond and blue-eyed, clad in cheap discount-store jeans and a floral shirt with ruffles, and the look on her face was one of terrified defiance.

"Hello," Meg said, forcing the words past her heart, which was beating in her throat.

The marvelous blue eyes narrowed.

"Carly," said Ted Ledger, "say hello."

"Hello," Carly complied grudgingly.

Looking at the child, Meg couldn't help thinking that the baby she'd lost would have been about this same age, if it hadn't been for the miscarriage.

She straightened her spine. Turned to the father who hadn't cared enough to send her so much as an e-mail, let alone be part of her life. "Where is my mother?" she asked evenly.

"Hiding out," Ledger said with a wisp of a grin. In his

youth, he'd probably been handsome. Now he was thin and gray-haired, with dark shadows under his pale blue eyes.

Carly looked Meg over again and jutted out her chin. "I don't want to live with her," she said. "She probably doesn't need a kid hanging around anyhow."

"Go in the kitchen," Ledger told the child.

To Meg's surprise, Carly obeyed.

"Live with me?" Meg echoed in a whisper.

"It's that or foster care," Ledger said. "Sit down."

Meg sat, not because her father had asked her to, but because all the starch had gone out of her knees. Questions battered at the back of her throat, like balls springing from a pitching machine.

Where have you been?

Why didn't you ever call?

If I kill my mother, could a dream-team get me off without prison time?

"I know this is sudden," Ted Ledger said, perching on the edge of the white velvet wingback chair Eve had had sent from her mansion in San Antonio, to make the place more "homey." "But the situation is desperate. *I'm* desperate."

Meg tried to swallow, but couldn't. Her mouth was too dry, and her esophagus had closed up. "I don't believe this," she croaked.

"Your mother and I agreed, long ago," Ledger went on, "that it would be best if I stayed out of your life. That's why she never brought you to visit me."

"Visit you?"

"I was in prison, Meg. For embezzlement."

"From McKettrickCo," Meg mused aloud, startled, but at the same time realizing that she'd known all along, on some half-conscious level.

"I told you he was a waste of hair and hide," Angus said. He stood over by the fake fireplace, one arm resting on the mantelpiece.

Meg took care to ignore him, not to so much as glance in his direction, though she could see him out of the corner of one eye. He was in old-man mode today, white-headed and wrinkled and John Wayne-tough, but dressed for the trail.

"Yes," Ledger replied. "Your mother saw that there was no scandal—easier to do in those days, before the media came into its own. I went to jail. She went on with her life."

"Where does Carly fit in?"

Ledger's smile was soft and sad. "While I was inside, I got religion, as they say. When I was released, I found a job, met a woman, got married. We had Carly. Then, three years ago, Sarah—my wife—was killed in a car accident. Things went downhill from there—I was diagnosed last month."

Tears burned in Meg's eyes, but they weren't for Ledger, or even for Sarah. They were for Carly. Although she'd grown up in a different financial situation, with all the stability that came with simply being a McKettrick, she knew what the child must be going through.

"You don't have any other family? Perhaps Sarah's people—"

Ledger shook his head. "There's no one. Your mother has generously agreed to pay my medical bills and arrange for a decent burial, but I'll be lucky if I live six weeks. And once I'm gone, Carly will be alone."

Meg pressed her fingertips to her temples and breathed slowly and deeply. "Maybe Mom could—"

"She's past the age to raise a twelve-year-old," Ledger interrupted.

He leaned forward slightly in his chair, rested his elbows

on his knees, intertwined his fingers and let his hands dangle. "Meg, you don't owe me a damn thing. I was no kind of father, and I'm not pretending I was. But Carly is your half sister. She's got your blood in her veins. And she doesn't have anybody else."

Meg closed her eyes, trying to imagine herself raising a resentful, grieving preadolescent girl. As much as she'd longed for her own child, nothing had prepared her for this.

"She won't go to foster care," she said. "Mother would never allow it."

"Boarding school, then," Ledger replied. "Carly would hate that. Probably run away. She needs a real home. Love. Somebody young enough to steer her safely through her teens, at least."

"You heard her," Meg said. "She doesn't want to live with me."

"She doesn't know what she wants, except for me to have a miraculous recovery, and that isn't going to happen. I can't ask you to do this for me, Meg—I've got no right to ask anything of you—but I can ask you to do it for Carly."

The room seemed to tilt. From the kitchen, Meg heard her mother's voice, and Carly's. What were they talking about in there?

"Okay," Meg heard herself say.

Ledger's once-handsome face lit with a smile of relief and what looked like sincere gratitude. "You'll do it? You'll look after your sister?"

My sister.

"Yes," Meg said. On the outside, she probably looked calm. On the inside, she was shaking. "What happens now?"

"I go into the hospital for pain control. Carly goes home

with you for a few days. When—and if—I get out, she'll come back to stay with me."

Meg nodded, her mind racing, groping, grasping for some handhold on an entirely new, entirely unexpected situation.

"We've got a room downstairs," Ledger said, rising painfully from the chair. "Carly and I will leave you alone with Eve for a little while."

Over by the fireplace, Angus scowled, powerful arms folded across his chest. Fortunately, he didn't say anything, because Meg would have told him to shut up if he had.

Her father left, Carly trailing after him.

Eve stepped into the kitchen doorway the moment they'd gone.

Angus vanished.

"Nice work, Mom," Meg said, still too shaken to stand up. Since a murder would be hard to pull off sitting down, her mother was off the hook. Temporarily.

"She's about the same age as your baby would have been," Eve said. "It's fate."

Meg's mouth fell open.

"Of course I knew," Eve told her, venturing as far as the white velvet chair and perching gracefully on the edge of its cushion. "I'm your mother."

Meg closed her mouth. Tightly.

Eve's eyes were on the door through which Ted Ledger and Carly had just passed. "I loved him," she said. "But when he admitted stealing all that money, there was nothing I could do to keep him out of prison. We divorced after his conviction, and he asked me not to tell you where he was."

Meg sagged back in her own chair, still dizzy. Still speechless.

"She's a beautiful child," Eve said, referring, of course, to Carly. "You looked just like her, at that age. It's uncanny, really."

"She's bound to have a lot of problems," Meg managed.

"Of course she will. She lost her mother, and now her father is at death's door. But she has you, Meg. That makes her lucky, in spite of everything else."

"I haven't the faintest idea how to raise a child," Meg pointed out.

"Nobody does, when they start out," Eve reasoned. "Children don't come with a handbook, you know."

Suddenly, Meg remembered the lunch she had scheduled with Cheyenne, the groceries she'd intended to buy. Instantaneous motherhood hadn't been on her to-do list for the day.

She imagined making a call to Cheyenne. *Gotta postpone lunch. You see, I just gave birth to a twelve-year-old in my mother's living room.*

"I had plans," she said lamely.

"Didn't we all?" Eve countered.

"There's no food in my refrigerator."

"Supermarket's right down the road."

"Where have they been living? What kind of life has she had, up to now?"

"A hard one, I would imagine. Ted's something of a drifter—I suspect they've been living out of that old car he drives. He claims he homeschooled her, but knowing Ted, that probably means she knows how to read a racing form and calculate the odds of winning at Powerball."

"Great," Meg said, but something motherly was stirring inside her, something hopeful and brave and very, very fragile. "Can I count on you for help, or just the usual interference?"

Eve laughed. "Both," she said.

Meg found her purse, fumbled for her cell phone, dialed Cheyenne's number.

It was something of a relief that she got her friend's voice mail.

"This is Meg," she said. "I can't make it for lunch. How about a rain check?"

Chapter Nine

Meg moved through the supermarket like a robot, programmed to take things off the shelves and drop them into the cart. When she got home and started putting away her groceries, she was surprised by some of the things she'd bought. There were ingredients for actual meals, not just things she could nuke in the microwave or eat right out of the box or bag.

She was brewing coffee when a knock sounded at the back door.

Glancing over, she saw her cousin Rance through the little panes of glass and gestured for him to come in. Tall and dark-haired, he looked as though he'd just come off a nineteenth-century cattle drive, in his battered boots, old jeans and Western-cut shirt. Favoring her with a lopsided grin, he removed his hat and hung it on one of the pegs next to the door.

"Heard you had a little shock this morning," he said.

Meg shook her head. She'd never gotten over how fast word got around in a place like Indian Rock. Then again, maybe Eve had called Rance, thinking Meg might need emotional support. "You could say that," she replied. "Who told you?"

Rance proceeded to the coffeemaker, which was still doing its steaming and gurgling number, took a mug down from the cupboard above and filled it, heedless of the brew dripping, fragrant and sizzling, onto the base. Of course, being a man, he didn't bother to wipe up the overflow.

"Eve," he said, confirming her suspicions.

Meg, not usually a neatnik, made a big deal of paper-toweling up the spill around the bottom of the coffeemaker. "It's no emergency, Rance," she told him.

He looked ruefully amused. "Your dad walks into your life after something like thirty years and it's not an emergency?"

"I suppose Mom told you about Carly."

Rance nodded. Ushered Meg to a seat at the table, set down his coffee mug and went back to pour a cup for her, messing up the counter all over again. "Twelve years old, something of an attitude," he confirmed, giving her the cup and then sitting astride the bench. "And coming to live with you. Is that going to screw up your love life?"

"I don't *have* a love life," Meg said. Sure, she'd spent the night tangling sheets with Brad O'Ballivan but, one, primal sex didn't constitute a relationship and, two, it was none of Rance's business anyway.

"Whatever," Rance said. "The point is, you've got a kid to raise, and she's a handful, by all accounts. I'm no authority on bringing up kids, but I do have two daughters. I'll do what I can to help, Meg, and so will Emma."

Rance's girls, Maeve and Rianna, were like nieces to Meg, and so was Keegan's Devon. While they were all younger than

Carly, they would be eager to include her in the family, and it was comforting to know that.

"Thanks," Meg said as her eyes misted over.

"You can do this," Rance told her.

"I don't seem to have a choice. Carly is my half sister, there's no one else, and blood is blood."

"If there's one concept a hardheaded McKettrick can comprehend right away, it's that."

"I don't know as we're all that hardheaded," Angus put in, after materializing behind Rance in the middle of the kitchen.

Meg didn't glance up, nor did she answer. She was close to Rance, Jesse and Keegan—always had been—but she'd never told them she saw Angus, dead since the early twentieth century, on a regular basis. Her mother knew, having overheard Meg talking to him, long after the age of entertaining imaginary playmates had passed, and for all the problems Eve had suffered after Sierra's kidnapping, she'd given her remaining daughter one inestimable gift. She'd believed her.

You're not the type to see things, Eve had said after Meg reluctantly explained. *If you say Angus McKettrick is here, then he is.*

Remembering, Meg felt a swell of love for her mother, despite an equal measure of annoyance.

"I'd better get back to punching cattle," Rance said, finishing his coffee and swinging a leg over the bench to stand. With winter coming on, he and his hired men were rounding up strays in the hills and driving the whole bunch down to the lower pastures. "If you need a hand over here, with the girl or anything else, you let me know."

Meg grinned up at him. He'd taken time out of a busy day to come over and check on her in person, and she appreciated that. "Once Carly's had a little time to settle in, we'll introduce her to Maeve and Rianna and Devon. I don't think she's got a clue what it's like to be part of a family like ours."

Rance laid a work-calloused hand on Meg's shoulder as he passed, carrying his empty coffee mug to the sink, then crossing to take his hat down from the peg. "Probably not," he agreed. "But she'll find out soon enough."

With that, Rance left again.

Meg turned to acknowledge Angus. "We *are* hardheaded," she told him. "Every last one of us."

"I'd rather call it 'persistent,'" Angus imparted.

"Your decision," Meg responded, getting up to dispose of her own coffee cup then heading for the backstairs. She didn't know when Carly would be arriving, but it was time to get a room ready for her. That meant changing sheets, opening windows to air the place out and equipping the guest bathroom with necessities like clean towels, a toothbrush and paste, shampoo and the like.

She'd barely finished, and returned to the kitchen to slap together a hasty lunch, when an old car rattled up alongside the house, backfired and shut down. As Meg watched from the window, Ted Ledger got out, keeping one hand to the car for balance as he rounded it, and leaned in on the opposite side, no doubt trying to persuade a reluctant Carly to alight.

Meg hurried outside.

By the time she reached the car, Carly was standing with a beat-up backpack dangling from one hand, staring at the barn.

"Do you have horses?" she asked.

Hallelujah, Meg thought. *Common ground.*

"Yes," she said, smiling.

"I hate horses," Carly said. "They smell and step on people."

Ted passed Meg a beleaguered look over the top of the old station wagon, his eyes pleading for patience.

"You do not," he said to Carly. Then, to Meg, "She's just being difficult."

Duh, Meg thought, but in spite of all her absent-father issues, she felt a pang of sympathy for the man. He was terminally ill, probably broke, and trying to find a place for his younger daughter to make the softest possible landing.

Meg figured it would be a fiery crash instead, complete with explosions, but she also knew she was up to the challenge. Mostly, that is. And with a lot of help from Rance, Keegan, Jesse and Sierra.

Oh, yeah. She'd be calling in her markers, all right.

Code-blue, calling all McKettricks.

"I'm not staying unless my dad can stay, too," Carly announced, standing her ground, there in the gravel of the upper driveway, knuckles white where she gripped the backpack.

Meg hadn't considered this development, though she supposed she should have. She forced herself to meet Ted's gaze, saw both resignation and hope in his eyes when she did.

"It's a big house," she heard herself say. "Plenty of room."

Rance's earlier question echoed in her mind. *Is that going to screw up your love life?*

There'd be no more overnight visits from Brad, at least not in the immediate future. To Meg, that was both a relief— things were moving too fast on that front—and a problem. Her body was still reverberating with the pleasure Brad had awakened in her, and already craving more.

"Okay," Carly said, moving a little closer to Ted. The two of them bumped shoulders in unspoken communication, and Meg felt a brief and unexpected stab of envy.

Meg tried to carry Ted's suitcase inside, but he wouldn't allow that. Manly pride, she supposed.

Angus watched from the back steps as the three of them

trailed toward the house, Meg in the lead, Ted following and Carly straggling at the rear.

"She's a good kid," Angus said.

Meg gave him a look but said nothing.

Just walking into the house seemed to wear Ted out, and as soon as Carly had been installed in her room, he expressed a need to lie down. Meg showed him to the space generations of McKettrick women—she being an exception—had done their sewing.

There was only a daybed, and Meg hadn't changed the sheets, but Ted waved away her offer to spruce up the room a little. She went out, closing the door behind her, and heard the bed-springs groan as if he'd collapsed onto them.

Carly's door was shut. Meg paused outside it, on her way to the rear stairway, considered knocking and decided to leave the poor kid alone, let her adjust to new and strange surroundings.

Downstairs, Meg went back to what she'd been doing when Ted and Carly arrived. She made a couple of extra sandwiches, just in case, wolfed one down with a glass of milk and eyeballed the phone.

Was Brad going to call, or was last night just another slam-bam to him? And if he *did* call, what exactly was she going to say?

Willie was surprisingly ambulatory, considering what he'd been through. When Brad came out of the upstairs bathroom, having showered and pulled on a pair of boxer-briefs and nothing else, the dog was waiting in the hall. Climbing the stairs must have been an ordeal, but he'd done it.

"You need to go outside, boy?" Brad asked. When Big John's health had started to decline, Brad had wanted to install an elevator, so the old man wouldn't have to manage a lot of steps, but he'd met with the usual response.

An elevator? Big John had scoffed. *Boy, all that fine Nashville livin' is goin' to your head.*

Now, with an injured dog on his hands, Brad wished he'd overridden his grandfather's protests.

He moved to lift Willie, intending to carry him downstairs and out the kitchen door to the grassy side yard, but a whimper from the dog foiled that idea. Carefully, the two of them made the descent, Willie stopping every few steps to rest, panting.

The whole process was painful to watch.

Reaching the kitchen at last, Brad opened the back door and waited as Willie labored outside, found a place in the grass after copious sniffing and did his business.

Once he was back inside, Brad decided another trip up the stairway was out of the question. He moved Willie's new dog bed into a small downstairs guest room, threw back the comforter on one of the twin-sized beds and fell onto it, face-first.

"Who's the old man?" Carly asked, startling Meg, who had been running more searches on Josiah McKettrick on the computer in the study, for more reasons than one.

"What old man?" Meg retorted pleasantly, turning in the chair to see her half sister standing in the big double doorway, looking much younger than twelve in a faded and somewhat frayed sleep shirt with a cartoon bear on the front.

"This house," Carly said implacably, "is haunted."

"It's been around a long time," Meg hedged, still smiling. "Lots of history here. Are you hungry?"

"Only if you've got the stuff to make grilled-cheese sandwiches," Carly said. She was in the gawky stage, but one day, she'd be gorgeous. Meg didn't see the resemblance Eve had commented on earlier, but if there was one, it was cause to feel flattered.

"I've got the stuff," Meg assured her, rising from her chair.

"I can do it myself," Carly said.

"Maybe we could talk a little," Meg replied.

"Or not," Carly answered, with a note of dismissal that sounded false.

Meg followed the woman-child to the kitchen, earning herself a few scathing backward glances in the process.

Efficiently, Carly opened the fridge, helped herself to a package of cheese and proceeded to the counter. Meg supplied bread and a butter dish and a skillet, but that was all the assistance Carly was willing to accept.

"Can you cook?" Meg asked, hoping to get some kind of dialogue going.

Carly shrugged one thin shoulder. Her feet were bare and a tiny tattoo of some kind of flower blossomed just above one ankle bone. "Dad's hopeless at it, so I learned."

"I see," Meg said, wondering what could have possessed her father to let a child get a tattoo, and if it had hurt much, getting poked with all those needles.

"You don't see," Carly said, skillfully preparing her sandwich, everything in her bearing warning Meg to keep her distance.

"What makes you say that?"

Another shrug.

"Carly?"

The girl's back, turned to Meg as she laid the sandwich in the skillet and adjusted the gas stove burner beneath, stiffened. "Don't ask me a bunch of questions, okay? Don't ask how it was, living on the road, or if I miss my mother, or what it's like knowing my dad is going to die. Just leave me be, and we'll get along all right."

"There's one question I have to ask," Meg said.

Carly tossed her another short, over-the-shoulder glower. "What?"

"Did it hurt a lot, getting that tattoo?"

Suddenly, a smile broke over Carly's face, and it changed everything about her. "Yes."

"Why did you do it?"

"That's *two* questions," Carly pointed out. "You said one."

"Was it because your friends got tattoos?"

Carly's smile faded, and she averted her attention again, spatula in hand, ready to turn her grilled-cheese sandwich when it was just right. "I don't have any friends," she said. "We moved around too much. And I didn't need them anyhow. Me and Dad—that was enough."

Meg's eyes burned.

"I got the tattoo," Carly said, catching Meg off-guard, "because my mom had one just like it, in the same place. It's a yellow rose—because Dad always called her his yellow rose of Texas."

Meg's throat went tight. How was she going to help this child face the loss of not one parent, but two? Sister or not, she was a stranger to Carly.

The phone rang.

Carly, being closest, picked up the receiver, peered at the caller ID panel, and went wide-eyed. *"Brad O'Ballivan?"* she whispered reverently, padding across the kitchen to give Meg the phone. *"The* Brad O'Ballivan?"

Meg choked out a laugh. Well, well, well. Carly was a fan. Just the opening Meg needed to establish some kind of bond, however tenuous, with her newly discovered kid sister. *"The* Brad O'Ballivan," she said before thumbing the talk button. "Hello?"

Brad's answer was an expansive yawn. Evidently, he'd

either just awakened or he'd gone to bed early. Either way, the images playing in Meg's mind were scintillating ones, and they soon rippled into other parts of her anatomy, like tiny tsunamis boiling under her skin.

"Willie's home," he said finally.

Carly was staring at Meg. "I have all his CDs," she said.

"That's good," Meg answered.

"We ought to celebrate," Brad went on. "I grill a mean steak. Six-thirty, my place?"

"Only if you have a couple of spares," Meg said. "I have company."

The smell of scorching sandwich billowed from the stove. Carly didn't move.

"Company?" Brad asked sleepily, with another yawn.

Meg pictured him scantily clothed, if he was wearing anything at all, with an attractive case of bed head. And she blushed to catch herself thinking lascivious thoughts with a twelve-year-old in the same room. "It's a lot to explain over the phone," she said diplomatically, gesturing to Carly to rescue the sandwich, which she finally did.

"The more the merrier," Brad said. "Whoever they are, bring them."

"We'll be there," Meg said.

Carly pushed the skillet off the burner and waved ineffectually at the smoke.

Meg said goodbye to Brad and hung up the phone.

"We're going to *Brad O'Ballivan's house?*" Carly blurted. *"For real?"*

"For real," Meg said. "If your dad feels up to it."

"He's your dad, too," Carly allowed. "And he likes Brad's music. We listen to it in the car all the time."

Meg let the part about Ted Ledger being her dad pass. He'd

been her sire, not her father. "Let's let him rest," she said, taking over the grilled cheese operation and feeling glad when Carly didn't protest, or try to elbow her aside.

"How long have you known him?" Carly demanded, almost breathless.

It was a moment before Meg realized the girl was talking about Brad, not Ted, so muddled were her thoughts. "Since junior high," she said.

"What's he like?"

"He's nice," Meg said carefully, slicing cheese, reaching for the butter dish and then the bread bag.

"'Nice'?" Carly looked not only skeptical, but a little disappointed. "He trashes hotel rooms. He pushed a famous actress into a swimming pool at a big Hollywood party—"

"I think that's mostly hype," Meg said, hoping the kid hadn't heard the notches-in-the-bedpost stuff. She started the new sandwich in a fresh skillet and carried the first one to the sink. When she glanced Carly's way, she was surprised and touched to see she'd taken a seat on the bench next to the table.

"Do you think he'd autograph my CDs?"

"I'd say there was a fairly good chance he will, yes." She turned the sandwich, got out a china plate, poured a glass of milk.

Carly glowed with anticipation. "If I had any friends," she said, "I'd call them all and tell them I get to meet Brad O'Ballivan *in the flesh*."

And what flesh it was, Meg thought, and blushed again. "Once you start school," she said, "you'll have all kinds of friends. Plus, there are some kids in the family around your age."

"It's not my family," Carly said, stiffening again.

"Of course it is," Meg argued, but cautiously, scooping a letter-perfect grilled-cheese sandwich onto a plate and presenting it to Carly with a flourish, along with the milk. She wished Angus had been there, to see her cooking. "You and I are sisters. I'm a McKettrick. So that means you're related to them, too, if only by association."

"I hate milk," Carly said.

"Brad drinks it," Meg replied lightly.

Carly reached for the glass, took a sip. Pondered the taste, and then took another. "You see him, too," the child observed. "The old man, I mean."

Before Meg could come up with an answer, Angus reappeared.

"I'm not that old," he protested.

"Yes, you are," Carly argued, looking right at him. "You must be a hundred, and that's *old.*"

Meg's mouth fell open.

"I *told* you I could see him," Carly said with a touch of smugness.

Angus laughed. "I'll be damned," he marveled.

Carly's brow furrowed. "Are you a ghost?"

"Not really," Angus said.

"What are you, then?"

"Just a person, like you. I'm from another time, that's all."

No big deal. I just step from one century to another at will. Anybody could do it.

Meg watched the exchange in amazement, speechless. Ever since she'd started seeing Angus, way back in her nursery days, she'd wished for one other person—just one— who could see him, too. Being different from other people was a lonely thing.

"When my dad dies, will he still be around?"

Angus approached the table, drew back Holt's chair, and sat down. His manner was gruff and gentle, at the same time, and Meg's throat tightened again, recalling all the times he'd comforted her, in his grave, deep-voiced way. "That's a question I can't rightly answer," he said solemnly. "But I can tell you that folks don't really die, in the way you probably think of it. They're just in another place, that's all."

Carly blinked, obviously trying hard not to cry. "I'm going to miss him something awful," she said very softly.

Angus covered the child's small hand with one of his big, work-worn paws. There was such a rough tenderness in the gesture that Meg's throat closed up even more, and her eyes scalded.

"It's a fact of life, missing folks when they go away," Angus said. "You've got Meg, here, though." He nodded his head slightly, in her direction, but didn't look away from Carly's face. "She'll do right by you. It's the McKettrick way, taking care of your own."

"But I'm not a McKettrick," Carly said.

"You could be if you wanted to," Angus reasoned. "You're not a Ledger, either, are you?"

"We've changed our name so many times," the child admitted, her eyes round and sad and a little hungry as she studied Angus, "I don't remember who I am."

"Then you might as well be a McKettrick as not," Angus said.

Carly's gaze slid to Meg, swung away again. "I'm not going to forget my dad," she said.

"Nobody expects you to do that," Angus replied. "Thing is, you've got a long life ahead of you, and it'll be a lot easier with a family to take your part when the trail gets rugged."

Upstairs, a door opened, then closed again.

"Your pa," Angus told Carly, lowering his voice a little, "is real worried about you being all right, once he's gone. You could put his mind at ease a bit, if you'd give Meg a chance to act like a big sister."

Carly bit her lower lip, then nodded. "I wish you wouldn't go away," she said. "But I know you're going to." She paused, and Meg grappled with the sudden knowledge that it was true—one day soon, Angus would vanish, for good. "If you see my mom—her name is Rose—will you tell her I've got a tattoo just like hers?"

"I surely will," Angus promised.

"And you'll look out for my dad, too?"

Angus nodded, his eyes misty. It was a phenomenon Meg had never seen before, even at family funerals. Then he ruffled Carly's hair and vanished just as Ted came down the stairs, moving slowly, holding tightly to the rail.

It was all Meg could do not to rush to his aid.

"Hungry?" she asked moderately.

"I could eat," Ted volunteered, looking at Carly. His whole face softened as he gazed at his younger child.

It made Meg wonder if he'd ever missed *her*, during all those years away.

As if he'd heard her thoughts, her father turned to her. "You turned out real well," he said after clearing his throat. "Your mom did a good job, raising you. But, then, Eve was always competent."

"We're going to meet Brad O'Ballivan," Carly said.

"Get out," Ted teased, a faint twinkle shining in his eyes. "We're not, either."

"Yes, we are," Carly insisted. "Meg knows him. He just called here. Meg says he might autograph my CDs."

Ted grinned, made his way to the table and sank into the chair Angus had occupied until moments before. Spent a few moments recovering from the exertion of descending the stairs and crossing the room.

Meg served up the extra sandwiches she'd made earlier,

struggling all the while with a lot of tangled emotions. Carly could see Angus. Ted Ledger might be a total stranger, but he was Meg's father, and he was dying.

Last but certainly not least, Brad was back in her life, and there were bound to be complications.

A strange combination of grief, joy and anticipation pushed at the inside walls of Meg's heart.

They arrived right on time, Meg and a young girl and a man who put Brad in mind of a faster-aging Paul Newman. Willie, who'd been resting on the soft grass bordering the flagstone patio off the kitchen, keeping an eye on his new master while he prepared the barbeque grill for action, gave a soft little woof.

Brad watched as Meg approached, thinking how delicious she looked in her jeans and lightweight, close-fitting sweater. She hadn't explained who her company was, but looking at them, Brad saw the girl's resemblance to Meg, and guessed the man to be the father she hadn't seen since she was a toddler.

He smiled.

The girl blushed and stared at him.

"Hey," he said, putting out a hand. "My name's Brad O'Ballivan."

"I know," the girl said.

"My sister, Carly," Meg told him. "And this is my—this is Ted Ledger."

Shyly, Carly slipped off her backpack, reached inside, took out a couple of beat-up CDs. "Meg said I could maybe get your autograph."

"No maybe about it," Brad answered. "I don't happen to have a pen on me at the moment, though."

Carly swallowed visibly. "That's okay," she said, her gaze straying to Willie, who was thumping his tail against the ground and grinning a goofy dog grin at her, hoping for friendship. "What happened to him?"

"He had a run-in with a pack of coyotes," Brad said. "He'll be all right, though. Just needs a little time to mend."

The girl crouched next to the dog, stroked him gently. "Hi," she said.

Meanwhile, Meg's father took a seat at the patio table. He looked bushed.

"I had to have stitches once," Carly told Willie. "Not as many as you've got, though."

"Brad's sister is a veterinarian," Meg said, finally finding her voice. "She fixed him right up."

"I'd like to be a veterinarian," Carly said.

"No reason you can't," Brad replied, turning his attention to Ted Ledger. "Can I get you a drink, Mr. Ledger?"

Ledger shook his head. "No, thanks," he said quietly. His gaze moved fondly between Meg and Carly, resting on one, then the other. "Good of you to have us over. I appreciate it. And I'd rather you called me Ted."

"Is there anything I can do to help?" Meg asked.

"I've got it under control," Brad told her. "Just relax."

Great advice, O'Ballivan, he thought. *Maybe you ought to take it.*

Meg went to greet Willie, who gave a whine of greeting and tried to lick her face. She laughed, and Brad felt something open up inside him, at the sound. When he'd conceived the supper idea, he'd intended to ply her with good wine and a thick steak, then take her to bed. The extra guests precluded that plan, of course, but he didn't regret it. When it finally registered that his and Meg's child might have looked a lot like Carly, though, he felt bruised all over again.

"Any news about Ransom?" Meg asked, stepping up

beside him when he turned his back to lay steaks on the grill, along with foil-wrapped baked potatoes that had been cooking for a while.

Brad shook his head, suddenly unable to look at her. If he did, she'd see all the things he felt, and he wasn't ready for that.

"According to the radio," Meg persisted, "the blizzard's passed, and the snow's melted."

Brad sighed. "I guess that means I'd better ride up and look for that stallion before Livie decides to do it by herself."

"I'd like to go with you," Meg said, sounding almost shy.

Brad thought about the baby who'd never had a chance to grow up. The baby Meg hadn't seen fit to tell him about. "We'll see," he answered noncommittally. "How do you like your steak?"

Chapter Ten

After the meal had been served and enjoyed, with Willie getting the occasional scrap, Brad signed the astounding succession of CDs Carly fished out of her backpack. Ted, who had eaten little, seemed content to watch the scene from a patio chair, and Meg insisted on cleaning up; since she'd had no part in the preparations, it only seemed fair.

As she carried in plates and glasses and silverware, rinsed them and put them into the oversize dishwasher, she reflected on Brad's mood change. He'd been warm to Ted, and chatted and joked with Carly, but when she'd mentioned that she'd like to accompany him when he went looking for Ransom again, it was as if a wall had slammed down between them.

She was just shutting the dishwasher and looking for the appropriate button to push when the screen door creaked open behind her. She turned, saw Brad hesitating on the threshold. It was past dusk—outside, the patio lights were burning brightly—but Meg hadn't bothered to flip a switch when she came in, so the kitchen was almost dark.

"Kid wants a T-shirt," he said, his face in shadow so she couldn't read his expression. "I think I have a few around here someplace."

Meg nodded, oddly stricken.

Brad didn't move right away, but simply stood there for a few long moments; she knew by the tilt of his head that he was watching her.

"You've gone out of your way to be kind to Carly," Meg managed, because the silence was unbearable. "Thank you."

He still didn't speak, or move.

Meg swallowed hard. "Well, it's getting late," she said awkwardly. "I guess we'd better be heading for home soon."

Brad reached out for a switch, and the overhead lights came on, seeming harsh after the previous cozy twilight in the room. His face looked bleak to Meg, his broad shoulders seemed to stoop a little.

"Seeing her—Carly, I mean—"

"I know," Meg said very softly. Of course Brad saw what she had, when he looked at Carly—the child who might have been.

"She's her own person," Brad said with an almost inaudible sigh. "It wouldn't be right to think of her in any other way. But it gave me a start, seeing her. She looks so much like you. So much like—"

"Yes."

"What's going on, Meg? You said you couldn't explain over the phone, and I figured out that Ledger had to be your dad. But there's more to this, isn't there?"

Meg bit her lower lip. "Ted is dying," she said. "And it turns out that Carly has no one else in the world except me."

Brad processed that, nodded. "Be careful," he told her quietly. "Carly is Carly. It would be all too easy—and completely unfair—to superimpose—"

"I wouldn't do that, Brad," Meg broke in, bristling. "I'm not pretending she's—she's our daughter."

"Guess I'll go rustle up that T-shirt," Brad said.

Meg didn't respond. For the time being, the conversation—at least as far as their lost child was concerned—was over.

Carly wore the T-shirt home—Brad's guitar-wielding profile was silhouetted on the front, along with the year of a recent tour and an impressive list of cities—practically bouncing in the car seat as she examined the showy signature on the face of each of her CDs.

"I bet he never trashed a single hotel room," she enthused, from the backseat of Meg's Blazer. "He's way too nice to do that."

Meg and Ted exchanged a look of weary amusement up front.

"It was quite an evening," Ted said. "Thanks, Meg."

"Brad did all the work," she replied.

"I like his dog, too," Carly bubbled. She seemed to have forgotten her situation, for the time being, and Meg could see that was a relief to Ted. "Brad said he'd change his name to Stitches, if he didn't already answer to Willie."

Meg smiled.

All the way home, it was Brad said this, Brad said that.

Once they'd reached the ranch house, Ted went inside, exhausted, while Carly and Meg headed for the barn to feed the horses. Despite her earlier condemnation of the entire equine species, Carly proved a fair hand with hay and grain.

"Is he your boyfriend?" Carly asked, keeping pace with Meg as they returned to the house.

"Is who my boyfriend?" Meg parried.

"You *know* I mean Brad," Carly said. "Is he?"

"He's a *friend*," Meg said. But a voice in her mind chided, *Right. And last night, you were rolling around on a mattress with him.*

"I may be twelve, but I'm not stupid," Carly remarked, as they reached the back door. "I saw the way he looked at you. Like he wanted to put his hands on you all the time."

Yeah, Meg thought wearily. *Specifically, around my throat.*

"You're imagining things."

"I'm very sophisticated for twelve," Carly argued.

"Maybe *too* sophisticated."

"If you think I'm going to act like some *kid,* just because I'm twelve, think again."

"That's exactly what I think. A twelve-year-old *is* a kid." Meg pushed open the kitchen door; Ted had turned on the lights as he entered, and the place glowed with homey warmth. "Go to bed."

"There's no TV in my room," Carly protested. "And I'm not sleepy."

"Tough it out," Meg replied. Crossing to the china cabinet on the far side of the room, she opened a drawer, found a notebook and a pen, and handed them to her little sister. "Here," she said. "Keep a journal. It's a tradition in the McKettrick family."

Carly hesitated, then accepted the offering. "I guess I could write about Brad O'Ballivan," she said. She held the notebook to her chest for a moment. "Are you going to read it?"

"No," Meg said, softening a little. "You can write anything you want to. Sometimes it helps to get feelings out of your head and onto paper. Then you can get some perspective."

Carly considered. "Okay," she said and started for the stairs, taking the notebook with her.

Meg, knowing she wouldn't sleep, tired as she was, headed for the study as soon as Carly disappeared, logged onto the Internet and resumed her research.

"You won't find him on that contraption," Angus told her.

She looked up to see him sitting in the big leather wingback chair by the fireplace. Like many other things in the house, the chair was a holdover from the Holt and Lorelei days.

"Josiah, I mean," Angus added, jawline hard again as he remembered the brother who had so disappointed him. "I told you he didn't use the McKettrick name." He gave a snort. "Sounded too Irish for him."

"Help me out, here," Meg said.

Angus remained silent.

Meg sighed and turned back to the screen. She'd been scrolling through names, intermittently, for days. And now suddenly, she had a hit, more an instinct than anything specific.

"Creed, Josiah *McKettrick,*" she said excitedly, clicking on the link. "I must have passed right over him dozens of times."

Angus materialized at her elbow, stooping and staring at the screen, his heavy eyebrows pulled together in consternation and curiosity.

"Captain in the United States Army," Meg read aloud, and with a note of triumph in her voice. "Founder of 'the legendary Stillwater Springs Ranch,' in western Montana. Owner of the Stillwater Springs *Courier,* the first newspaper in that part of the territory. On the town council, two terms as mayor. Wife, four sons, active member of the Methodist Church." She stopped, looked up at Angus. "Doesn't sound like an anti-Irish pirate to me." She tapped at Josiah's solemn photograph on the home page. Bewhiskered, with a thick head of white hair he looked dour and prosperous in his dark suit, the coat fastened with one button at his breastbone, in that curious nineteenth-century way. "There he is, Angus," she said. "Your brother, Josiah McKettrick Creed."

"I'll be hornswoggled," Angus said.

"Whatever that is," Meg replied, busily copying information onto a notepad. The Web site was obviously the work of a skillful amateur, probably a family member with a genealogical bent, and there was no "contact us" link, but the name of the town, and the ranch if it still existed, was information enough.

"Looks like you missed something," Angus said.

Meg peered at the screen, trying to see past Angus's big index finger, scattering a ring of pixels around its end.

She pushed his hand gently aside.

And saw a tiny link at the bottom of the page, printed in blue letters.

A press of a mouse button and she and Angus were looking at the masthead of Josiah's newspaper, the *Courier*.

The headline was printed in heavy type. *MURDER AND SCANDAL BESET STILLWATER SPRINGS RANCH.*

Something quivered in the pit of Meg's stomach, a peculiar combination of dread and fascination. The byline was Josiah's own, and the brief obituary beneath it still pulsed with the staunch grief of an old man, bitterly determined to tell the unflinching truth.

Dawson James Creed, 21, youngest son of Josiah McKettrick Creed and Cora Dawson Creed, perished yesterday at the hand of his first cousin, Benjamin A. Dawson, who shot him dead over a game of cards and a woman. Both the shootist and the woman have since fled these parts. Services tomorrow at 2:00 p.m., at the

First Street Methodist Church. Viewing this evening at the Creed home. Our boy will be sorely missed.

"Creed," Angus repeated, musing. "That was my mother's name, before she and my pa hitched up."

"So maybe Josiah *wasn't* a McKettrick," Meg ventured. "Maybe your mother was married before, or—"

Angus stiffened. "Or nothing," he said pointedly. "Back in those days, women didn't go around having babies out of wedlock. Pa must have been her second husband."

Meg, feeling a little stung, didn't comment. Nor did she argue the point, which would have been easy to back up, that premarital pregnancies weren't as uncommon in "his day" as Angus liked to think.

"Where's that old Bible Georgia set such store by?" he asked now.

Georgia, his second wife, mother of Rafe, Kade and Jeb, had evidently been her generation's record-keeper and family historian. "I suppose Keegan has it," she answered, "since he lives in the main ranch house."

"Ma wrote all the begats in that book," Angus recalled. "I never thought to look at it."

"She never mentioned being married before?"

"No," Angus admitted. "But folks didn't talk about things like that much. It was a private matter and besides, they had their hands full just surviving from day to day. No time to sit around jawing about the past."

"I'll drop in on Keegan and Molly in the morning," Meg said. "Ask if I can borrow the Bible."

"I want to look at it *now.*"

"Angus, it's late—"

He vanished.

Meg sighed. There were no more articles on the Web site—just that short, sad obituary notice—so she logged off the computer. She was brewing a cup of herbal tea in the microwave, hoping it would help her sleep, when Ted came down the backstairs, wearing an old plaid flannel bathrobe and scruffy slippers.

Lord, he wanted to talk.

Now, from the look on his face.

She wasn't ready, and that didn't matter.

The time had come.

Dragging back a chair at the table, Ted crumpled into it.

"Tea?" Meg asked, and immediately felt stupid.

"Sit down, Meg," Ted said gently.

She took the mug from the microwave, grateful for its citrusy steamy scent, and joined him, perching on the end of one of the benches.

"There's no money," Ted said.

"I gathered that," Meg replied, though not flippantly. And the dizzying thought came to her that maybe this was all some kind of con—a *Paper Moon* kind of thing, Ted playing the Ryan O'Neal part, while Carly handled Tatum's role. But the idea fizzled almost as quickly as it had flared up in her mind—a scam would have been so much easier to take than the grim reality.

Ted ran a tremulous hand through his thinning hair. "I wish things had happened differently, Meg," he said. "I wanted to come back a hundred times, say I was sorry for everything that happened. I convinced myself I was being noble—you were a McKettrick, and you didn't need an ex-yardbird complicating your life. The truth gets harder to deny when you're toeing up to the pearly gates, though. I was a coward, that's all. I tried to make up for it by being the best father I could to Carly." He paused, chuckled ruefully. "I won't take any prizes for that, either. After Rose died, it was as if somebody had greased the bottom of my feet. I just couldn't stay put, and it was mostly downhill, a slippery slope, all the way. The worst part is, I dragged Carly right along with me. Last job I had, I stocked shelves in a discount store."

"You don't have to do this," Meg said, blinking back tears she didn't want him to see.

"Yes," Ted said, "I do. I loved your mother and she loved me. You need to know how happy we were when you were born—that you were welcome in this big old crazy world."

"Okay," Meg allowed. "You were happy." She swallowed. "Then you embezzled a lot of money and went to prison."

"Like most embezzlers," Ted answered, "I thought I could put it back before it was missed. It didn't happen that way. Your mother tried to cover for me at first, but there were other McKettricks on the board, and they weren't going to tolerate a thief."

"Why did you do it?" The question, more breathed than spoken, hovered in the otherwise silent room.

"Before I met Eve, I gambled. A lot. I still owed some people. I was ashamed to tell Eve—and I knew she'd divorce me—so I 'borrowed' what I needed and left as few tracks as possible. That got my creditors off my back—they were knee-breakers, Meg, and they wouldn't have stopped at hurting me. They'd have gone after you and Eve, too."

"So you stole the money to protect Mom and me?" Meg asked, not bothering to hide her skepticism.

"Partly. I was young and I was scared."

"You should have told Mom. She would have helped you."

"I know. But by the time I realized that, it was too late." He sighed. "Now it's too late for a lot of things."

"It's not too late for Carly," Meg said.

"Exactly my point. She's going to give you some trouble, Meg. She won't want to go to school, and she's used to being a loner. I'm all the family she's had since her mother was killed. Like I said before, I've got no right to ask you for anything. I don't expect sympathy. I know you won't grieve when I'm gone. But Carly *will,* and I'm hoping you're McKettrick enough to stand by her till she finds her balance. My worst fear is that she'll go down the same road I did, drifting from place to place, living by her wits, always on the outside looking in."

"I won't let that happen," Meg promised. "Not because of you, but because Carly is my sister. And because she's a child."

They'd been over this before, but Ted seemed to need a lot of reassurance. "I guess there is one other favor I could ask," he said.

Meg raised an eyebrow. Waited.

"Will you forgive me, Meg?"

"I stopped hating you a long time ago."

"That isn't the same as forgiving me," Ted replied.

She opened her mouth, closed it again. A glib, "Okay, I forgive you" died on her tongue.

Ted smiled sadly. "While you're at it, forgive your mother, too. We were both wrong, Eve and I, not to tell you the whole truth from the beginning. But she was trying to protect you, Meg. And it says a lot about the other McKettricks, that none of them ever let it slip that I was a thief doing time in a Texas prison while you were growing up. A lot of people would have found that secret too juicy to keep to themselves."

Meg wondered if Jesse, Rance and Keegan had known, and decided they hadn't. Their parents had, though, surely. All three of their fathers had been on the company board with

Eve, back in those days. Meg thought of them as uncles—and they'd looked after her like a daughter, taken her under their powerful wings when she summered on the Triple M, and so had her "aunts." Stirred her right into the boisterous mix of loud cousins, remembered her birthdays and bought gifts at Christmas. All the while, they'd been conspiring to keep her in the dark about Ted Ledger, of course, but she couldn't resent them for it. Their intentions, like Eve's, had been good.

"Who are you, really?" Meg asked, remembering Carly's remark about changing last names so many times she was no longer sure what the real one was. And underlying the surface question was another.

Who am I?

Ted smiled, patted her hand. "When I married your mother, I was Ted Sullivan. I was born in Chicago, to Alice and Carl Sullivan. Alice was a homemaker, Carl was a finance manager at a used car dealership."

"No brothers or sisters?"

"I had a sister, Sarah. She died of meningitis when she was fifteen. I was nineteen at the time. Mom never recovered from Sarah's death—she was the promising child. I was the problem."

"How did you meet Mom?" She hadn't thought she needed, or even wanted, to know such things. But, suddenly, she did.

Ted grinned at the memory, and for just a moment, he looked young again, and well. "After I left home, I took college courses and worked nights as a hotel desk clerk. I moved around the country, and by the time I wound up in San Antonio, I was a manager. McKettrickCo owned the chain I worked for, and one of your uncles decided I was a bright young man with a future. Hired me to work in the home office. Where, of course, I saw Eve every day."

Meg imagined how it must have been, both Ted and Eve still young, and relatively mistake-free. "And you fell in love."

"Yes," Ted said. "The family accepted me, which was decent of them, considering they were rich and I had an old car and a couple of thousand dollars squirreled away in a low-interest savings account. The McKettricks are a lot of things, but they're not snobs."

Having money doesn't make us better than other people, Eve had often said as Meg was growing up. *It just makes us luckier.*

"No," she agreed. "They're not snobs." She tried to smile and failed. "So I would have been Meg Sullivan, not Meg McKettrick—if things hadn't gone the way they did?"

Ted chuckled. "Not in a million years. You know the McKettrick women don't change their names when they marry. According to Eve, the custom goes all the way back to old Angus's only daughter."

"Katie," Meg said. Her mind did a time-warp thing—for about fifteen seconds, she was nineteen and pregnant, having her last argument with Brad before he got into his old truck and drove away. Late that night, he would board a bus for Nashville.

We'll get married when I get back, Brad had said. *I promise.*

You're not coming back, Meg had replied, in tears.

Yes, I am. You'll see—you'll be Meg O'Ballivan before you know it.

I'll never be Meg O'Ballivan. I'm not taking your name.

Have it your way, Ms. McKettrick. You always do.

"Meg?" Ted's voice brought her back to the kitchen on the Triple M. Her tea had grown cold, sitting on the tabletop in its heavy mug.

"You're not the first person who ever made a mistake," she told her father. "I hereby confer upon you my complete forgiveness."

He laughed, but his eyes were glossy with tears.

"You're tired," Meg said. "Get some rest."

"I want to hear your story, Meg. Eve sent me a few pictures, the occasional copy of a report card, when I was on the inside. But there are a lot of gaps."

"Another time," Meg answered. But even as Ted stood to make his way back upstairs, and she disposed of her cold tea and put the mug into the dishwasher, she wondered if there would *be* another time.

Phil was back.

Brad, accompanied to the barn by an adoring Willie, tossed the last flake of hay into the last feeder when he heard the distinctive purr of a limo engine and swore under his breath.

"This is getting old," he told Willie.

Willie whined in agreement and wagged his tail.

Phil was walking toward Brad, the stretch gleaming in the early morning light, when he and Willie stepped outside.

"Good news!" Phil cried, beaming. "I spoke to the Hollywood people, and they're willing to make the movie right here at Stone Creek!"

Brad stopped, facing off with Phil like a gunfighter on a windswept Western street. "No," he said.

Phil, being Phil, was undaunted. "Now, don't be too hasty," he counseled. "It would really give this town a boost. Why, the jobs alone—"

"Phil—"

Just then, Livie's ancient Suburban topped the hill, started down, dust billowing behind. Brad took a certain satisfaction in the sight when the rig screeched to a halt alongside Phil's limo, covering it in fine red dirt.

Livie sprang from the Suburban, smiling. "Good news,"

she called, unknowingly echoing Phil's opening line. "The Iversons' cattle aren't infected."

Phil nudged Brad in the ribs and said in a stage whisper, "She could be an extra. Bet your sister would like to be in a movie."

"In a what?" Livie asked, frowning. She crouched to examine Willie briefly, and accept a few face licks, before straightening and putting out a hand to Phil Meadowbrook. "Olivia O'Balli-van," she said. "You must be my brother's manager."

"*Former* manager," Brad said.

"But still with his best interests at heart," Phil added, placing splayed fingers over his avaricious little ticker and looking woebegone, long-suffering and misunderstood. "I'm offering him a chance to make a *feature film,* right here on the ranch. Just *look* at this place! It's perfect! John Ford would salivate—"

"Who's John Ford?" Livie asked.

"He made some John Wayne movies," Brad explained, beginning to feel cornered.

Livie's dusty face lit up. She had hay dust in her hair—probably acquired during an early morning visit to the Iversons' dairy barn. "Wait till I tell the twins," she burst out.

"Hold it," Brad said, raising both hands, palms out. "There isn't going to *be* any movie."

"Why not?" Livie asked, suddenly crestfallen.

"Because I'm retired," Brad reminded her patiently.

Phil huffed out a disgusted sigh.

"I don't see the problem if they made the movie right here," Livie said.

"At last," Phil interjected. "Another voice of reason, besides my own."

"Shut up, Phil," Brad said.

"You always talked about making a movie," Livie went on,

watching Brad with a mischievous light dancing in her eyes. "You even started a production company once."

"Cynthia got it in the divorce," Phil confided, as though Brad wasn't standing there. "The production company, I mean. I think that soured him."

"Will you stop acting as if I'm not here?" Brad snapped.

Willie whimpered, worried.

"See?" Phil was quick to say. "You're upsetting the dog." Another patented Phil Meadowbrook grin flashed. "Hey! He could be in the movie, too. People eat that animal stuff up. We might even be able to get Disney in on the project—"

"No," Brad said, exasperated. "No Disney. No dog. No petite veterinarian with hay in her hair. *I don't want to make a movie."*

"You could build a library or a youth center or something with the money," Phil said, trailing after Brad as he broke from the group and strode toward the house, fully intending to slam the door on his way in.

"We could use an animal shelter," Livie said, scrambling along at his other side.

"Fine," Brad snapped, slowing down a little because he realized Willie was having trouble keeping up. "I'll have my accountant cut a check."

The limo driver gave the horn a discreet honk, then got out and tapped at his watch.

"Plane to catch," Phil said. "Big Hollywood meeting. I'll fax you the contract."

"Don't bother," Brad warned.

Livie caught at his arm, sounding a little breathless. "What is the *matter* with you?" she whispered. "That movie would be the biggest thing to happen in Stone Creek since that pack of outlaws robbed the bank in 1907!"

Brad stopped. Thrust his nose right up to Livie's. "I. Am. *Retired.*"

Livie set her hands on her skinny hips. She really needed to put some meat on those fragile little bones of hers. "I think you're chicken," she said.

Willie gave a cheery little yip.

"You stay out of this, Stitches," Brad told him.

"Chicken," Livie repeated, as the now-dusty limo made a wide turn and started swallowing up dirt road.

"Not," Brad argued.

"Then what?"

Brad shoved a hand through his hair as the answer to Livie's question settled over him, like the red dust that had showered the limo. He was making some headway with Meg, slowly but surely, but Meg and show business mixed about as well as oil and water. Deep down, she probably believed, as Livie had until this morning, that he'd go back to being that other Brad O'Ballivan, the one whose name was always written in capital letters, if the offer was good enough.

Too, if he agreed to do the movie, Phil would never get off his back. He'd be back, before the cameras stopped rolling, with another offer, another contract, another big idea.

"I used to be a performer," Brad said finally. "Now I'm a rancher. I can't keep going back and forth between the two."

"It's one movie, Brad, not a world concert tour. And you wanted to do a movie for so long. What happened? *Was* it losing the production company to Cynthia, like your manager said?"

"No," Brad said. "This is a Pandora's box, Livie. It's the proverbial can of worms. One thing will lead to another—"

"And you'll leave again? For good, this time?"

He shook his head. "No."

"Then just think about it," Livie reasoned. "Making the movie, I mean. Think about the money it would bring into Stone Creek, and how excited the local people would be."

"And the animal shelter," Brad said, sighing.

"Small as Stone Creek is, there are a lot of strays," Livie said. "Did you come out here for a reason?"

"Yes, to see my big brother and check up on Willie."

"Well, here I am, and Willie's fine. Go or stay, but I don't want to talk about that damn movie anymore, understood?"

Livie smirked. "Understood," she said sweetly.

At four-thirty that afternoon, the movie contract sputtered out of the fax machine in Brad's study.

He read it, signed it and faxed it back.

Chapter Eleven

Carly sat hunched in the front passenger seat of the Blazer, arms folded, glowering as kids converged on Indian Rock Middle School, colorful clothes and backpacks still new, since class had only been in session for a little over a month. It was Monday morning and Ted was scheduled to enter the hospital in Flagstaff for "treatment" the following day. Meg's solemn promise to take Carly to visit him every afternoon, admittedly small comfort, was nonetheless all she had to offer.

"I don't want to go in there," Carly said. "They're going to give me some stupid test and put me with the little kids. I just know it."

Ted had homeschooled Carly, for the most part, and though she was obviously a very bright child, there was no telling what kind of curriculum he'd used, or if the process had involved books at all. Her scores would determine her placement, and she was understandably worried.

"Everything will be all right," Meg said.

"You keep saying that," Carly protested. "Everybody says that. *My dad is going to die.* How is that 'all right'?"

"It isn't. It totally bites."

"You could homeschool me."

Meg shook her head. "I'm not a teacher, Carly."

"Neither is my dad, and he did fine!"

That, Meg thought, *remains to be seen.* "More than anything in the world, your dad wants you to have a good life. And that means getting an education."

Tears brimmed in Carly's eyes. "*My* dad? He's *your* dad, too."

"Okay," Meg said.

"You hate him. You don't care if he dies!"

"I *don't* hate him, and if there was any way to keep him alive, I'd do it."

Carly's right hand went to the door handle; with her left, she gathered up the neon pink backpack Meg had bought for her over the weekend, along with some new clothes. "Well, not hating somebody isn't the same as *loving* them."

With that, she shoved open the car door, unfastened her seat belt and got out to stand on the sidewalk, facing the long brick schoolhouse, her small shoulders squared under more burdens than any child ought to have to carry.

Meg waited, her eyes scalding, until Carly disappeared into the building. Then she drove to Sierra's house, where she found her other sister on the front porch, deadheading the flowers in a large clay pot.

The bright October sunshine gilded Sierra's chestnut hair; she looked like Mother Nature herself in her floral print maternity dress.

Meg parked the Blazer in the driveway and approached, slinging her bag over her shoulder as she walked.

Sierra beamed, delighted, and straightened, one hand resting protectively on her enormous belly, the other shading her eyes. "I just made a fresh pot of coffee," she called. "Come in, and we'll catch up."

Meg smiled. She'd lived her life as an only child; now she had two sisters. She and Sierra had had time to bond, but establishing a relationship with Carly was going to be a major challenge.

"I suppose Mom told you the latest," Meg said, referring to Ted and Carly's arrival.

"Some of it. The gossip lasted about twenty minutes, though—you got beat out by the news that Brad O'Ballivan is making a movie over at Stone Creek. Everybody in the county wants to be an extra."

Meg stopped in the middle of the sidewalk. Brad hadn't called since the barbeque, and she hadn't heard about the movie. That hurt, and though she regained her composure quickly, Sierra was quicker.

"You didn't know?" she asked, holding the front door open and urging Meg through it.

Meg sighed, shook her head.

Sierra patted her shoulder. "Let's have that coffee," she said softly.

For the next hour, she and Meg sat in the sunny kitchen, catching up. Meg told her sister what she knew about Ted's condition, Carly, and *most* of what had happened between her and Brad.

Sierra chuckled at the account of Jesse and Keegan's helicopter rescue the day of the blizzard. Got tears in her eyes when Meg related Willie's story.

Although Sierra was one of the most grounded people Meg knew, her emotions had been mercurial since the beginning of her last trimester.

"So when is this baby going to show up, anyhow?" Meg inquired cheerfully when she was through with the briefing. It was definitely time to change the subject.

"I was due a week ago," Sierra answered. "The nursery is all ready, and so am I. Apparently, the baby isn't."

Meg touched her sister's hand. "Are you scared?"

Sierra shook her head. "I'm past that. Mostly, I feel like a bowling-ball smuggler."

"You know," Meg teased, "if you'd spilled the beans about whether this kid is a boy or a girl, you wouldn't have gotten so many yellow layettes at your baby shower."

Sierra laughed, crying a little at the same time. "The sonogram was inconclusive," she said. "The little dickens drew one leg up and hid the evidence."

Meg sobered, looked away briefly. "Would you hate me if I admitted I'm a little envious? Because the baby's coming, I mean, and because you already have Liam, and Travis loves you so much?"

"You know I couldn't hate you," Sierra answered gently, but there was a worried expression in her blue eyes. Long ago, Meg and Travis had dated briefly, and they were still very good friends. While Sierra surely knew neither of them would deceive her, ever, she might think she'd stolen Travis's affections and broken Meg's heart in the process. "Truth time. Do you still have feelings for Travis?"

"The same kind of feelings I have for Jesse and Keegan and Rance," Meg replied honestly. She drew a deep breath and puffed it out. "Truth time? Here's the whole enchilada. I fell hard for Brad O'Ballivan when I was in high school, and I don't think I'm over it."

"Is that a bad thing?"

Meg remembered the way Brad had looked as they stood in his kitchen, after the steak dinner on the patio. She'd seen sorrow, disappointment and a sense of betrayal in his eyes, and the set of his face and shoulders. "I'm not sure," she said. Then she stood, carried her empty cup and Sierra's to the sink. "I'd better get home. Ted's there alone, and he wasn't feeling well when I left to take Carly to school."

Sierra nodded, remaining in her chair, squirming a little and looking anxious.

"You're okay, right?" Meg asked, alarmed.

"Just a few twinges," Sierra said. "It's probably nothing."

Meg was glad she'd already set the cups down, because she'd have dropped them to the floor if she hadn't. *"Just a few twinges?"*

"Would you mind calling Travis?" Sierra asked. "And Mom?"

"Oh, my God," Meg said, grabbing her bag, scrabbling through it for her cell phone. "You've been sitting there listening to my tales of woe and all the time you've been *in labor?*"

"Not the whole time," Sierra said lamely. "I thought it was indigestion."

Meg speed-dialed Travis. "Come home," she said before he'd finished his hello. "Sierra's having the baby!"

"On my way," he replied, and hung up in her ear.

Next, she called Eve. "It's happening!" she blurted. "The baby—"

"For heaven's sake," Sierra protested good-naturedly, "you make it sound as though I'm giving birth on the kitchen floor."

"Margaret McKettrick," Eve instructed sternly, "calm

yourself. We have a plan. Travis will take Sierra to the hospital, and I will pick Liam up after school. I assume you're with Sierra right now?"

"I'm with her," Meg said, wondering if she'd have to deliver her niece or nephew before help arrived. She'd watched calves, puppies and colts coming into the world, but *this* was definitely in another league.

"Did you call Travis?" Eve wanted to know.

"Yes," Meg watched Sierra anxiously as she spoke.

"My water just broke," Sierra said.

"Oh, my God," Meg ranted. "Her water just broke!"

"Margaret," Eve said, "get a grip—and a towel. I'll be there in five minutes."

Travis showed up in four flat. He paused to bend and kiss Sierra soundly on the mouth, then dashed off, returning momentarily with a suitcase, presumably packed with things his wife would need at the hospital.

Meg sat at the table, with her head between her knees, feeling woozy.

"I think she's hyperventilating," Sierra told Travis. "Do we have any paper bags?"

Just then, Eve breezed in through the back door. She tsk-tsked Meg, but naturally, Sierra was her main concern. As her younger daughter stood, with some help from Travis, Eve cupped Sierra's face between her hands and kissed her on the forehead.

"Don't worry about a thing," she ordered. "I'll see to Liam."

Sierra nodded, gave Meg one last worried glance and allowed Travis to steer her out the back door.

"Shouldn't we have called an ambulance or something?" Meg fretted.

"Oh, for heaven's sake," Eve replied. "You don't need an ambulance!"

"Not for *me,* Mother. For Sierra."

Eve soaked a cloth at the sink, wrung it out and slapped it onto the back of Meg's neck. "Breathe," she said.

Brad watched from a front window as Livie parked the Suburban, got out and headed for the barn. "Here we go," he told Willie, resigned. "She's on the hunt for Ransom again, and that means I'll have to go. You're going to have to stay behind, buddy."

Willie, curled up on a hooked rug in front of the living room fireplace, simply sighed and closed his eyes for a snooze, clearly unconcerned. Some of the advance people from the movie studio had already arrived in an RV, to scout the location, and the kid with the backward baseball cap was a dog-lover. If necessary, Brad would press him into service.

Brad had been up half the night going over the script, faxed by Phil, penning in the occasional dialogue change. For all his reluctance to get involved in the project, he liked the story, tentatively titled *The Showdown,* and he was looking forward to trying his hand at a little acting.

The truth was, though, he'd had to read and reread because his mind kept straying to Meg. He'd been so sure, right along, that they could make things work. But seeing Carly—a younger version of Meg, and most likely of the daughter they might have had—brought up a lot of conflicting feelings, ones he wasn't sure how to deal with.

It wasn't rational; he knew that. Meg's explanation was believable, even if it stung, and her reasons for keeping the secret from him made sense. Still, a part of him was deeply resentful, even enraged.

Livie was saddling Cinnamon when he reached the barn.

"Where do you think you're going?" he asked.

She gave him a look. "Three guesses, genius," she said pleasantly. "And the first two don't count."

"I guess you didn't hear about the blizzard that blew up in about five minutes when Meg and I were up in the hills trying to find that damn horse?"

"I heard about it," Livie said. She put her shoulder to Cinnamon's belly and pulled hard to tighten the cinch. "I just want to check on him, that's all. Just take a look."

Brad leaned one shoulder against the door frame, arms folded, letting his body language say he wasn't above blocking the door.

Livie's expression said *she* wasn't above riding right over him.

"I'll see if I can talk one of Meg's cousins into taking you up in the helicopter," Brad said.

"Oh, right," Livie mocked. "And scare Ransom to death with the noise."

"Livie, will you listen to reason? That horse has survived all this time without a lick of help from you. What's different now?"

"Will you stop calling him 'that horse'? His name is Ransom and he's a *legend,* thank you very much."

"Being a legend," Brad drawled, "isn't all it's cracked up to be."

Livie led Cinnamon toward him; he moved into the center of the doorway and stood his ground.

"What's different, Livie?" he repeated.

She sighed, seemed even smaller and more fragile than usual. "You wouldn't believe me if I told you."

"Give it a shot," Brad said.

"Dreams," Livie said. "I have these dreams—"

"Dreams."

"I knew you wouldn't—"

"Hold it," Brad interrupted. "I'm listening."

"Just get out of my way, please."

Brad shook his head, shifted so his feet were a little farther apart, kept his arms folded. "Not gonna happen."

"He talks to me," Livie said, her voice small and exasperated and full of the O'Ballivan grit that was so much a part of her nature.

"A horse talks to you." He tried not to sound skeptical, but didn't quite succeed.

"In dreams," Livie said, flushing.

"Like Mr. Ed, in that old TV show?"

Livie's temper flared in her eyes, then her cheekbones. "No," she said. "Not 'like Mr. Ed in that old TV show'!"

"How, then?"

"I just hear him, that's all. He doesn't move his lips, for pity's sake!"

"Okay."

"You believe me?"

"I believe that you believe it, Liv. You have a lot of deep feelings where animals are concerned—sometimes I wish you liked people half as much—and you've been worried about that—about Ransom for a long time. It makes sense that he'd show up in your dreams."

Livie let Cinnamon's reins dangle and set her hands on her hips. "What did you do, take an online shrink course or something? Jungian analysis in ten easy lessons? Next, you'll be saying Ransom is a symbol with unconscious sexual connotations!"

Brad suppressed an urge to roll his eyes. "Is that really so far beyond the realm of possibility?"

"Yes!"

"Why?"

"Because Ransom isn't the only animal I dream about, that's why. And it isn't a recent phenomenon—it's been happening since I was little! Remember Simon, that old sheepdog we had when we were kids? He told me he was leaving—and three days later, he was hit by a car. I could go on, because there are a whole lot of other stories, but frankly, I don't have time. Ransom is in trouble."

Surprise was too mild a word for what Brad felt. Livie had always been crazy about animals, but she was stone practical, with a scientific turn of mind, not given to spooky stuff. And she'd never once confided that she got dream messages from four-legged friends.

"Why didn't you tell me? Did Big John know?"

"You'd have packed me off to a therapist. Big John had enough to worry about without Dr. Doolittle for a granddaughter. Now—will you please move?"

"No," Brad said. "I won't move, please or otherwise. Not until you tell me what's so urgent about tracking down a wild stallion on top of a damn mountain!"

Tears glistened in Livie's eyes, and Brad felt a stab to his conscience.

Livie's struggle was visible, and painful to see, but she finally answered. "He's in pain. There's something wrong with his right foreleg."

"And you plan to do what when—and if—you find him? Shoot him with a tranquilizer gun? Livie, this is Stone Creek, Arizona, not the *Wild Kingdom*. And dream or no dream, that horse—" He raised both hands to forestall the impatience brewing in her face. "*Ransom* is not a character in a Disney movie. He's not going to let you walk up to him, examine his foreleg and give him a nice little shot. If you *did* get close, he'd probably stomp you down to bone fragments and a bloodstain!"

"He wouldn't," Livie said. "He knows I want to help him."

"Livie, suppose—just *suppose,* damn it—that you're wrong."

"I'm not wrong."

"Of *course* you're not wrong. You're a freaking O'Balli-van!" He paused, shoved a hand through his hair. Tried another tack. "There aren't that many hours of daylight left. You're not going up that mountain alone, little sister—not if I have to hog-tie you to keep you here."

"Then you can come with me."

"Oh, that's noble of you. I'd *love* to risk freezing to death in a freaking blizzard. Hell, I've got nothing *better* to do, besides nurse a wounded dog that *you* brought to me, and make a freaking *movie*—also your idea—"

Livie's mouth twitched at one corner. She fought the grin, but it came anyway. "Do you realize you've used the word 'freaking' three times in the last minute and a half? Have you considered switching to decaf?"

"Very funny," Brad said, but he couldn't help grinning back. He rested his hands on Livie's shoulders, squeezed lightly. "You're my little sister. I love you. If you insist on tracking a wild stallion all over the mountain, at least wait until morning. We'll saddle up at dawn."

Livie looked serious again. "You promise?"

"I promise."

"Okay," she said.

"Okay? That's it? You're giving up without a fight?"

"Don't be so suspicious. I said I'd wait until dawn, and I will."

Brad raised one eyebrow. "Shake on it?"

Livie put out a hand. "Shake," she said.

He had to be satisfied with that. In the O'Ballivan family, shaking hands on an agreement was like taking a blood oath— Big John had drilled that into them from childhood. "Since we're leaving so early, maybe you'd better spend the night here."

"I can do that," Livie said, turning to lead Cinnamon back to his stall. "But since I'm not going tonight, I might as well make my normal rounds first. I conned Dr. Summers into covering for me, but he wasn't too happy about it." Her eyes took on a mischievous twinkle as he approached, took over the process of unsaddling the horse. "How are things going with Meg?"

Brad didn't look at her. "Not all that well, actually."

"What's wrong?"

"I'm not sure I could put it into words."

Livie nudged him before pushing open the stall door to leave. "It's a long ride up the mountain," she said. "Plenty of time to talk."

"I might take you up on that," he answered.

"I'll just look in on Willie, then go make my rounds. See you later, alligator."

Brad's eyes burned. Like the handshake, "See you later, alligator" was a holdover from Big John. "In a while, crocodile," he answered on cue.

By the time he got back to the house, Livie had already examined Willie, climbed into the Suburban and driven off. A note stuck to the refrigerator door read, *Are you making supper, Mr. Movie Star? Or should I pick up a pizza?*

Brad chuckled and took a package of chicken out of the freezer.

The phone rang.

"Yea or nay on the double Hawaiian deluxe with extra ham, cheese and pineapple?" Livie asked.

"Forget the pizza," Brad replied. "I'm not eating anything you've handled. You stick your arm up cows' butts for a living, after all."

She laughed, said goodbye and hung up.

He started to replace the receiver, but Meg was still on his mind, so he punched in the digits. Funny, he reflected, how he remembered her number at the Triple M after all this time. He couldn't have recited the one he'd had in Nashville to save his life.

Voice mail picked up. "You've reached 555-7682," Meg said cheerily. "Leave a message and, if it's appropriate, I'll call you back."

Brad moved to disconnect, then put the receiver back to his ear. "It's Brad. I was just—a—calling to see how things are going with your dad and Carly—"

She came on the line, sounding a little breathless. "Brad?"

His heart did a slow backflip. "Yeah, it's me," he said.

"I hear you're making a movie in Stone Creek."

He closed his eyes. He'd blown it again—Meg should have heard the news from him, not via the local grapevine. "I thought maybe Carly could be an extra," he said.

"She'd love that, I'm sure," Meg said with crisp formality.

"Meg? The movie thing—"

"It's all right, Brad. I'm happy for you. Really."

"You sound thrilled."

"You could have mentioned it. Not exactly an everyday occurrence, especially in the wilds of northern Arizona."

"I wanted to talk about it in person, Meg."

"You know where I live, and clearly, you know my telephone number."

"I know where your G-spot is, too," he said.

He heard her draw in a breath. "Dirty pool, O'Ballivan."

"All's fair in lust and war, McKettrick."

"Is that what this is? Lust?"

"You tell me."

"I'm not the one who took a step back," she reminded him.

He knew what she was talking about, of course. He'd been pretty cool to her the night of the steak dinner. "Livie and I are riding up the mountain again tomorrow, to look for Ransom. Do you still want to go?"

She sighed. He hoped she was thawing out, but with Meg, it could go either way. Ice or fire. "I wish I could. Ted's being admitted to the hospital tomorrow morning, and I promised to take Carly to visit him as soon as school lets out for the day."

"She's having a pretty rough time," he said. "If there's anything I can do to help—"

"The T-shirt was a hit. So is having your autograph on all those CDs. Your kindness means a lot to her, Brad." A pause. "On a happier note, Sierra went into labor today. I'm expecting to be an aunt again at any moment."

"That is good news," Brad said, but he put one hand to his middle, as though he'd taken a fist to the stomach.

"Yeah," Meg said, and he knew by the catch in her voice that, somehow, she'd picked up on his reaction. "Well, anyway, congratulations on the movie, and thanks for getting in touch. Oh, and be careful on the mountain tomorrow."

The invisible fist moved from his solar plexus to his throat, squeezing hard. *Congratulations on the movie...thanks for getting in touch...so long, see you around.*

She'd hung up before he could get out a goodbye.

He thumbed the off button, leaned forward and rested his head against a cupboard door, eyes closed tight.

Willie nuzzled him in the thigh and gave a soft whine.

* * *

Two hours later, Livie returned, freshly showered and wearing a dress.

"Got a hot date?" Brad asked, trying to remember the last time he'd seen his sister in anything besides boots, ragbag jeans and one of Big John's old shirts.

She ignored the question and, with a flourish, pulled a bottle of wine from her tote bag and set it on the counter, sniffing the air appreciatively. "Fried chicken? Is there no end to your talents?"

"Not as far as I know," he joked.

Livie elbowed him. "We should have invited the twins to join us. It would be like old times, all of us sitting down together in this kitchen."

Not quite like old times, Brad thought, missing Big John with a sudden, piercing ache, as fresh as if he'd just gotten the call announcing his grandfather's death.

Livie was way too good at reading him. She snatched a cucumber slice from the salad and nibbled at it, leaning back against the counter and studying his face. "You really miss Big John, don't you?"

He nodded, not quite trusting himself to speak.

"He was so proud of you, Brad."

He swallowed. Averted his eyes. "Keep your fingers out of the salad," he said.

Livie laid a hand on his arm. "I know you think you disappointed him at practically every turn. That you should have been here, instead of in Nashville or on the road or wherever, and maybe all of that's true, but he *was* proud. And he was grateful, too, for everything you did."

"He'd raise hell about this movie," Brad said hoarsely.

"He'd brag to everybody who would let him bend their ear," Livie replied.

"Do you know what I'd give to be able to talk to Big John just one more time? To say I'm sorry I didn't visit—call more often?"

"A lot, I guess. But you can still talk to him. He'll hear you." She stood on tiptoe, kissed Brad lightly on the cheek. "Tell me you've already fed the horses, because I'd hate to have to swap out this getup for barn gear."

Brad laughed. "I've fed them," he said. He turned, smiled down into her upturned face. "I never would have taken you for a mystic, Doc. Do you talk to Big John? Or just wild stallions and sheepdogs?"

"All the time," Livie said, plundering a drawer for a corkscrew, which Brad immediately took from her. "I don't think he's really gone. Most of the time, it feels as if he's in the next room, not some far-off heaven—sometimes, I even catch the scent of his pipe tobacco."

Since Brad had taken over opening the cabernet, Livie got out a couple of wineglasses. Willie poked his nose at her knee, angling for attention.

"Yes," she told the dog. "I know you're there."

"Does he talk to you, too?" Brad asked, only half kidding.

"Sure," Livie replied airily. "He likes you. You're a little awkward, but Willie thinks you have real potential as a dog owner."

Grinning, Brad sloshed wine into Livie's glass, then his. Raised it in a toast. "To Big John," he said, "and King's Ransom, and Stone Creek's own Dr. Doolittle. And Willie."

"To the movie and Meg McKettrick," Livie added, and clinked her glass against Brad's.

Brad hesitated before he drank. "To Meg," he said finally.

During supper, they chatted about Livie's preliminary plans for the promised animal shelter—it would be state of the art, offering free spaying and neutering, inoculations, etc.

They cleaned up the kitchen together afterward, as they had done when they were kids, then took Willie out for a brief walk. He was still sore, though the pain medication helped, and couldn't make it far, but he managed.

Since he hadn't slept much the night before, Brad crashed in the downstairs guest room early, leaving Livie sitting at the kitchen table, absorbed in his copy of the script.

Hours later, sleep-grogged and blinking in the harsh light of the bedside lamp, he awakened to find Livie standing over him, fully dressed—this time in the customary jeans—and practically vibrating with anxiety.

He yawned and dragged himself upright against the headboard, "Liv, it's the middle of the night."

"Ransom's cornered," Livie blurted. "We have to get to him, and quick. Call a McKettrick and borrow that helicopter!"

Chapter Twelve

The whole thing was crazy.

It was two in the morning.

He'd have to swallow his pride to roust Jesse or Keegan at that hour, and ask for a monumental favor in the bargain. *My sister had this dream, involving a talking horse,* he imagined himself saying.

But the look of desperation in Livie's eyes made the difference.

"Here's a number," she said, shoving a bit of paper at him and handing him the cordless phone from the kitchen.

"Where did you get this?" Brad asked as Willie, curled at the foot of his bed, stood, made a tight circle and laid himself down again.

Livie answered from the doorway, plainly exasperated.

Jesse and I used to go out once in a while," she said. "Make he call and get dressed!"

She didn't give him a chance to suggest that *she* make the request, since she and Jesse had evidently been an item at one time, but hurried out.

As soon as the door shut behind her, Brad sat up, reached for his jeans, which had been in a heap on the floor, and got into them while he thumbed Jesse's number.

McKettrick answered on the second ring, growling, "This had better be good."

Brad closed his eyes for a moment, used one hand to button his fly while keeping the receiver propped between his ear and his right shoulder. "It's Brad O'Ballivan," he said. "Sorry to wake you up, but there's an emergency and—" He paused only briefly, for the last words had to be forced out. "I need some help."

Barely forty-five minutes later, the McKettrickCo helicopter landed, running lights glaring like something out of *Close Encounters of the Third Kind,* in the field directly behind the ranch house. Jesse was at the controls.

"Hey, Liv," he said with a Jesse-grin once she'd scrambled into the small rear seat and put on a pair of earphones.

"Hey," Livie replied. There was no stiffness about either of them—the dating scenario must have ended affably, or not been serious in the first place.

Brad sat up front, next to Jesse, with a rifle between his knees, dreading the moment when he'd have to explain what his moonlight odyssey was all about.

But Jesse didn't ask for an explanation. All he said was, "Where to?"

"Horse Thief Canyon," Livie answered. "On the eastern rim."

Jesse nodded, cast one sidelong glance at Brad's rifle, and lifted the copter off the ground.

I might have to get one of these things, Brad thought, still sleep-jangled.

Within fifteen minutes, they were high over the mountain, spot-lighting the canyon, so named for being the place where Sam O'Ballivan and some of his Arizona Rangers had once cornered a band of horse rustlers.

"There he is!" Livie shouted, fairly blowing out Brad' eardrums. He leaned for a look and what he saw made his heart swoop to his boot heels.

Ransom gleamed in the glare of the searchlight, rearing and pawing the ground with his powerful forelegs. Behind him, against a rock face, were his mares—Brad counted three, but it was hard to tell how many others might be in the shadows—and before him, a pack of nearly a dozen wolves was closing in. They were hungry, focused on their cornered prey, and they paid no attention whatsoever to the copter roaring above their heads.

"Set this thing down!" Livie ordered. "Fast!"

Jesse worked the controls with one hand and hauled a second rifle out from under the pilot's seat with the other Clearly, he'd spotted the wolves, too.

He landed the copter on what looked like a ledge, too narrow for Brad's comfort. The wait for the blades to slow seemed endless.

"Showtime," Jesse said, shoving open his door, rifle in hand. "Keep your heads down. The updraft will be pretty strong."

Brad nodded and pushed open the door, willing Livie to stay behind, knowing she wouldn't.

Just fifty yards away, Ransom and the wolf pack were still facing off. The mares screamed and snorted, frantic with fear their rolling eyes shining white in the darkness.

With only the moon for light now, the scene was eerie.

The small hairs rose on the back of Brad's neck and one

of the wolves turned and studied him with implacable amber
eyes. His gray-white ruff shimmered in the silvery glow of
cold, distant stars.

Some kind of weird connection sparked between man and
beast. Brad was only vaguely aware of Jesse coming up
behind him, of Livie already fiddling with her veterinary kit.

I'm a predator, the wolf told Brad. *This is what I do.*

Brad cocked the rifle. *I'm a predator, too,* he replied
silently. *And you can't have these horses.*

The wolf pondered a moment, took a single stealthy step
toward Ransom, the stallion bloody-legged and exhausted
from holding off the pack.

Brad took aim. *Don't do it, Brother Wolf. This isn't a bluff.*

Tilting his massive head back, the wolf gave a chilling howl.

Ransom was stumbling a little by then, looking as though
he'd go down. That, of course, was exactly what the pack was
waiting for. Once the great steed was on the ground, they'd
have him—and the mares. And the resultant carnage didn't
bear considering.

Jesse stood at Brad's side, his own rifle ready. "I wouldn't
have believed he was real," McKettrick said in a whisper,
though whether he was referring to Ransom or the old wolf was
anybody's guess, "if I hadn't seen him with my own eyes."

The wolf yowled again, the sound raising something primitive in Brad.

And then it was over.

The leader turned, moving back through the pack at a trot,
and they rounded, one by one, with a lethal and hesitant
grace, to follow.

Brad let out his breath, lowered his rifle. Jesse relaxed, too.

Livie, carrying her kit in one hand, headed straight for
Ransom.

Brad moved to stop her, but Jesse put out his arm.

"Easy," he said. "This is no time to spook that horse."

It would be the supreme irony, Brad reflected grimly, if they had to shoot Ransom in the end, after going to all this trouble to save his hide. If the stallion made one aggressive move toward Livie, though, he'd do it.

"It's me, Olivia," Livie told the legendary wild stallion in a companionable tone. "I came as soon as I could."

Brad brought his rifle up quickly when Ransom butted Livie with his massive head, but Jesse forced the barrel down, murmuring, "Wait."

Ransom stood, lathered and shining with sweat and fresh blood, and allowed Livie to stroke his long neck, ruffle his mane. When she squatted to run her hands over his forelegs, he allowed that, too.

"I'll be damned," Jesse muttered.

The vision was surreal—Brad wasn't entirely convinced he wasn't dreaming at home in his bed.

"You're going to have to come in," Livie told the horse, "at least long enough for that leg to heal."

Unbelievably, Ransom nickered and tossed his head as though he were nodding in agreement.

"How the hell does she expect to drive a band of wild horses all the way down the mountain to Stone Creek Ranch?" Brad asked. He wasn't looking for an answer from Jesse—he was just thinking out loud.

Jesse whacked him on the shoulder. "You've been in the big city too long, O'Ballivan," he said. "You stay here, in case the wolves come back, and I'll go gather a roundup crew. It'll be a few hours before we get here, though—keep your eye out for the pack and pray for good weather. About the last thing we need is another of those blizzards."

By that time, Livie had produced a syringe from her kit, and was preparing to poke it through the hide on Ransom's neck.

Brad moved a step closer.

"Stay back," Livie said. "Ransom's calm enough, but these mares are stressed out. I'd rather not find myself at the center of an impromptu rodeo, if it's all the same to you."

Jesse chuckled, handed Brad his rifle, and turned to sprint back to the copter. Moments later, it was lifting off again, veering southwest.

Brad stood unmoving for a long time, still not sure he wasn't caught up in the aftermath of a nightmare, then leaned his and Jesse's rifles against the trunk of a nearby tree.

Ransom stood with his head down, dazed by the drug Livie had administered minutes before. The mares, still fitful but evidently aware that the worst danger had passed, fanned out to graze on the dry grass.

In the distance, the old wolf howled with piteous fury.

Pinkish-gold light rimmed the eastern hills as Meg returned to the house, after feeding the horses, and the phone was ringing.

She dived for it, in case it was Travis calling to say Sierra had had the baby.

In case it was Brad.

It was Eve.

"You're an aunt again," Meg's mother announced, with brisk pride. "Sierra had a healthy baby boy at four-thirty this morning. I think they're going to call him Brody, for Travis's brother."

Joy fluttered inside Meg's heart, like something trying delicate wings, and tears smarted in her eyes. "She's okay? Sierra, I mean?"

"She's fine, by all reports," Eve answered. "Liam and I are heading for Flagstaff right after breakfast. He's beside himself."

After washing her hands at the kitchen sink, Meg poured herself a cup of hot coffee. By habit, she'd set it brewing before going out to the barn. Upstairs, she heard Ted's slow step as he moved along the corridor.

"Ted's checking in today," she said, keeping her voice down. "I'll stop by to see Sierra and the baby after I get him settled." She drew a breath, let it out softly. "Mother, Carly is not handling this well."

Eve sighed sadly. "I'm sure she isn't, the poor child," she said. "Why don't you keep her out of school for the day and let her come along with you and Ted?"

"I suggested that," Meg replied, as her father appeared on the back stairs, dressed, with a shaving kit in one hand.

Their gazes met.

"And?" Eve prompted.

"And Ted said he wants her to attend class and visit later, when school's out for the day."

Ted nodded. "Is that Eve?"

"Yes," Meg said.

He gestured for the phone, and Meg handed it to him.

"This is Ted," he told Meg's mother. While he explained that Carly needed to settle into as normal a life as possible, as soon as possible, Carly herself appeared on the stairs, looking glum and stubborn.

She wore jeans and the souvenir T-shirt Brad had given her, in spite of the fact that it reached almost to her knees. The expression in her eyes dared Meg to object to the outfit—or anything else in the known universe.

"Hungry?" Meg asked.

"No," Carly said.

"Too bad. In this house, we eat breakfast."

"I might puke."

"You might."

Ted cupped a hand over one end of the phone. "Carly," he said sternly, "you *will* eat."

Scowling, Carly swung a leg over the bench next to the table and plunked down, angrily bereft. Meg poured orange juice, carried the glass to the table, set it down in front of her sister.

It was a wonder the stuff didn't come to an instant boil, considering the heat of Carly's glare as she stared at it.

"This bites," she said.

"Okay, I'll pass the word," Ted told Eve. "See you later."

He hung up. "Eve's hoping you can have lunch with her and Liam after you visit Sierra and the baby."

Meg nodded, distracted.

"It bites," Carly repeated, watching Ted with thunderous eyes. "You're going to the *hospital,* and I have to go to that stupid school, where they'll probably put me in *kindergarten* or something. I'm *supposed* to be in seventh grade."

Meg had no idea how Carly had fared on the tests she'd taken the day before, but it seemed safe to say things probably wouldn't go as badly as all that.

She got a frown for her trouble.

"This time next week," Ted told his younger daughter, "you'll probably be a sophomore at Harvard. Drink your orange juice."

Carly took a reluctant sip and eyeballed Meg's jeans, which were covered with bits of hay. "Don't you have like a *job* or something?"

"Yeah," Meg said, putting a pan on the stove to boil water for oatmeal. "I'm a ranch hand. The work's hard, the pay is lousy, there's no retirement plan and you have to shovel a lot of manure, but I love it."

Breakfast was a dismal affair, one Carly did her best to drag out, but, finally, the time came to leave.

Meg remained in the house for a few extra minutes while Ted and Carly got into the Blazer, giving them time to talk privately.

When she joined them, Carly was in tears, and Ted looked weary to the center of his soul.

Meg gave him a sympathetic look, pushed the button to roll up the garage door and backed out.

When they reached the school, Ted climbed laboriously out of the Blazer and stood on the sidewalk with Carly. They spoke earnestly, though Meg couldn't hear what they said, and Carly dashed at her cheeks with the back of one hand before turning to march staunchly through the colorful herd of kids toward the entrance.

Ted had trouble getting back into the car, but when Meg moved to get out and come around to help him, he shook his head.

"Don't," he said.

She nodded, thick-throated and close to tears herself.

When they reached the hospital in Flagstaff, Eve was waiting in the admittance office.

"I'll take over from here," she told Meg, standing up extra-straight as she watched a nurse ease Ted into a waiting wheelchair. "You go upstairs and see your sister and your new nephew. Room 502."

Meg hesitated, nodded. Then, surprising even herself, she bent and kissed Ted on top of the head before walking purposefully toward the nearest elevator.

Sierra glowed from the inside, as though she'd distilled sunlight to a golden potion and swallowed it down. The room was bedecked in flowers, splashes of watercolor pink, blue and yellow shimmered all around.

"Aunt Meg!" Liam cried delightedly, zooming out of the teary blur. "I've got a brand-new brother and his name is Brody Travis Reid!"

With a choked laugh, Meg hugged the little boy, almost displacing his Harry Potter glasses in the process. "Where *is* this Brody yahoo, anyhow?" she teased. "His legend looms large in this here town, but so far, I haven't seen hide nor hair of him."

"Silly," Liam said. "He's in the *nursery,* with all the other babies!"

Meg ruffled his hair. Went to give Sierra a kiss on the forehead.

"Congratulations, little sister," she said.

"He's so beautiful," Sierra whispered.

"Boys are supposed to be *handsome,* not beautiful," Liam protested, dragging a chair up on the other side of Sierra's bed and standing in the seat so he could be eye to eye with his mother. "Was I handsome?"

Sierra smiled, squeezed his small hand. "You're *still* handsome," she said gently. "And Dad and I are counting on you to be a really good big brother to Brody."

Liam turned to Meg, beaming. "Travis is going to adopt me. I'll be Liam McKettrick Reid, and Mom's changing her name, too."

Meg lifted her eyebrows slightly.

"Somebody had to break the tradition," Sierra said. "I've already told Eve."

Sierra would be the first McKettrick woman to take her husband's last name in generations.

"Mom's okay with that?" Meg asked.

Sierra grinned. "Timing is everything," she said. "If you want to break disturbing news to her, be sure to give birth first."

Meg chuckled. "You are a brave woman," she told Sierra. Then, turning to her nephew, she held out a hand. "How about showing me that brother of yours, Liam McKettrick Reid?"

Jesse returned at midmorning, as promised, with a dozen mounted cowboys. To Brad, the bunch looked as though they'd ridden straight out of an old black-and-white movie, their clothes, gear and horses only taking on color as they drew within hailing distance.

Brad was bone-tired, and Livie, her doctoring completed for the time being, had fallen asleep under a tree, bundled in his coat as well as her own. He'd built a fire an hour or so before dawn, but he craved coffee something fierce, and he was chilled to his core.

Before bedding down in the wee small hours, Livie had cheerfully informed her brother that while he ought to keep watch for the wolf pack, he didn't need to worry that Ransom and the mares would run off. They knew, she assured him, that they were among friends.

He'd kept watch through what remained of the night, pondering the undeniable proof that his sister *had* received an SOS from Ransom.

Now, with riders approaching, Livie wakened and got up off the ground, smiling and dusting dried pine needles and dirt off her jeans.

Jesse, Keegan and Rance were in the lead, ropes coiled around the horns of their saddles, rifles in their scabbards.

Rance nodded to Brad, dismounted and walked over to Ransom. He checked the animal's legs as deftly as Livie had.

"Think he can make it down the mountain to the ranch?" Rance asked.

Livie nodded. "If we take it slowly," she said. Her smile took in the three McKettricks and the men they'd rallied to help. "Thanks, everybody."

Most of the cowboys stared at Ransom as though they expected him to sprout wings, like Pegasus, and take to the blue-gold morning sky. One rode forward, leading mounts for Livie and Brad.

Livie took off Brad's coat and handed it to him, then swung up into the saddle with an ease he couldn't hope to emulate. He kicked dirt over the last embers of the campfire while Rance handed up Livie's veterinary kit.

The ride down the mountain would be long and hard, though thank God the weather had held. The sky was blue as Meg's eyes.

Brad took a deep breath, jabbed a foot into the stirrup and hauled himself onto the back of a pinto gelding. He was still pretty sore from the *last* trip up and down this mountain.

The cowboys went to work, starting Ransom and his mares along the trail with low whistles to urge them along.

Livie rode up beside Brad and grinned. "You look like hell," she said.

"Gosh, thanks," Brad grimaced, shifting in the saddle in a vain attempt to get comfortable.

She chuckled. "Think of it as getting into character for the movie."

Seeing Brody for the first time was the high point of Meg's day, but from there, it was all downhill.

Ted's tests were invasive, and he was drugged.

Liam was hyper with excitement, and didn't sit still for a

second during lunch, despite Eve's grandmotherly reprimands. The food in the cafeteria tasted like wood shavings, and she got a call from the police in Indian Rock on her way home.

Carly had ditched school, and Wyatt Terp, the town marshal, had picked her up along Highway 17. She'd been trying to hitchhike to Flagstaff.

Meg sped to the police station, screeched to a stop in the parking lot and stormed inside.

Carly sat forlornly in a chair near Wyatt's desk, looking even younger than twelve.

"I just wanted to see my dad," she said in a small voice, taking all the bluster out of Meg's sails.

Meg pulled up a chair alongside Carly's and sat down, taking a few deep breaths to center herself. Wyatt smiled and busied himself in another part of the station house.

"You could have been kidnapped, or hit by a car, or a thousand other things," Meg said carefully.

"Dad and I thumbed it lots of times," Carly said defensively, "when our car broke down."

Meg closed her eyes for a moment. Waited for a sensible reply to occur to her. When that didn't happen, she opened them again.

"Will you take me to see him now?" Carly asked.

Meg sighed. "Depends," she said. "Are you under arrest, or just being held for questioning?"

Carly relaxed a little. "I'm not busted," she answered seriously. "But Marshal Terp says if he catches me hitchhiking again, I'll probably do hard time."

"You pull any more stupid tricks like this one, kiddo," Meg said, "and *I'll* give you all the 'hard time' you can handle."

Wyatt approached, doing his best to look like a stern

lawman, but the effect was more Andy-of-Mayberry. "You can go, young lady," he told Carly, "but I'd better not see you in this office again unless you're selling Girl Scout cookies or 4-H raffle tickets or something. Got it?"

"Got it," Carly said meekly, ducking her head slightly.

Meg stood, motioned for her sister to head for the door.

Carly didn't move until the lawman raised an eyebrow at her.

"Is it the badge that makes her mind?" she whispered to Wyatt, once Carly was out of earshot. "And if so, do you happen to have a spare?"

He needed to see Meg.

It was seven-thirty that night before Ransom and his band were corralled at Stone Creek Ranch, and the McKettricks and their helpers had unsaddled all their horses, loaded them into trailers and driven off. Livie had greeted Willie, taken a hot shower and, bundled in one of Big John's ugly Indian-blanket bathrobes, gobbled down a bologna sandwich before climbing the stairs to her old room to sleep.

Brad was tired.

He was cold and he was hungry and he was saddle sore.

The only sensible thing to do was shower, eat and sleep like a dead man.

But he still needed to see Meg.

He settled for the shower and clean clothes.

Calling first would have been the polite thing to do, but he was past that. So he scrawled a note to Livie—*Feed the dog and the horses if I'm not back by morning*—and left.

The truck knew its way to the Triple M, which was a good thing, since he was in a daze.

Lights glowed warm and golden from Meg's windows, and

his heart lifted at the sight, at the prospect of seeing her. The McKettricks, he recalled, tended to gather in kitchens. He parked the truck in the drive and walked around to the back of the house, knocked at the door.

Carly answered. She looked wan, as worn-out and used-up as Brad felt, but her face lit up when she saw him.

"I get to stay in seventh grade," she said. "According to my test scores, I'm gifted."

Brad rustled up a grin and resisted the urge to look past her, searching for Meg. "I could have told you that," he said as she stepped back to let him in.

"Meg's upstairs," Carly told him. "She has a sick headache and I'm supposed to leave her alone unless I'm bleeding or there's a national emergency."

Brad hid his disappointment. "Oh," he said, because nothing better came to him.

"I heard you were making a movie," Carly said. Clearly she was lonesome, needed somebody to talk to.

Brad could certainly identify. "Yeah," he answered, and this time the grin was a little easier to find.

"Can I be in it? I wouldn't have to have lines or anything. Just a costume."

"I'll see what I can do," Brad said. "My people will call your people."

Carly laughed, and the sound was good to hear.

He was about to excuse himself and leave when Meg appeared on the stairs wearing a cotton nightgown, with her hair all rumpled and shadows under her eyes.

"Rough day?" he asked, a feeling of bruised tenderness stealing up from his middle to his throat, like thick smoke from a smudge fire.

She tried to smile, pausing a moment on the stairs.

"Time for me to get lost," Carly said. "Can I use your computer, Meg?"

Meg nodded.

Carly left the room and Brad stood still, watching Meg.

"I guess I should have called first," he said.

"Sit down," Meg told him. "I'll make some coffee."

"I'll make the coffee," Brad replied. "*You* sit down."

For once, she didn't give him any back talk. She just padded over to the table and plunked into the big chair at the head of it.

"Did you find Ransom?" she asked, while Brad opened cupboard doors, scouting for a can of coffee.

"Yes," he said, pleased that she'd remembered, given everything else that was going on in her life. "He and the mares have the run of my best pasture." He told Meg the rest of the story, or most of it, leaving out the part about Livie's dreams, not because he was afraid of what she might think of his sister's strange talent, but because the tale was Livie's to tell or keep to herself.

Meg grinned as she listened, shaking her head. "Rance and Keegan and Jesse must have been in their element, driving wild horses down the mountain like they were back in the old West."

"Maybe," Brad agreed, leaning back against the counter as he waited for the coffee to brew. "As for me—if I never have to do that again, it'll be too soon."

Meg laughed, but her eyes misted over in the next moment. She'd looked away too late to keep him from seeing. "Sierra—my other sister—had a baby this morning. A boy. His name is Brody."

Brad ached inside. It had been hard for Meg to share that news, and it shouldn't have been. Given the way he'd shut her out after meeting Carly, he couldn't blame her for being wary.

He went to her, crouched beside her chair, took one of her

hands in both of his. "I'm sorry about the other night, Meg. I was just—I don't know—a little rattled by Carly's age, and her resemblance to you."

"It's okay," Meg said, but a tear slipped down her cheek.

Brad brushed it away with the side of one thumb. "It isn't okay. I acted like a jerk."

She sniffled. Nodded. "A *major* jerk."

He chuckled, blinked a couple of times because his eyes burned. Rose to his full height again. "I was hoping to spend the night," he said. "Until I remembered Carly's living here now."

Meg bit her lip. "I have guest rooms," she told him.

She didn't want him to leave, then.

Brad's spirits rose a notch.

"But what about Willie, and your horses?"

"Livie's at the house," he said, moving away from her, getting mugs down out of a cupboard. If he'd stayed close, he'd have hauled her to her feet and laid a big sloppy one on her, complete with tongue, and with a twelve-year-old in practically the next room, that was out. "She'll take care of the livestock."

After that, they sat quietly at the venerable old McKettrick table and talked about ordinary things. It made him surprisingly happy, just being there with Meg, doing nothing in particular.

In fact, life seemed downright perfect to him.

Which just went to show what *he* knew.

Chapter Thirteen

Brad blinked awake, sprawled on his back on the big leather couch in Meg's study, fully dressed and covered with an old quilt.

Carly stood looking down at him, a curious expression on her face, probably surprised that he hadn't slept with Meg.

"What time is it?" he asked, yawning.

"Six-thirty," Carly answered. She was wearing jeans and the T-shirt he'd given her, and it looked a little the worse for wear. "Have you decided if I get to be in your movie?"

Brad chuckled, yawned again. "I haven't heard from your agent," he teased.

She frowned. "I don't have an agent," she replied. "Is that a problem?"

"No," he relented, smiling. "I can promise you a walk-on. Beyond that, it's out of my hands. Deal?"

"Deal!" Carly beamed. But then her face fell. "I hope my dad makes it long enough to see me on the big screen," she said.

Brad's heart slipped, caught itself with a lurch that was almost painful. "We could show him the rushes," he said after swallowing once. "Right in his hospital room."

"What are rushes?"

"Film clips. They're not edited, and there's no music—not even sound, sometimes. But he'd see you."

Meg appeared in the doorway of the study, clad in chore clothes.

"I get to be in the movie," Carly informed her excitedly. "Even though I don't have an agent."

"That's great," Meg said softly, her gaze resting with tender gratitude on Brad. "Coffee's on, if anybody's interested."

Brad threw back the quilt, sat upright, pulled on his boots. "Somebody's interested, all right," he said. "I'll feed the horses if you'll make breakfast."

"Sounds fair," Meg answered, turning her attention back to Carly. "Nix on the T-shirt, Ms. Streep. You've worn it for three days in a row now—it goes in the laundry."

On her way to certain stardom, Carly apparently figured she could give ground on the T-shirt edict. "Okay," she said, and headed out of the room, ostensibly to go upstairs and change clothes.

"Carly got arrested yesterday," Meg announced, looking wan.

Brad stood, surprised. And not surprised. "What happened?"

"She decided to cut school and hitchhike to Flagstaff to see Ted in the hospital. Thank God, Wyatt happened to be heading up Highway 17 and spotted her from his squad car."

Brad approached Meg, took her elbows gently into his hands. "Having doubts about being an instant mother, McKettrick?" he asked quietly. She seemed uncommonly fragile, and knowing she'd been flattened by a headache the night before worried him.

"Yes," she said after gnawing at her lower lip for a couple of seconds. "I've always wanted a child, more than anything, but I didn't expect it to happen this way."

He drew her close, held her, buried his face in her hair and breathed in the flower-and-summer-grass scent of it. "I know you don't think of Ted as a father," he said close to her ear, "but a reunion with him this late in the game, especially with a terminal diagnosis hanging over his head, has to be a serious blow. Maybe you need to acknowledge that Carly isn't the only one with some grieving to do."

She tilted her head back, her blue eyes shining with tears. "Damn him," she whispered. "Damn him for coming back here to die! Where was he when I took my first steps— lost my front teeth—broke my leg at horseback riding camp—graduated from high school and college? Where was he when you—"

"When I broke your heart?" Brad finished for her.

"Well—" Meg paused to sniffle once. "Yeah."

"I'd do anything to make that up to you, Meg. Anything for a do over. But the world doesn't work that way. Maybe besides finding a place for Carly, where he knows she'll be loved and she'll be safe, Ted's looking for the same thing I am. A second chance with you."

She looked taken aback. "Maybe," she agreed. "But he sure took his sweet time putting in an appearance, and so did you."

Brad gave her another hug. They were on tricky ground, and he knew it. Carly could be heard clattering down the stairs at the back of the house, into the kitchen.

They needed privacy to carry the conversation any further.

"I'll go feed the horses," he reiterated. "You make breakfast."

He kissed her forehead, not wanting to let her go. "Once you've dropped Carly off at school, you could drop in at my place."

He held his breath, awaiting her answer. Both of them knew what would happen if he and Meg were alone at Stone Creek Ranch.

"I'll let you know," she said at long last.

He hesitated, nodded once and left her to feed the horses.

Breakfast turned out to be toaster waffles and micro-wave bacon.

"Next time," Brad told Meg, after they'd exchanged a light kiss next to her Blazer, with Carly watching avidly from the passenger seat, "I'll cook and *you* feed the horses."

He sang old Johnny Cash favorites all the way home, at the top of his lungs, with the truck windows rolled down.

But the song died in his throat when he topped the rise and saw a sleek white limo waiting in the driveway. Some gut instinct, as primitive as what he'd felt facing down the leader of the wolf pack up at Horse Thief Canyon, told him this wasn't Phil, or even a bunch of movie executives on an outing.

The chauffer got out, opened the rear right-hand door of the limo as Brad pulled to a stop next to it, buzzing up the truck windows and frowning.

A pair of long, shapely legs swung into view.

Brad swore and slammed out of the truck to stand like a gunfighter, his hands on his hips.

"I'd be perfect for the female lead in this movie," Cynthia Donnigan said, tottering toward him on spiked heels that sank into the dirt. Her short, stretchy skirt rode up on her gym-toned thighs, and she didn't bother to adjust it.

He stared at her in amazement and disbelief, literally speechless.

Cynthia lowered her expensive sunglasses and batted her

lashes—as fake as her breasts—and her collagen-enhanced lips puckered into a pout. "Aren't you glad to see me?"

Her hair, black as Ransom's coat, was arranged in artfully careless tufts stiff enough to do damage if she decided to head butt somebody.

"What do you think?" he growled.

Luck, Big John had often said, was never so bad that it couldn't get worse. At that moment, Meg's Blazer came over the rise, dust spiraling behind it.

"I think you're not very forgiving," Cynthia said, following his gaze and then zeroing in on his face with a smug little twist of her mouth. "Bygones are bygones, baby. I'm ideal for the part and you know it."

Brad took a step back as she teetered a step forward. "Not a chance," he said, aware of Meg coming to a stop behind him, but not getting out of the Blazer.

Cynthia smiled and did a waggle-fingered wave in Meg's direction. "I've checked into a resort in Sedona," she said sweetly. "I can wait until you come to your senses and agree that the part of the lawman's widow was written for me."

Brad turned, approached the Blazer and met Meg's wide eyes through the glass of the driver's-side window. He opened the door and offered a hand to help her down.

"The second wife?" Meg asked, more mouthing the words than saying them.

Brad nodded shortly.

Meg peered around him as she got out of the Blazer. Then, with a big smile, she walked right up to Cynthia with her hand out. "I think I've seen you in several feminine hygiene product commercials," she said.

That made Brad chuckle to himself.

Cynthia simmered. "Hello," she responded, in a dangerous purr. "You must be the girl Brad left behind."

Meg had grown up rough-and-tumble, with a bunch of mischievous boy cousins, and served on the executive staff of a multinational corporation. She wasn't easy to intimidate. To Brad's relief—and amusement—she hooked an arm through his, smiled winningly and said, "It's sort of an on-again, off-again kind of thing with Brad and me. Right now, it's definitely on."

Cynthia blinked. She was strictly a B-grade celebrity, but as Brad's ex-wife and sole owner of an up-and-coming production company, she was used to deference of the Beverly Hills variety.

But this was Stone Creek, Arizona, not Beverly Hills.

And the word *deference* wasn't in Meg's vocabulary.

Temporarily stymied, Cynthia pushed her sunglasses back up her nose, minced back toward the waiting limo. The driver stood waiting, still holding her door open and staring off into space as though oblivious to everything going on in what was essentially the barnyard.

Brad followed. "If you manage to wangle your way into this movie," he said, "I'm out."

Cynthia plopped her scantily clad butt onto the leather seat, but didn't draw her killer legs inside. "Read your contract, Brad," she said. "You signed with Starglow Productions. *My* company."

The shock that made his stomach go into a free fall must have shown in his face, because his ex-wife smiled.

"Didn't I tell you I changed the name of the company?" she asked. "No me, no movie, cowboy."

"No movie," Brad said, feeling sick. The whole county was excited about the project—they'd have talked about it for years to come. Carly and a lot of other people would be disappointed—not least of all, himself.

"Back to Sedona," Cynthia told the driver, with a lofty gesture of one manicured hand.

"Yes, ma'am," he replied. But he gave Brad a sympathetic glance before getting behind the wheel.

Brad stood still, furious not only with Cynthia, and with Phil, who had to have known who owned Starglow Productions, but with himself. He'd been too quick to sign on the dotted line, swayed by his own desire to play big-screen cowboy, and by Livie's suggestion that he build an animal shelter with the proceeds. If he tried to back out of the deal now, Cynthia's lawyers would be all over him like fleas on an old hound dog, and he didn't even want to think of the potential publicity.

"So that's the second wife," Meg said, stepping up beside him and watching as the sleek car zipped away.

"That's her," he replied gloomily. "And I am royally, totally screwed."

She moved to stand in front of him, looking up into his face. "I was trying hard not to eavesdrop," she said, "but I couldn't help gathering that she wants to be in the movie."

"She *owns* the movie," Brad said.

"And this is so awful because—?"

"Because she's a first-class, card-carrying bitch. And because I can hardly stand to be in the same room with her, let alone on a movie set for three or four months."

Meg took his hand, gave him a gentle tug in the direction of the house. "Can't you break the contract?"

"Not without getting sued for everything I have, including this ranch, and bringing so many tabloid stringers to Stone Creek that they'll be swinging from the telephone poles."

"Then maybe you should just bite the proverbial bullet and make the movie."

"You haven't read the script," Brad said. "I have to kiss her. And there's a love scene—"

Meg's eyes twinkled. "You sound like a little boy, balking at being in the school play with a *girl*." She tugged him up the back steps, toward the kitchen door.

Willie met them on the other side, wagging cheerfully.

Brad let him out, scowling, and he and Meg waited on the porch while the dog attended to his duties.

"You have no idea what she's like," Brad said.

Meg gave him a light poke with her elbow. "I know you must have loved her once. After all, you married her."

"The truth is a lot less flattering than that," he replied, unable, for a long moment, to meet Meg's eyes. What he had to say was going to upset her, for several reasons, and there was no way to avoid it. "We hooked up after a party. Six weeks later, she called and told me she was pregnant, and the baby was mine. I married her, because she said she was going to get an abortion if I didn't. I went on tour—she wanted to go along and I refused. Frankly, I wasn't ready to present Cynthia to the world as my adored bride. She called the press in, gave them pictures of the 'wedding.' And then, just to make sure I knew what it meant to cross her, she had the abortion anyway."

The pain was there in Meg's face—she had to be thinking that, had she told him about *their* baby, he'd have married her with the same singular lack of enthusiasm—but her words took him by surprise. "I'm sorry, Brad," she said softly. "You must have really wanted to be a dad."

He whistled for Willie, since speaking was beyond him for the moment, and the dog, obviously on the mend, made it up the porch steps with no help. "Yeah," he said.

"I have an idea," Meg said.

He glanced at her. "What?"

"We could rehearse your love scene. Just to be sure you get it right."

In spite of everything, he chuckled. The sound was raw and hurt his throat, but it was genuine. "Aren't you the least bit jealous?" he asked.

She looked honestly puzzled. "Of what?"

"I'm going to have to kiss Cynthia. Get naked with her on the silver screen. This doesn't bother you?"

"I'll cover my eyes during that part of the movie," she joked, with a little what-the-hell motion of her shoulders. Then her expression turned serious. "Of course, there's a fine line between hatred and passion. If you care for Cynthia, you need to tell me—now."

He laid his hands on her shoulders, remembered the satiny smoothness of her bare skin. "I care for *you*, Meg McKettrick," he said. "I tried hard—with Valerie, even with Cynthia—but it never worked. I was always thinking about you—reading about you in the business pages of newspapers, getting what news I could through my sisters, checking the McKettrickCo Web site. Whenever I read or heard your name, I got this sour ache in the pit of my stomach, because I was scared a wedding announcement would follow."

Meg stiffened slightly. "What would you have done if one had?"

"Stopped the wedding," he said. "Made a scene Indian Rock and Stone Creek would never forget." He smiled crookedly. "Kind of a sticky proposition, given that I could have been married at the time."

"Not to mention that my cousins would have thrown you

bodily out of the church," Meg huffed, but there was a smile beginning in her eyes, already tugging at the corners of her mouth.

"I said it would have been an unforgettable scene," he reminded her, grinning. "I would have fought back, you see, and yelled your name, like Stanley yelling for Stella in *A Streetcar Named Desire.*"

She pretended to punch him in the stomach. "You're impossible."

"I'm also horny. And a lot more—though I'm not sure you're ready to hear that part."

"Try me."

"Okay. I love you, Meg McKettrick. I always have. I always will."

"You're right. I wasn't ready."

"Then I guess rehearsing the love scene is out?"

She smiled, stood on tiptoe and kissed the cleft in his chin. "I didn't say that. Hardworking actors should know their scenes cold."

He bent his head, nibbled at her delectable mouth. "Oh, I'll know the scene," he breathed. "But there won't be anything 'cold' about it."

Meg hauled herself up onto her elbows, out of a sated sleep, glanced at the clock on the table next to Brad's bed and screamed.

"What?" Brad asked, bolting awake.

"Look at the time!" Meg wailed. "Carly will be out of school in fifteen minutes!"

Calmly, Brad reached for the telephone receiver, handed it to her. "Call the school and tell them you've been detained and you'll be there soon."

"Detained?"

"Would you rather say you've been in bed with me all afternoon?"

"No," she admitted, and dialed 411, asking to be connected to Indian Rock Middle School.

When she arrived at the school forty-five minutes later, Carly was waiting glumly in the principal's office. Her expression softened, though, when she saw that Brad had come along.

"Oh, great," she said. "Brad O'Ballivan shows up at my school, *in person,* and nobody's around to see but the geek-wads in detention. Who'd believe a word *they* said?"

Brad laughed. "Did I ever tell you I was one of those 'geek-wads' once upon a time, always in detention?"

"Get out," Carly said, intrigued.

"Don't get the idea that being in detention is cool," Meg warned.

Carly rolled her eyes.

The three of them made the drive to Flagstaff in Brad's truck. Carly chattered nonstop for the first few miles, pointing out the place where she'd been "busted" for trying to hitch a ride, but as they drew nearer to their destination, she grew more and more subdued.

It didn't help that Ted was worse than he'd been the day before. He looked shrunken, lying there in his bed with tubes and monitors attached to every part of his body.

Looking at her father, it seemed to Meg that he'd used up the last of his personal resources to fling himself over an invisible finish line—getting Carly to her for safekeeping. For the first time it was actually real to Meg: he *was* dying.

Brad gave her a nudge toward the bed, an unspoken reminder of what he'd said about her having grieving to do, just as Carly did.

"How about a milk shake in the cafeteria?" Meg heard Brad say to Carly.

In the next moment, the two of them were gone, and Meg was alone with the man who had abandoned her so long ago that she didn't even remember him.

"That young man," Ted said, "is in love with you."

"He left me, too," Meg said without meaning to expose the rawest nerve in her psyche. "It's a pattern. First you, then Brad."

"Do yourself a favor and don't superimpose your old man over him," Ted struggled to say. "And when Carly gets old enough, don't let her make that mistake, either. I don't have time to make it up to you, what I did and didn't do, but he does. You give him the chance."

Tears welled in Meg's eyes, thickened her throat. "I hate it that you're dying," she said.

Ted put out his left hand, an IV tube dangling from it. "Me, too," he ground out. "Come here, kid."

Meg let him pull her closer, lowered her forehead to rest against his.

She felt moisture in the gray stubble on his cheeks and didn't know if the tears were hers or her father's. Or both.

"If I could stay around a little longer, I'd find a way to prove that you're still my little girl and I've always loved you. Since I'm not going to get that chance, you'll have to take my word for it."

"It isn't fair," Meg protested, knowing the remark was childish.

"Not much is, in this life," Ted answered, as Meg raised her head so she could look into his face. "Know what I'd tell you if I'd been around all this time like a regular father, and had the right to say what's on my mind?"

Meg couldn't answer.

"I'd tell you not to let Brad O'Ballivan get away. Don't let your damnable McKettrick pride get in the way of what he's offering, Meg."

"He told me he loves me," she said.

"Do you believe him?"

"I don't know."

"All right, then, do you love him?"

Meg bit her lower lip, nodded.

"Have you told him?"

"Sort of," Meg said.

"Take it from me, kid," Ted countered, trying to smile. "'Sort of' ain't good enough." His faded eyes seemed to memorize Meg, take her in. "Get the nurse for me, will you? This pain medication isn't working."

Meg immediately rang for the nurse, and when help came, rushed to the elevators and punched the button for the cafeteria. By the time she got back with Carly and Brad, the room was full of people in scrubs.

Carly broke free and rushed to her dad's bedside, squirming through until she caught hold of his hand.

The medical team, in the midst of an emergency, would have pushed Carly aside if Brad hadn't spoken in a voice of calm but unmistakable authority.

"Let her stay," he said.

"Dad?" Carly whispered desperately. "Dad, don't go, okay? Don't go!"

A nurse eased Carly back from the bedside, and the work continued, but it was too late, and everyone knew it.

The heartbeat monitor blipped, then flatlined.

Carly turned, sobbing, not into Meg's arms, but into Brad's.

He held her and drew Meg close against his side at the same time.

After that, there were papers to sign. Meg would have to call her mother later, but at the moment, she simply couldn't say the words.

Carly seemed dazed, allowing herself to be led out of the hospital, back to Brad's truck. She'd been inconsolable in Ted's hospital room, but now she was dry-eyed and the only sound she made was the occasional hiccup.

Brad didn't take them back to the Triple M, but to his own ranch. There, he called Eve, then Jesse. Vaguely, as if from a great distance, Meg heard him ask her cousin to make sure her horses got fed.

There were other calls, too, but Meg wasn't tracking. She simply sat at the kitchen table, watching numbly while Carly knelt on the floor, both arms around a sympathetic Willie, her face buried in his fur.

Olivia arrived—Brad must have summoned her—and brought a stack of pizza boxes with her. She set the boxes on the counter, washed her hands at the sink and immediately started setting out plates and silverware.

"I'm not hungry," Carly said.

"Me, either," Meg echoed.

"Humor me," Olivia said.

The pizza tasted like cardboard, but it filled a hole, if only a physical one, and Meg was grateful. Following her example, Carly ate, too.

"Are we staying here tonight?" Carly asked Brad, her eyes enormous and hollow.

Olivia answered for him. "Yes," she said.

"Who are you?"

"I'm Livie—Brad's sister."

"The veterinarian?"

Olivia nodded.

"My dad died today."

Olivia's expressive eyes filled with tears. "I know."

Meg swallowed, but didn't speak. Next to her, Brad took her hand briefly, gave it a squeeze.

"Do you like being an animal doctor?" Carly asked. She'd said hardly a word to Meg or even Brad since they'd left the hospital, but for some reason, she was reaching out to Olivia O'Ballivan.

"I love it," Olivia said. "It's hard sometimes, though. When I try really hard to help an animal, and they don't get better."

"I kept thinking my dad would get well, but he didn't."

"Our dad died, too," Olivia said after a glance in Brad's direction. "He was struck by lightning during a roundup. I kept thinking there must have been a mistake—that he was just down in Phoenix at a cattle auction, or looking for strays up on the mountain."

Meg felt a quick tension in Brad, a singular alertness, gone again as soon as it came. Her guess was he hadn't known his sister, a child when the accident happened, had secretly believed their father would come home.

"Does it ever stop hurting?" Carly asked, her voice small and fragile.

Meg squeezed her eyes shut. Does *it ever stop hurting?* she wondered.

"You'll never forget your dad, if that's what you mean," Olivia said. "But it gets easier. Brad and our sisters and I, we were lucky. We had our grandfather, Big John. Like you've got Meg."

Brad pushed his chair back, left the table. Stood with his back to them all, as if gazing out the darkened window over the sink.

"Big John passed away, too," Olivia explained quietly. "But we were all grown up by then. He was there when it counted, and now we've got each other."

Carly turned imploring eyes on Meg. "You won't die, too? You won't die and leave me all alone?"

Meg got up, went to Carly, gathered her into her arms. "I'll be here," she promised. *"I'll be here."*

Carly clung to her for a long time, then, typically, pulled away. "Where am I going to sleep?" she asked.

"I thought maybe you'd like to stay in my room," Olivia said. "It has twin beds. You can have the one by the window, if you'd like."

"You're going to stay, too?"

"For tonight," Olivia answered.

Carly looked relieved. Maybe, for a child, it was a matter of safety in numbers—herself, Meg, Brad, Olivia and Willie, all huddled in the same house, somehow keeping the uncertain darkness at bay. "I think I'd like to sleep now," she said. "Can Willie come, too?"

"He'll need to go outside first, I think," Olivia said.

Brad took Willie out, without a word, returned and watched as the old dog climbed the stairs, Carly leading the way, Olivia bringing up the rear.

"Thanks," Meg said when she and Brad were alone. "You've been wonderful."

Brad began clearing the table, disposing of pizza boxes.

Meg caught his arm. "Brad, what—?"

"My grandfather," he said. "I just got to missing him. Regretting a lot of things."

She nodded. Waited.

"I'm sorry, Meg," he told her. "That your dad's gone, and you didn't get a chance to know him. That you've got a rough time ahead with Carly. And most of all, I'm sorry there's nothing I can do to make this better."

"You could hold me," Meg said.

He pulled her into an easy, gentle embrace. Kissed her forehead. "I could hold you," he confirmed.

She wanted to ask if he'd meant it, when—was it only a few hours ago?—he'd said he loved her. The problem was, she knew if he took the words back, or qualified them somehow, she wouldn't be able to bear it. Not now, while she was mourning the father she'd lost years ago.

They stood like that for a while, then, by tacit agreement, finished tidying up the kitchen. Before they started up the backstairs, Brad switched out the lights, and Meg stood waiting for him, blinded, not knowing her way around the house, but unafraid. As long as Brad was there, no gloom would have been deep enough to swallow her.

In his room upstairs, they undressed, got into bed together, lay enfolded in each other's arms.

I love you, Meg thought with stark clarity.

They didn't make love.

They didn't talk.

But Meg felt a bittersweet gratification just the same, a deep shift somewhere inside herself, where spirit and body met.

On the edge of sleep, just before she tumbled helplessly over the precipice, Angus crossed her mind, along with a whisper-thin wondering.

Where had he gone?

Chapter Fourteen

The snows came early that year, to the annoyance of the movie people, and Brad was away from the ranch a lot, filming scenes in a studio in Flagstaff. He'd grudgingly admitted that Cynthia had been right—she *was* perfect for the part of Sarah Jane Stone—and while Meg visited the set once or twice, she stayed away when the love scenes were on the schedule.

She had a lot of other things on her mind, as it happened. She and Carly were bonding, slowly but surely, but the process was rocky. With the help of a counselor, they felt their way toward each other—backed off—tried again.

When the day came for Carly's promised scene—she played a nameless character in calico and a bonnet who brought Brad a glass of punch at a party and solemnly offered it. She'd endlessly practiced her single line—a "you're welcome, mister" to his "thank you"—telling Meg very seriously that there were no small parts, only small actors.

The movie part gave Carly something to hold on to in the dark days after Ted's passing, and Meg was eternally grateful for that. Both she and Carly spent a lot of time at Brad's house, even when he wasn't around, looking after Willie and gradually becoming a part of the place itself.

Ransom and his mares occupied the main pasture at Stone Creek Ranch, and the job of driving hay out to them usually fell to Olivia and Meg, with Carly riding in the back of the truck, seated on the bales. During that time, Meg and Olivia became good friends.

In the spring, when there would be fresh grass in the high country, and no snow to impede their mobility, Ransom and the mares would be turned loose.

"You'll miss him," Meg said once, watching Olivia as she stood in the pickup bed, tossing bales of grass hay to the ground after Carly cut the twine that held them together.

Olivia swallowed visibly and nodded, admiring the stallion as he stood, head turned toward the mountain, sniffing the air for the scents of spring and freedom. On warmer days, he was especially restless, prancing back and forth along the farthest fence, tail high, mane flying in the breeze.

Meg knew there had been many opportunities to sell Ransom for staggering amounts of money, but neither Olivia nor Brad had even considered the idea. In their minds, Ransom wasn't theirs to sell—he belonged to himself, to the high country, to legend. With his wounds healed, he'd have been able to soar over any fence, but he seemed to know the time wasn't right. There in the O'Ballivans' pasture, he had plenty of feed and easily accessible water, hard to find in winter, especially up in the red peaks and canyons, and he'd be at a disadvantage with the wolves. Still, there was a palpable, restless air of yearning about him that bruised Meg's heart.

It would be a sad and wonderful day when the far gate was opened.

Olivia cheered herself, along with Meg and Carly, with the fact that Brad had decided to make the ranch a haven for displaced mules, donkeys and horses, including unwanted Thoroughbreds who hadn't made the grade as racers, studs or broodmares. At the first sign of spring, the adoptees would begin arriving, courtesy of the Bureau of Land Management and various animal-rescue groups.

In the meantime, the ranch, like the larger world, seemed to Meg to be hibernating, practically in suspended animation. Like Ransom, she longed for spring.

It was after one of their visits to Brad's, while they were attending to their own horses on the Triple M, that Carly brought up a subject Meg had been troubled by, but hadn't wanted to raise.

"Where do you suppose Angus is?" the child asked. "I haven't seen him around in a couple of months."

"Hard to know," Meg said carefully.

"Maybe he's busy on the other side," Carly suggested. "You know, showing my dad around and stuff."

"Could be," Meg allowed. Until his last visit—the night he'd been so anxious for a look at the McKettrick family Bible—Meg had seen and spoken to her illustrious ancestor almost every day of her life. She hadn't had so much as a glimpse of him since then, and while there had been countless times she'd wished Angus would stay where he belonged, so she could be a normal person, she missed him.

Surely he wouldn't have simply stopped visiting her without even saying goodbye. It appeared, though, that that was exactly what he'd done.

"I wish he'd come," Carly said somewhat wistfully. "I want to ask him if he's seen my dad."

Meg slipped an arm around her sister, held her close against her side for a second or two. "I'm sure your—our—dad is fine," she said softly.

Carly smiled, but sadness lingered in her eyes. "For a while, I hoped Dad would come back, the way Angus did. But I guess he's busy or something."

"Probably," Meg agreed. It went without saying that the Angus phenomenon was rare, but there were times when she wondered if that was really true. How many children, prattling about their imaginary playmates, were actually seeing someone real?

They started back toward the house, two sisters, walking close.

Inside, they both washed up—Meg at the kitchen sink, Carly in the downstairs powder room—and began preparing supper. After the meal, salad and a tamale pie from a recently acquired cookbook geared to the culinarily challenged, Meg cleared the table and loaded the dishwasher while Carly settled down to her homework.

Like most kids, she had a way of asking penetrating questions with no preamble. "Are you going to marry Brad O'Ballivan?" she inquired now, looking up from her math text. "We spend a lot of time at his place, and I know you sleep over when I'm visiting Eve. Or he comes here."

Things were good between Brad and Meg, probably because he was so busy with the movie that they rarely saw each other. When they *were* together, they took every opportunity to make love.

"He hasn't asked," Meg said lightly. "And you're in some pretty personal territory, here. Have I mentioned lately that you're twelve?"

"I might be twelve," Carly replied, "but I'm not stupid."

"You're definitely not stupid," Meg agreed good-naturedly, but on the inside, she was dancing to a different tune. Her period, always as regular as the orbit of the moon, was two weeks late. She'd bought a home pregnancy test at a drugstore in Flagstaff, not wanting word of the purchase to get around Indian Rock as it would have if she'd made the purchase locally, but she hadn't worked up the nerve to use it yet.

As much as she'd wanted a child, she almost hoped the results would be negative. She knew what would happen if the plus sign came up, instead of the minus. She'd tell Brad, he'd insist on marrying her, just as he'd done with both Valerie and Cynthia, and for the rest of her days, she'd wonder if he'd proposed out of honor, or because he actually loved her.

On the other hand, she wouldn't dare keep the knowledge from him, not after what had happened before, when they were teenagers. He'd never forgive her if something went wrong; even the truest, deepest kind of love between a man and a woman couldn't survive if there was no trust.

All of which left Meg in a state of suspecting she was carrying Brad's child, not knowing for sure, and being afraid to find out.

Carly, whose intuition seemed uncanny at times, blindsided her again. "I saw the pregnancy-test kit," she announced.

Meg, in the process of wiping out the sink, froze.

"I didn't mean to snoop," Carly said quickly. By turns, she

was rebellious and paranoid, convinced on some level that living on the Triple M as a part of the McKettrick family was an interval of sorts, not a permanent arrangement. In her experience, everything was temporary. "I ran out of toothpaste, and I went into your bathroom to borrow some, and I saw the kit."

Sighing, Meg went to the table and sat down next to Carly, searching for words.

"Are you mad at me?" Carly asked.

"No," Meg said. "And I wouldn't send you away even if I was, Carly. You need to get clear on that."

"Okay," Carly said, but she didn't sound convinced. Meg guessed it would take time, maybe a very long time, for her little sister to feel secure. Her face brightened. "It would be so cool if you had a baby!" she spouted.

"Yes," Meg agreed, smiling. "It would."

"So what's the problem with finding out for sure?"

"Brad's really busy right now. I guess I'm looking for a chance to tell him."

Just then, as if by the hand of Providence, a rig drove up outside, a door slammed.

Carly rushed to the window, gave a yip of excitement. "He's here!" she crowed. "And Willie's with him!"

Meg closed her eyes. So much for procrastination.

Carly hurried to open the back door, and Brad and the dog blew in with a chilly wind.

"Here," Brad said, handing Carly a DVD case. "It's your big scene, complete with dialogue and music."

Carly grabbed the DVD and fled to the study, which contained the only TV set in the house, fairly skipping and Willie, now almost wholly recovered from his injuries, dashed after her, barking happily.

Meg was conscious, in those moments, of everything that

was at stake. The child and even the dog would suffer if the conversation she and Brad were about to have went sour.

"Sit down," she said, turning to watch Brad as he shed his heavy coat and hung it from one of the pegs next to the door.

"Sounds serious," Brad mused. "Carly get into trouble at school again?"

"No," Meg answered, after swallowing hard.

Brad frowned and joined her at the table, sitting astraddle the bench while she occupied the chair at the end. "Meg, what's the trouble?" he asked worriedly.

"I bought a kit—" she began, immediately faltering.

His forehead crinkled. "A kit?" The light went on. "A *kit!*"

"I think I might be pregnant, Brad."

A smile spread across his face, shone in his eyes, giving her hope. But then he went solemn again. "You don't sound very happy about it," he said, looking wary. "When did you do the test?"

"That's just it. I haven't done it yet. Because I'm afraid."

"Afraid? Why?"

"Things have been so good between us, and—"

Gently, he took her hand. Turned it over to trace patterns on her palm with the pad of his thumb. "Go on," he said, his voice hoarse, obviously steeling himself against who knew what.

"I know you'll marry me," Meg forced herself to say. "If the test is positive, I mean. And I'll always wonder if you feel trapped, the way you did with Cynthia."

Brad considered her words, still caressing her palm. "All right," he said presently. "Then I guess we ought to get married *before* you take the pregnancy test. Because either way, Meg, I want you to be my wife. Baby or no baby."

She studied him. "Maybe we should live together for a while. See how it goes."

"No way, McKettrick," Brad replied instantly. "I know lots of good people share a house without benefit of a wedding these days, but when it comes down to it, I'm an old-fashioned guy."

"You'd really do that? Marry me without knowing the results of the test? What if it's negative?"

"Then we'd keep working on it." Brad grinned.

Meg bit her lower lip, thinking hard.

Finally, she stood and said, "Wait here."

But she only got as far as the middle of the back stairway before she returned.

"The McKettrick women don't change their names when they get married," she reminded him, though they both knew Sierra had already broken that tradition, and happily so.

"Call yourself whatever you want," Brad replied. "For a year. At the end of that time, if you're convinced we can make it, then you'll go by O'Ballivan. Deal?"

Meg pondered the question. "Deal," she said at long last.

She went upstairs, slipped into her bathroom and leaned against the closed door, her heart pounding. Her reflection in the long mirror over the double sink stared back at her.

"Pee on the stick, McKettrick," she told herself, "and get it over with."

Five minutes later, she was staring at the little plastic stick, filled with mixed emotion. There was happiness, but trepidation, too. *What-ifs* hammered at her from every side.

A light knock sounded at the door, and Brad came in.

"The suspense," he said, "is killing me."

Meg showed him the stick.

And his whoop of joy echoed off every wall in that venerable old house.

"I think I have a future in show business," Carly confided to Brad later that night when she came into the kitchen to say good-night. She'd watched her scene on the study TV at least fourteen times.

"I think you have a future in the eighth grade," Meg responded, smiling.

"What if I end up on the cutting-room floor?" Carly fretted. Clearly, she'd been doing some online research into the movie-making process.

"I'll see that you don't," Brad promised. "Go to bed, Carly. A movie star needs her beauty sleep."

Carly nodded, then went upstairs, DVD in hand. Willie, who had been following her all evening, sighed despondently and lay down at Brad's feet, muzzle resting on his forepaws.

Brad leaned down to stroke the dog's smooth, graying back. "Looks like Carly's already got one devoted fan," he remarked.

Meg chuckled. "More than one," she said. "I certainly qualify, and so do you. Eve spoils her, and Rance's and Keegan's girls think of her as the family celebrity."

Brad grinned. "Carly's a pro," he said. "But you're wise to steer her away from show business, at least for the time being. It's hard enough for adults to handle, and kids have it even worse."

The topics of the baby and marriage pulsed in the air between them, but they skirted them, went on talking about other things. Brad was comfortable with that—there would be time enough to make plans.

"According to her teachers," Meg said, "Carly has a near-genius affinity for computers, or anything technical. Last week she actually got the clock on the DVD player to stop blinking twelves. This, I might add, is a skill that has eluded presidents."

"Lots of things elude presidents," Brad replied, finishing his coffee. "We're wrapping up the movie next week," he added. "The indoor scenes, at least. We'll have to do the stagecoach robbery and all the rest next spring. Think you could pencil a wedding into your schedule?"

Meg's cheeks colored attractively, causing Brad to wonder what *other* parts of her were turning pink. She hesitated, then nodded, but as she looked at him, her gaze switched to something just beyond his left shoulder.

Brad turned to look, but there was nothing there.

"I hate leaving you," he said, turning back, frowning a little. "But I've got an early call in the morning." Neither of them were comfortable sleeping together with Carly around, but that would change after they were married.

"I understand," Meg said.

"Do you, Meg?" he asked very quietly. "I love you. I want to marry you, and I would have, even if the test had been negative."

She said them then, the words he'd been waiting for. Before that, she'd spoken them only in the throes of passion.

"I love you right back, Brad O'Ballivan."

He stood, drew her to her feet and kissed her. It was a lingering kiss, gentle but thorough.

"But there's still one thing I haven't told you," she choked out, when their mouths parted.

Brad braced himself. Waited, his mind scrambling over possibilities—there was another man out there somewhere after all, one with some emotional claim on her, or more she hadn't told him about the first pregnancy, or the miscarriage...

"Ever since I was a little girl," she said, "I've been seeing Angus McKettrick. In fact, he's here right now."

Brad recalled the glance she'd thrown over his shoulder a few minutes before, the odd expression in her eyes. First

Livie, with her Dr. Doolittle act—now Meg claimed she could see the family patriarch, who had been dead for over a century.

He thrust out a sigh.

She waited, gnawing at her lip, her eyes wide and hopeful.

"If you say so," he said at last, "I believe you."

Joy suffused her face. "Really?"

"Really," he said, though the truth was more like: *I'm* trying *to believe you.* As with Livie, he would believe if it killed him, despite all the rational arguments crowding his mind.

She stood on tiptoe and kissed him. "I'd insist that you stay, since we're engaged," she whispered, "but Angus is even more old-fashioned than you are."

He laughed, said good-night and looked down at Willie.

The dog was standing, wagging his tail and grinning, looking up at someone who wasn't there.

There were indeed, Brad thought, as he and Willie made the lonely drive back to Stone Creek Ranch in his truck, more things in heaven and earth than this world dreams of.

"Where have you been?" Meg demanded, torn between relief at seeing Angus again, and complete exasperation.

"You always knew I wouldn't be around forever," Angus said. He looked older than he had the last time she'd seen him, even careworn, but somehow serene, too. "Things are winding down, girl. I figured you needed to start getting used to my being gone."

Meg blinked, surprised by the stab of pain she felt at the prospect of Angus's leaving for good. On the other hand, she *had* always known the last parting would come.

"I'm going to have a baby," she said, struggling not to cry. "I'll need you. The baby and Carly will need you."

Angus seldom touched her, but now he cupped one hand under her chin. His skin felt warm, not cold, and solid, not ethereal. "No," he said gruffly. "You only need yourselves and each other. Things are going to be fine from here on out, Meg. You'll see."

She swallowed, wanting to cling to him, knowing it wouldn't be right. He had a life to live, somewhere else, beyond some unseen border. There were others there, waiting for him.

"Why did you come?" she asked. "In first place, I mean?"

"You needed me," he said simply.

"I did," she confirmed. For all the nannies and "aunts and uncles," she'd been a lost soul as a child, especially after Sierra was kidnapped and Eve fell apart in so many ways. She'd never blamed her mother, never harbored any resentment for the inevitable neglect she'd suffered, but she knew now that, without Angus, she would have been bereft.

He was carrying a hat in his left hand, and now he put it on, the gesture somehow final. "You say goodbye to Carly for me," he said. "And tell her that her pa's just fine where he is."

Meg nodded, unable to speak.

Angus leaned in, planted a light, awkward kiss on Meg's forehead. "When you get to the end of the trail," he said, "and that's a long ways off, I promise, I'll be there to say welcome."

Still, no words would come. Not even ones of farewell. So Meg merely nodded again.

Angus turned his back and, in the blink of an eye, he was gone.

She cried that night, for sorrow, for joy and for a thousand other reasons, but when the morning came, she knew Angus had been right.

She didn't need him anymore.

The wedding was small and simple, with only family and a few friends present. Meg still considered the marriage provisional, and went on calling herself Meg McKettrick, although she and Carly moved in at Stone Creek Ranch right away. All the horses came with them, but Meg still paid regular visits to the Triple M, always hoping, on some level, for just one more glimpse of Angus.

It didn't happen, of course.

So she sorted old photos and journals when she was there, and with some help from Sierra, catalogued them into something resembling archives. Eve, tired of hotel living, planned on moving back in. A grandmother, she maintained, with Eve-logic, ought to live in the country. She ought to bake pies and cookies and shelter the children of the family under broad, sturdy branches, like an old oak tree.

Meg smiled every time she pictured her rich, sophisticated, well-traveled mother in an apron and sensible shoes, but she had to admit Eve had pulled off a spectacular country-style Christmas. There had been a massive tree, covered in lights and heirloom ornaments, bulging stockings for Carly and Liam and little Brody, and a complete turkey dinner, only partly catered.

She'd already taken over the master bedroom, and she'd brought her two champion jumpers from the stables in San Antonio, and installed them in the barn. She rode every chance she got, often with Brad and Carly and sometimes with Jesse, Rance and Keegan.

Meg, being pregnant and out of practice when it came to horseback riding, usually watched from a perch on the pasture fence. She didn't believe in being overly cautious—it wasn't the McKettrick way—but this baby was precious to her, and to Brad. She wasn't taking any chances.

Dusting off an old photograph of Holt and Lorelei, Meg stepped back to admire the way it looked on the study mantle. She heard her mother at the back of the house.

"Meg? Are you here?"

"In the study," Meg called back.

Eve tracked her down. "Feeling nostalgic?" she asked, eyeing the picture.

Meg sighed, sat down in a high-backed leather chair, facing the fireplace. "Maybe it's part of the pregnancy. Hormones, or something."

Eve, always practical, threw off her coat, draping it over the back of the sofa, marched to the fireplace and started a crackling, cheerful blaze. She let Meg's words hang, all that time, finally turning to study her daughter.

"Are you happy, Meg? With Brad, I mean?"

When it came to happiness, she and Brad were constantly charting fresh territory. Learning new things about each other, stumbling over surprises both profound and prosaic. For all of that, there was a sense of fragility to the relationship.

"I'm happy," she said.

"But?" Eve prompted. She stood with her back to the fireplace, looking very ungrandmotherly in her tailored slacks and silk sweater.

"It feels—well—too good to be true," Meg admitted.

Eve crossed to drag a chair closer to Meg's and sit beside her. "You're holding back a part of yourself, aren't you? From Brad, from the marriage?"

"I suppose I am," Meg said. "It's sort of like the first day we were allowed to swim in the pond, late in the spring, when Jesse and Rance and Keegan and I were kids. The water was always freezing. I'd stick a toe in and stand shivering on the bank while the boys cannonballed into the water, howling and whooping and trying to splash me. Finally, more out of shame than courage, I'd jump in." She shuddered. "I still remember that icy shock— it always knocked the wind out of me for a few minutes."

Eve smiled, probably remembering similar swimming fests from her own childhood, with another set of McKettrick cousins. "But then you got used to the temperature and had as much fun as the boys did."

Meg nodded.

"It's not smart to hold yourself apart from the shocks of life, Meg—the good ones or the bad. They're all part of the mix, and paradoxically, shying away from them only makes things harder."

Meg was quiet for a long time. Then she said quietly, "Angus is gone."

Eve waited.

"I miss him," Meg confessed. "When I was a teenager, especially, I used to wish he'd leave me alone. Now that he's gone—well—every day, the memories seem less and less real."

Eve took her hand, squeezed. "Sometimes," she said very softly, "just at twilight, I think I see them—Angus and his four sturdy, handsome sons—riding single-file along the creek bank. Just a glimpse, a heartbeat really, and then they're gone. It's odd, because they don't look like ghosts. Just men on horseback, going about their ordinary business. I could almost convince myself that, for a fraction of a moment, a curtain had opened between their time and ours."

"Rance told me the same thing once," Meg said. "He used different words, but he saw the riders, traveling one behind the other beside the creek, and he knew who they were."

The two women sat in thoughtful silence for a while.

"It's a strange thing, being a McKettrick," Meg finally said.

"You're an O'Ballivan now," Eve surprised her by saying. "And your baby will be an O'Ballivan, too."

Meg looked hard at her mother, startled. Eve had been

miffed when Sierra took Travis's last name, and made a few remarks about tradition not being what it once was.

"What about the McKettrick way?" she asked.

"The McKettrick way," Eve said, giving Meg's hand another squeeze, "is living at full throttle, holding nothing back. It's taking life—and change—as they come. Anyway, lots of women keep their last names these days—taking their husbands' is the novelty now." She paused, studying Meg with loving, intelligent eyes. "It's what's standing in your way," she said decisively. "You're afraid that if you're not Meg McKettrick anymore, you'll lose some part of your identity, and have to get to know yourself as a new person."

Meg realized that she *was* a new person—though of course still herself in the most fundamental ways. She was a wife now, a mother-figure as well as a sister to Carly. When the baby came, there would be yet another new level to who she was.

"I've been hiding behind the McKettrick name," she mused, more to herself than Eve.

"It's a fine name," Eve said. "We take a lot of pride in it—maybe too much, sometimes."

"Would *you* take your husband's name, if you remarried?" Meg ventured.

Eve thought about her answer before shaking her head from side to side. "No," she said. "I don't think so. I've been a McKettrick for so long, I wouldn't know how to be anything else."

Meg smiled. "And you don't want me to follow in your footsteps?"

"I want you to be *happy.* Don't stand on the bank shivering, Meg. *Jump in. Get wet.*"

"Were *you* happy, Mom?" The reply to that question seemed terribly important; Meg held her breath to hear it.

"Most of the time, yes," Eve said. "When Hank took Sierra

and vanished, I was shattered. I don't think I could have gone on if it hadn't been for you. Though I realize it probably didn't seem that way to you, that you were my main reason for living, you and the hope of getting Sierra back. I'm so sorry, Meg, for coming apart at the seams the way I did. For not being there for you."

"I've never resented that, Mom. As young as I was, I knew you loved me, and that the things that were happening didn't change that for a moment. Besides, I had Angus."

The clock on the mantelpiece ticked ponderously, marking off the hours, the minutes, the seconds, as it had been doing for over a hundred years. It had ticked and tocked through the lives of Holt and Lorelei and their children, and the generations to follow.

The sound reminded Meg of something she'd always known, at least unconsciously. Life seemed long, but it was finite, too. One day, some future McKettrick would sit listening to that same clock, and Meg herself would be a memory. An ancestor in a photo.

"Gotta go pick Carly up at school," she said, standing up.

Time to find Brad, she added silently, *and introduce him to his wife.*

"Hello," I'll say, as if we're meeting for the first time. "My name is Meg O'Ballivan."

Chapter Fifteen

That late March day was blustery and cold, but there was a fresh, piney tinge to the air. Brad, Meg and Carly stood watching from a short distance as Olivia squared her shoulders, walked to the far gate, sprung the latch and opened the way for Ransom to go.

A part of Meg hoped he'd choose to stay, but it wasn't to be.

Ransom approached the path to freedom cautiously at first, the mares straggling behind him, still shaggy with their winter coats.

When the great stallion drew abreast of Olivia, he paused, nickered and tossed his magnificent head once, as if to bid her goodbye. Tears slipped down Olivia's cheeks, and she made no attempt to wipe them away. She'd arrived during breakfast that morning and said Ransom had told her it was time.

Meg, who had after all seen a ghost from childhood, didn't question her sister-in-law's ability to communicate with animals. Even Brad, quietly skeptical about such things, couldn't write it all off to coincidence.

Carly, her own face wet, leaned into Brad a little. Meg sniffled, trying to be brave and philosophical.

He put one arm around her shoulders and one around Carly's. Glancing up at him, Meg didn't see the sorrow she and Carly and Olivia were feeling, but an expression of almost transported wonder and awe.

Ransom walked through the gate, turned a little way beyond and reared onto his hind legs, a startlingly beautiful sight against the early-spring sky, summoning his mares with a loud whinny.

"I guess being in a couple of movie scenes went to his head," Brad joked, a rasp in his voice. "He thinks he's Flicka." The filming was over now, and things were settling down on the ranch, and around town. Local attention had turned to the new animal shelter, now under construction just off Main Street.

Meg's throat was so clogged with emotion, she couldn't speak. She rested her head against Brad's shoulder and watched, riveted, as Ransom shot off across the meadow, headed back up the mountain.

The mares followed, tails high.

Olivia watched them out of sight. Then, with a visible sigh and another squaring of her shoulders, she slowly closed the gate.

Meg started toward her, but Brad caught hold of her hand and held her back.

Olivia passed them by as if they were invisible, climbed agilely over the inside fence, and moved toward her perennially dusty Suburban.

"She'll be all right," Brad assured Meg quietly, watching his sister go.

Together, Brad, Carly and Meg returned to the house, saying little.

Life went on. Willie needed to go out. The phone was ringing. The fax machine in Brad's study was spewing paper.

Business as usual, Meg thought, quietly happy, despite her sadness over the departure of Ransom and the mares. She knew, as Brad did, and certainly Olivia, that they might never see those horses again.

"I don't suppose I could stay home from school, just for today?" Carly ventured, as Brad answered the phone and Meg started a fresh pot of coffee.

Outside, the toot of a horn announced the arrival of the school bus, and Brad cocked a thumb in that direction and gave Carly a mock stern look.

She sighed dramatically, still angling for an Oscar, as Brad had once observed, but grabbed up her backpack and left the house.

"No, Phil," Brad said into the telephone receiver, "I'm *still* not doing that gig in Vegas. I don't *care* how good the buzz is about the movie—"

Meg smiled.

Brad rolled his eyes, listening. "I am so not over the way you stuck me with Cynthia for a leading lady," he went on. "You owe me for that one, big-time."

When the call was over, though, Brad found his guitar and settled into a chair in the living room, looking out over the land, playing soft thoughtful chords.

Meg knew, without being told, that he was writing a new song. She loved listening to him, loved being his wife. While he was still adamant about not doing concert tours, they'd been drawing up plans for weeks for a recording studio to be constructed out behind the house. Brad O'Ballivan was filled with music, and he had to have some outlet for it.

He didn't seem to long for the old life, though. First and foremost, he was a family man. He and Meg had legally adopted Carly, though he was still Brad to her, and Ted would always be Dad. He looked forward to the baby's birth as much as Meg did, and had even gone so far as to have the first sonogram framed.

Their son, McKettrick "Mac" O'Ballivan, was strong and sturdy within Meg's womb. He was due on the Fourth of July.

Meg paused by Brad's chair, bent to kiss the top of his head.

He looked up at her, grinned and went on strumming and murmuring lyrics.

When a knock came at the front door, Willie growled half-heartedly but didn't get up from his favorite lounging place, the thick rug in front of the fire.

Meg went to answer, and felt a strange shock of recognition as she gazed into the face of a stranger, somewhere in his midthirties.

His hair was dark, and so were his eyes, and yet he bore a striking resemblance to Jesse. Dressed casually in clean, good-quality Western clothes, he took off his hat and smiled, and only then did Meg remember Angus's prediction.

One of them's about to land on your doorstep, he'd said.

"Meg McKettrick?" the man asked, showing white teeth as he smiled.

"Meg O'Ballivan," she clarified. Brad was standing behind her now, clearly curious.

"My name is Logan Creed," said the cowboy. "And I believe you and I are kissin' cousins."

* * * * *

SPECIAL EDITION™

THE BILLIONAIRE AND HIS BOSS
by *PATRICIA KAY*

When philanthropist Alex Hunt takes a
blue-collar job, he forms an instant attraction
to his new boss P.J. Kincaid—but is she also
pretending to be someone she is not?

YOURS, MINE...OR OURS?
by *KAREN TEMPLETON*

Ex-cop Rudy Vaccaro buys a New Hampshire
inn, and when he finds out that Violet Kildare
had been promised the property, he offers
her a job...and his heart.

Both available December 26
wherever you buy books

REQUEST YOUR FREE BOOKS!
2 FREE NOVELS PLUS 2 FREE GIFTS!

SPECIAL EDITION®
Life, Love and Family!

YES! Please send me 2 FREE Silhouette Special Edition® novels and my 2 FREE gifts. After receiving them, if I don't wish to receive any more books, I can return the shipping statement marked "cancel." If I don't cancel, I will receive 6 brand-new novels every month and be billed just $4.24 per book in the U.S., or $4.99 per book in Canada, plus 25¢ shipping and handling per book and applicable taxes, if any*. That's a savings of at least 15% off the cover price! I understand that accepting the 2 free books and gifts places me under no obligation to buy anything. I can always return a shipment and cancel at any time. Even if I never buy another book from Silhouette, the two free books and gifts are mine to keep forever.

235 SDN EEYU   335 SDN EEY6

Name	(PLEASE PRINT)
Address	Apt.
City	State/Prov.	Zip/Postal Code

Signature (if under 18, a parent or guardian must sign)

Mail to the **Silhouette Reader Service™:**
IN U.S.A.: P.O. Box 1867, Buffalo, NY 14240-1867
IN CANADA: P.O. Box 609, Fort Erie, Ontario L2A 5X3

Not valid to current Silhouette Special Edition subscribers.

Want to try two free books from another line?
Call 1-800-873-8635 or visit www.morefreebooks.com.

* Terms and prices subject to change without notice. NY residents add applicable sales tax. Canadian residents will be charged applicable provincial taxes and GST. This offer is limited to one order per household. All orders subject to approval. Credit or debit balances in a customer's account(s) may be offset by any other outstanding balance owed by or to the customer. Please allow 4 to 6 weeks for delivery.

Your Privacy: Silhouette is committed to protecting your privacy. Our Privacy Policy is available online at www.eHarlequin.com or upon request from the Reader Service. From time to time we make our lists of customers available to reputable firms who may have a product or service of interest to you. If you would prefer we not share your name and address, please check here. ☐

SSE07

COMING NEXT MONTH

#1873 FALLING FOR THE M.D.—Marie Ferrarella
The Wilder Family
When Walnut River General Hospital received a takeover offer
from a large corporation, Dr. Peter Wilder butted heads with board
member Bethany Holloway, a staunch supporter of the merger. But
soon Peter realized he had a takeover target of his own: Bethany's
heart.

#1874 HIS SECOND-CHANCE FAMILY—RaeAnne Thayne
The Women of Brambleberry House
Returning to her seaside hometown was hard on widowed fifth-
grade teacher Julia Blair. But then she saw the For Rent sign on the
rambling Victorian and knew she and her twins had found home. Of
course, it helped when she realized the workman in the backyard was
Will Garrett, her childhood sweetheart all grown up....

#1875 THE BILLIONAIRE AND HIS BOSS—Patricia Kay
The Hunt for Cinderella
Philanthropist Alex Hunt needed to find a bride within a year or
his wealthy father would disinherit him and jeopardize his charity
work. So, to avoid the gold diggers, Alex took a fake name and a
blue-collar job...and formed an instant attraction to his new boss
P. J. Kincaid. But was P.J. also pretending to be someone she wasn't?

#1876 YOURS, MINE...OR OURS?—Karen Templeton
Guys and Daughters
For ex-cop Rudy Vaccaro, buying a 150-year-old New Hampshire
inn was a dream come true. But his preteen daughter felt very
differently about the matter—as did Violet Kildare, the former
owner's maid, who'd been promised the property. Sympathetic, Rudy
let Violet keep her job...not knowing he was getting a new lease on
life and love in return.

#1877 YOU, AND NO OTHER—Lynda Sandoval
Return to Troublesome Gulch
Police officer Cagney Bishop had always lived in the shadow of
her bullying police chief father—especially when he ran her first
love Jonas Eberhardt out of town. Now Jonas was back, a wealthy
man, funding the local teen center to show that Troublesome Gulch
hadn't defeated him. But would Jonas's true gift be to offer Cagney a
second chance?

#1878 FOR JESSIE'S SAKE—Kate Welsh
Abby Hopewell felt betrayed by men—especially her only true love,
Colin McCarthy. When they were young, he'd callously left her in
the lurch and split town. Or so Abby thought. Now Colin was back,
his daughter, Jessie, in tow, and Abby's bed-and-breakfast was the
only place to stay. It was time to revisit the past....